CW01213502

Book of Silence

Christine Andain

authorHOUSE®

AuthorHouse™ UK Ltd.
500 Avebury Boulevard
Central Milton Keynes, MK9 2BE
www.authorhouse.co.uk
Phone: 08001974150

This book is a work of fiction. People, places, events, and situations are the product of the author's imagination. Any resemblance to actual persons, living or dead, or historical events, is purely coincidental.

© 2008 Christine Andain. All rights reserved.

No part of this book may be reproduced, stored in a retrieval system, or transmitted by any means without the written permission of the author.

First published by AuthorHouse 5/8/2008

ISBN: 978-1-4343-7328-1 (sc)

Printed in the United States of America
Bloomington, Indiana

This book is printed on acid-free paper.

To Ian for his support

Acknowledgements

Special thanks to Hilary Green, Lynda Kirby, Maureen King, Avril Senior and Elaine Stump - all members of my writing group, whose advice and criticisms have always, if not sometimes painful, been invaluable, to Mr. Ahmet Erdengiz, Director of Political Affairs and the members of the Missing Persons Team of Northern Cyprus, who returned early from an excavation in order that they could help me with my research, to my father, Frank Eccles, who enthused me as a child to write and last of course my agent Darin Jewell.

Northern Cyprus, 2004

Chapter One

Inspector Osman Zahir stared down into the open grave at the three hands. The flesh had gone, leaving the bones yellowed and clenched like claws. Two of the hands were linked, the fingers bent around each other and the third lay a few centimetres away, as if rejected by the other two.

Os could hear the heavy panting of Tramps just behind him. The dog's paw prints where it had leapt into the hole, added more chaos to that caused by the mechanical digger.

'Do you think it's part of the Bronze cemetery down the hill, sir?' Sener, his sergeant, nodded in the direction of the historical site.

Os squinted across to the hillock.

'I wouldn't have thought so. It must be over a kilometre away. I'm no expert but these bones look as if they haven't been in the earth as long as that.'

He felt Roisin's hand brush his as she moved to stand close by him. He wanted to take hold of it but he resisted. The driver of the digger was standing on the other side of the hole by his machine and his sergeant had eyes like a hawk. Os could tell that she was shaken. Not that it was surprising. It wasn't every day that you came across the contents of an unmarked grave. He looked down at her pale face.

'Why don't you go and have a cup of tea? It's getting hot out here and there's nothing more you can do. I'll drop in on my way back to the station.'

She hesitated and he waited for her to refuse, but then she nodded and, calling the dog, walked off in the direction of home.

Sener said nothing, instead he skirted around the disturbed ground to talk to the workman. Os hunkered down and stared at the mess of bones, semi-submerged in soil. There was something that resembled a skull, though only the jaw was visible. If this was an archaeological site, like the one that had recently been disturbed in Ozankoy, then it wouldn't be long before the foreigners turned up to protect it. He took his mobile out of his pocket and keyed in a number. When Os had finished talking, Sener joined him.

'What did he have to say?'

'Nothing different from your friend,' the sergeant answered. 'He was sent out by Oztec Construction this morning to start clearing the site. They're building ten houses here.' He pulled a face. 'His boss is on his way up now.'

Os looked around him. He'd only lived in these hills for five months but he had quickly come to love the quietness of the area. It took ten minutes to drive up here from the main road but it was worth it. Until this morning, he had looked out onto land that was shrub with the occasional olive tree. Now it was going to all disappear under concrete. Well, not today it wasn't. The 'Missing Persons Team' would close the area down for several days at least but after that? Os pushed aside the image of the destruction ahead. It was happening everywhere and no one in authority appeared to have any control.

'So we're in for an argument, are we?' Os replied, turning back to his sergeant. Well, he was ready for anything some aggressive contractor could throw at him. The law was exact, about what should happen if human remains were discovered, so the company would just have to wait.

'I don't like to be reminded how we'll end up,' Sener said as he stood balanced at the edge of the hole staring gloomily in to its depths.

Os grunted, having no desire to get into such a macabre subject.

They stared silently at the human remains until a squawk made Os glance up into the clear blue sky. Two large birds were circling above them. Os squinted, trying to recognise the species. Were they scavengers of some kind? He shivered. If they were after a meal they were going to be disappointed. He suddenly felt in need of some action.

'Can I leave you in charge? I'll just call in and see how she is before I go back to the station?' Os glanced in the direction of their house.

Sener shrugged his shoulders. 'No problem. It was a good thing she was out here when the digger unearthed this. I bet they would've carried on if they could've got away with it. What do you want me to do?'

Os checked his watch. 'The 'Missing Persons Team' should be here by eleven at the latest - perhaps earlier. I'm not sure what they'll need from us but ring the station and get a constable - and organise a rota. I presume they'll want a policeman on duty for as long as they're here - through the night as well.' He glanced at the workman who had climbed back into his digger and was smoking another cigarette. 'Call me if his boss causes any trouble. Are you sure you can handle this on your own?'

'No problem.' Sener took a packet of cigarettes out of his pocket and selected one. 'You still giving up, sir?' he asked, offering the packet to the Inspector.

Os nodded, aware that he was staring as the sergeant placed the cigarette in his mouth. He glanced one more time into the hole, noticing that several flies were now crawling over the jaw of the skull. An image of his own corpse covered in bloated maggots flashed into his head. He turned away.

He took the less steep route back up to where he had parked his car. Six large modern houses stretched out on the hill above the road. Each house was separated from its neighbour by a large plot of cultivated garden. The people, in the nearby Karaman village, sarcastically called it Millionaire's row but although this wasn't true, the properties were more expensive than many other areas on the island. They were paying for the tremendous views of the mountains behind them and the sea in front and of course the stillness that had always been prevalent until this morning.

They lived in a bungalow. Steep steps went from the road up to a wrought iron gate that opened onto a patio. The building was L-shaped, the missing area providing the space for a large swimming pool. To the left, a canvas awning jutted off from the outside wall of the sitting room and in the shade was a plastic table and chairs. Although an empty glass had been left on the white surface, there was no sign of anyone.

Os stepped into the cool, tiled hall. The study door was open but Roisin was not at her desk. Then the en-suite toilet flushed and there was the sound of a door opening. He caught sight of himself in the large mirror at the end of the hallway. His highly polished shoes were now covered in dust. Perhaps it was time to change his dark wool suits for the linen ones he preferred in the summer. Roisin was already wearing shorts but then she hadn't yet experienced how hot it became here in the summer. He loosened his silk tie as he walked into the bedroom.

'So what's happening?'

She stood five foot tall in the doorway of the bathroom, her long red hair an explosion of curls. She had changed into shorts and a T- shirt and the sun had brought out a sprinkling of freckles on her arms and chest. But, unlike the rest of her tanned body, her face was pale. He walked over and put his arms around her as he would have liked to when he had first arrived at the scene. She snuggled into his chest.

'Not a very pleasant thing to find, though I should imagine Tramps would disagree with me.'

Her body shook with giggles. He leaned back and looked down into her vivid green eyes. He was used to brown and he was still fascinated by the colour.

'I wouldn't have known anything about it if he hadn't brought me a bone. I thought it was from a dead sheep at first.' Roisin pulled a face as she revisited the experience.

He told her about the phone call he had made and then said, 'Shall I make you a cup of tea?'

She nodded. 'Have you left your sergeant down there?'

'He's waiting for the Team to arrive. All we've got to do then is keep a policeman on duty until they've finished.' He ran a finger over her lips, pleased to see colour coming back into her cheeks. 'I'll have to go back to the office after this. You go outside now - I'll bring the tea out.'

Os went into the kitchen. The home and the mongrel had been left to Roisin by her aunt. They had met at a neighbour's party, when she had been in the process of selling the bungalow and finding a home for the dog. It had been during a rare period when there hadn't been a woman in his life and they had been instantly attracted to each other. He still thanked Allah that Roisin's neighbour had been a colleague of his and that Os had, at the last minute, decided to take up his invitation instead of staying at home to watch the football. After two weeks he had persuaded her not to go back to Liverpool and had moved in with her after a month; that had been five months ago.

He turned on the kettle and then leaned against the black marble kitchen top. She had made an effort to clear away her aunt's clutter but somehow it had been replaced by her own. It was the same throughout the house; it was her least attractive trait. Placing three dirty glasses, a knife and plate into the sink he took out two clean mugs from a cupboard.

He joined Roisin by the garden wall. They both looked down at Sener talking to two men in suits while the workman hung back. On the road was a white van, the name, Oztec Construction blazoned on the side. Os handed her a mug and took a sip of his own black tea. She continued to stare at the scene below her.

'Is your sergeant going to be all right on his own?'

Os nodded. 'He knows he can ring me but he'll be enjoying himself. What are you going to do for the rest of the day?'

She balanced the mug on the wall and turned around so that she could lean back against the white stone and look up at him. 'I'm going to finish the chapter on colons and semicolons. I've been fiddling around with it for days. Living with you has distracted me.' She grinned up at him. 'If I don't get this book finished by the beginning of June, I'll be in trouble.'

'You've got three weeks then.' He bent to kiss her but she had other things on her mind.

'What's this Team that you were talking about?'

He grinned. She was obviously back to her old self.

'A group of anthropologists, archaeologists and detectives. They first work out the identity of any skeletons found on the island and then give the remains to the relatives so that they can be buried. Dr Pehlivan - who's in charge - gave a talk at a conference I went to. I had his number on my mobile because he offered me a job on his team.' He smiled as Roisin's eyes widened. 'I decided to stay where I was. You know about the Civil War that took place here in the sixties and seventies, Greeks against Turks?' She nodded and he continued. 'Pehlivan will be able to tell us how old the bones are - whether they actually were from the Bronze Age Cemetery or much later.' He placed his now empty mug next to hers. 'I'm going - I'll see you tonight.'

When he reached his car, he again looked down the hill. The men in suits were now standing on their own, both talking into their separate mobiles. Sener was leaning against the wheel hub of the digger, the perpetual cigarette in his hand. He saw Os and raised his fist in a salute.

Fifteen minutes later, as Os waited to turn right onto the main Karalangalou - Girne road, a large white van drew alongside, heading in the direction Os had just come from. The driver, a man in his late fifties in white overalls, caught Os's eye and they stared at each other before he put his foot down and roared up the hill. Os knew that he had seen the man before, he just didn't know from where.

Chapter Two

It was seven o'clock when Os arrived home. He found Roisin in the kitchen.

'Another bad day?'

'Is it that obvious?'

She grinned. 'You look as if you've been dragging your hands through your hair.'

He glanced over her head at his reflection in the window. His thick, black hair was in need of a comb and his brown eyes showed the strain of the afternoon.

He sighed. 'Atak is driving me insane.'

'What's he done now?'

'Nothing, that's the problem. I want to press a computer button for my information but he prefers to have everything written on paper. He says we can't afford the man - power to transfer it all.' Os took a tiny tomato from a full bowl and popped it into his mouth. 'Cross referencing takes hours.'

'You know he's an eegit! Did you get my message?'

He nodded and took a beer out of the fridge.

'Did you find anything out?'

Enjoying her impatience, Os pulled back the ring of the can. 'I did.'

'And?'

'They found a silver cross, a chain and a ring.'

Roisin stared at him. 'I don't suppose there was any inscription on anything?'

'They didn't say. One of the team rang me back just as I was leaving.'

'A wedding ring?'

Os shook his head. 'I doubt it, not if it was silver. What made you think of it anyway?'

'Martha and I went for a coffee in Endremit this afternoon. She wanted to know what had happened this morning.' Roisin grinned. 'Apparently all the village are talking about it.'

She wiped her hands on a tea towel and then took an opened bottle of white wine from the fridge. He waited as she poured herself a glass and then put the bottle back.

'I thought the bone looked in too good a state to be from the Bronze Age. So I thought the most likely alternative would be that they had died during the Civil War. And if that was the case then there might still be someone around who remembered something.' She stopped as if expecting him to give an opinion. He didn't, intrigued by what she was going to say next. 'Martha told me that Endremit village had been predominantly Turkish Cypriot about that time. She knows the man who owns the local bar and he's lived there all his life. I thought he'd be worth talking to.' She came to stand by him and slipped her hand under his jacket, running it up his back. He shivered. She smiled. 'Anyway, when we got there, Martha took over.'

Os took a sip of his beer. Even though she was a Liverpudlian, somehow the traces of her parents' Irish ancestry were still in her voice. He never tired of listening to her. When she realised he wasn't going to say anything, she continued.

'He wasn't any help really – Hassan his name is- just asked if anything had been found by the body, something which could help with identification.' Roisin moved away and began to peel an onion. 'Martha asked him what he meant and he said that he had read in the papers that a team from

Lefkosa sometimes identified bodies through a lighter or a piece of jewellery. It must be the same people who are down there now.'

Os raised an eyebrow. 'Does Martha want a job down the station?'

This time she didn't smile back at him. Instead he heard irritation in her voice.

'So are you going to make some enquiries now?'

'It's not my job.'

He had seen the tent when he'd arrived back from work. The large white van, that he had passed that morning, was still parked on the road above the site. He had briefly considered going down to see how they were getting on but it had been a long frustrating day. He would talk to them tomorrow.

'They'll take everything they find back to their laboratory. If they want our help they'll contact us.' He broke off as an overwhelming need hit him. 'I could kill for a cigarette.'

As if suddenly remembering that she was preparing the evening meal or perhaps because she was annoyed, she attacked the onion with a sharp knife until the vegetable collapsed in fine slivers. She then broke open a garlic bulb. Sighing, he took a stick of chewing gum from his pocket and peeled off the silver wrapping.

'I saw my mother when I was in Lefkosa today.'

She stood still for a second then began to mash the garlic against the chopping board.

'I had to make an appearance in court so I dropped in for my lunch.'

Roisin's voice sounded falsely bright. 'How was she?'

'Fine. A few aches and pains.'

She was now concentrating on making a garlic paste, which despite its smooth consistency, continued to be crushed and scraped alternatively against the blade of the knife.

She finally asked, 'What did you eat?'

He kept his voice even. 'Kebabs and salad. She baked her own bread this morning.'

'Sounds lovely to be sure. I don't suppose you'll want anything tonight then?'

'She wants us to go for Sunday lunch. I said we were going to the Saris' on Friday night.'

'Are we?' Her face brightened and he couldn't help but feel hurt by the transformation. 'You didn't tell me.'

'I only saw Aka this morning in court.'

'It's ages since I talked to Cassey.'

'They want us there for seven o'clock.' He put down his can. 'I'm going for a swim.'

From the far end of the pool he watched her lay the patio table. 'Are you coming in?'

She shook her head. Os put his head back into the water and did a slow crawl then twisted around and returned in the direction he had just come. His stomach was still knotted. Roisin made no effort with his parents; she had no interest in visiting them and had only invited them back here, once. It was her house, so it was difficult to demand what he thought was common courtesy. Okay, his mother was overpowering at times, but she had his best interests at heart and his father was charming. To be fair to Roisin, he knew she liked the cultured Professor of History but they always skirted around the subject of his mother.

'The pasta's ready.'

Os pulled himself out of the water and, after wrapping a towel around his waist, joined her at the table. She had put out another beer for him and lit a candle.

They avoided the previous sensitive topic. He made an effort to eat, keeping to himself that after his large lunch, he wasn't hungry. Roisin appeared to be as preoccupied as him. Then, when she asked him why he thought the bodies had been buried on the hillside, he didn't answer. He had enough work without theorising about things that no longer concerned him. The report that Atak had instructed him to compile on the growing number of burglaries, continued to niggle him. The man was over delegating, which wouldn't be so annoying if the data was easy to get hold of. The habitual negative feelings he felt towards his boss, flooded back and he pushed his unfinished meal away.

Os sensed her hurt in the way she cleared the dishes and then disappeared into her study, leaving him sitting alone outside with a brandy and his packet of chewing gum.

He stared into the night, his moodiness lying heavily on him like a wet overcoat. His attempt to give up smoking wasn't helping but when he'd found out how much she disliked it, he felt he had no choice. In a flash of irritation he picked up the brandy bottle and two glasses from the kitchen and collecting the torch and the dog, made his way down the hillside in the direction of the tent. A light glowed inside the canvas. Fikri was doing the first part of the night shift and he knew that the sergeant would be delighted to have company.

As Os approached he heard low voices. The flap to the front of the tent was rolled up and two men sat on canvas chairs facing out to sea. They were engrossed in conversation, so it was not until the dog appeared in front of them that they noticed the newcomer. Fikri got to his feet.

'Hello sir. This is Sergeant Derya.'

Os glanced at the other man who had also stood up. Os recognised him as the driver of the van which had passed him that morning. But more importantly, he now remembered why he had looked so familiar. He had worked with Derya in the Lefkosa station several years ago.

'Inspector now, I believe,' the older man said, coming forward and shaking Os's hand. 'You've done well since I last saw you.'

Os grinned. He'd liked this man, who had been a sergeant when Os had joined the force. He was what Os would call a solid copper, perhaps not over imaginative but thorough, and as far as Os knew, honest.

'So what are you up to? Obviously not still working for Lefkosa Police?'

Derya shook his head. 'I was seconded to the Team not long after you left. Hopefully I'll be with them until I retire – I much prefer the work.' He went into the back of the tent and reappeared with another canvas chair. 'Here, sit down. Do you want one?'

Os chose not to think about the reasons why he helped himself to a cigarette and why he avoided looking in Fikri's direction. He held up the brandy bottle and the two glasses. 'Have you got another glass?'

Derya picked up a plastic mug. Os poured out generous measures and then wandered over to stand by the open grave. A great deal of soil had been removed since that morning. Os had never looked at a real skeleton before and in the moon light the bones seemed to glow. Because there had only been three hands on view that morning, Os had expected other bones to be missing; but from this viewpoint the skeletons seemed, apart from a hand, to be complete. Os shivered again, as he had done that morning when the birds seemed to be waiting to pounce. He pushed aside an inexplicable feeling that something evil had happened here. Derya joined him.

'It's interesting work. I'm the only detective - the oldest member by about thirty years - besides Dr. Pehlivan.' He grinned.

'The majority of them are women, aren't they?' Fikri called from his chair. There was no envy in Fikri's voice, women were not one of his vices. Os smiled and the action raised his spirits. He turned back and lowered himself into one of the canvas chairs. 'So tell me what you do now.'

Os sat at his desk nursing a black coffee. He had drunk too much brandy the previous night and his head ached. He was also feeling guilty that he had been such bad company. Roisin had been in bed, either asleep, or pretending when he had staggered home. Aware that he stunk of smoke and alcohol he had thought it best not to wake her and they had spent the night on opposite sides of the bed. A member of the admin - staff knocked on the open door interrupting his black thoughts.

'A phone message was left for you sir. One of the 'M.P. Team' that are working out at Karaman.'

Os took the note. It was from the anthropologist who had told him about the jewellery the day before. It confirmed that they were excavating the remains of a male and female persons and that they had definitely not been in the ground long enough to be part of the Bronze Age Cemetery. He was well aware that this wasn't anything to do with the Girne police; it was for the 'M. P. Team' to investigate; but he was more than bored with what he was supposed to be doing. He had spent months on the Homicide Training Course and now here he was, interviewing workmen about petty theft. And perhaps more importantly, if he found out something more about these skeletons, he might appease Roisin. Recalling Roisin's account of their American neighbour's conversation with the Endremit bar owner, he picked up the phone and keyed in a number. A few minutes later two men stood in front of him.

Both men carried the same rank but that was where the similarity ended. Sener was in his late thirties, dark brown, thick hair, cut short, as was his moustache. His brown eyes smiled at his boss and there was an eagerness about him which Os always found uplifting.

His colleague did not have the same enthusiastic attitude to his work. He moved more ponderously; partly because of the extra weight he carried around his waist and partly because he had no interest in adding to his workload. His hair was worn longer but its thinness and lack of colour did nothing to enhance his lined face. Os noticed with some satisfaction that Fikri looked worse than him this morning.

'Shut the door and take a seat.' Os straightened his back, suddenly feeling this that there was more of a purpose to the day. The two sergeants, though appearing surprised, pulled out two chairs that were stacked against the wall.Os waited a few seconds for them to settle before saying, 'We're going to have a break today from what we've been doing. I want us to go up to Endremit. Ask a few questions.' He waved the note in the air. 'I've had some new information from the excavations. We don't know the ages yet of the couple found up there but they've been in the ground between thirty to forty years.' He paused, waiting for some kind of reaction but the two men were silent. 'Their deaths could have been from natural causes but as they appear to have been dumped, it seems unlikely.' Os chose to ignore Fiki's sullen face and re-directed his words towards Sener. 'The relatives could have used the cemetery just outside Endremit village but instead the bodies were left in unmarked graves. It seems likely that we've got a murder case here.' Fikri took out a cigarette and lit up. This time Os was not tempted to join him.'Yesterday afternoon they also found a silver ring, cross and chain by the bodies.'

Fikri pulled a face. 'We don't know if they were Greeks or Turks. Shouldn't we be leaving it to these people from the Government? They normally deal with everything don't they?'

'If there was a cross, it's likely to have been Greeks, sir. In those days, Karaman was Karmi, a Greek village. Someone from the village could've done the killing.'

Os looked at Sener and nodded. He could always be relied on. Os had recently had him promoted to sergeant. 'Perhaps but Endremit village was mainly Turkish so there might still be someone there who remembers something. We can spare a few hours from what we're doing here.' Os lifted up some papers from his desk and let them fall. 'We're not getting very far with this spate of burglaries anyway. It might do us good to have a break, see things with new eyes.' Os wondered whether he sounded convincing. He omitted to tell them the other reason for his interest in Endremit, besides his own boredom.

'So how are we going to handle this sir? Do you envisage us questioning every one in the village?'

Again Os heard the flatness in Fikri's voice. He was a man in his late fifties, waiting for retirement, who liked to work on one case at a time.

'I'll tell Halil to do some research on who was around forty years ago - still living in Endremit village now. Sener, give him a hand. I'd like to get out there this afternoon and it would be useful if we had a list of people to interview.'

Sener nodded and stood up to leave. Os turned to his other sergeant.

'You carry on with what you were doing but be ready to leave at two o'clock.'

Os waited for a negative response but the sergeant merely nodded and left the room. Os looked at his watch. It was ten o'clock. He had four hours to complete the paper work that was piled up on his desk.

The phone rang and a feeling of foreboding settled on him as he picked up the receiver. His new-found enthusiasm disappeared. Sighing, he pushed back his chair and went in search of his boss.

The door to Aziz Atak's office was open. Relieved that he didn't have to go through the office of the man's secretary, Os knocked on the door. The room was twice the size of his own. The floor area was polished parquet and a large desk was placed centrally in the room; as usual the dark wooden surface was covered with paperwork. Every time he was here, Os wondered how his boss found anything. Aziz stood with his back to the window which faced the gardens of the neighbouring private hospital. He could smell the strong aftershave that Atak insisted on wearing which became more pungent when the man sweated.

'Osman! Come in. Take a seat.'

Os did as he was requested, fighting back the familiar irritation he felt for a man who held such different views from his own. Aziz Atak waved the local newspaper that he had presumably had time to read that morning.

'The press are having a field day. They're blaming the politicians for allowing the flood of mainland Turks onto the island - saying it's them who're increasing our crime figures.' He wiped a drop of spittle from his chin with a handkerchief that had already seen some use. Os kept his face blank and waited for the real reason for his summons. 'How are your investigations coming on?' Atak growled. He pulled out his chair and sat down, creating a gush of escaping air from the leather upholstery. 'I had dinner with the Interior Minster and his wife last night and he's far from happy. He thinks that we should be doing more and I have to say I agree with him.'

Os forced himself not to snap back. How typical of the man. He had been promoted by the politicians and now here he was keeping his part of the deal with his sycophantic behaviour. Os had no doubt that money was being exchanged between the new construction millionaires and the less wealthy, elected members. But that was something he was not senior enough to investigate. Anyway, he knew that Atak wouldn't allow him to delve into such a cesspool. The prolific building programme had meant that an enormous number of unskilled labourers had been allowed into the country without work permits. Unsurprisingly, the results of all this corruption was increased crime.

Instead Os replied, 'We've brought in several men for questioning but at the moment we've no strong leads.' The big man glowered at his Inpsector but said nothing.

'They're taking things that are easy to get rid of - jewellery, electrical equipment, money that people leave around, bedding - kitchen utensils.' Os sighed. 'The culture of the island has changed but the politicians have to take some responsibility.'

He attempted to put as much respect as he could into his voice. 'But then I'm sure you defended our position, sir.'

His superior officer stared at him for a few moments then dropped his newspaper on the desk.'Of course, Osman. I understand how hard you're all working, I told the Minister myself. Last week I was in Lefkosa, asking for a bigger budget but you already know their answer. There's no money for more staff and,' he glanced down at the offending newspaper, '…it doesn't help that the press are calling us incompetent.'

Os turned a smile into a grimace. He suspected that Aziz Atak's concern was about whether he would be blamed for what outsiders saw as police stagnation. He decided not to admit that he was about to spend valuable, police time investigating something that was likely to have no bearing on the crime figures. Sensing that his boss was temporarily mollified, he stood up.

'If that's all, I'd better get back to work, sir.'

Atak nodded. 'Don't forget, Osman, I need those burglary figures on my desk for next week.'

As Os reached the door he glanced back and saw that the older man had resumed his position by the window but now he was staring out at the gardens below. The man's indolence erased any sense of guilt that Os might have had about his plans for that afternoon. No doubt the Commandant was passing his time before getting ready for another lunchtime engagement.

On his way back to his office, he made a short detour to the administration room. Halil and Sener were both bent over ledgers, copying names onto sheets of paper. Os left them to it. One day they might have all this information at the touch of a computer button but for now they had to make do. Meanwhile he would finish that report.

At ten minutes to two, Sener came into his office waving several sheets of paper.

'There are only fifteen people who fit the criteria.'
'Who's the Muhtar?' Os asked.
'Hassan Kartal. He owns the village bar.'

Os took the sheets of paper, scanning the information. The Endremit bar owner was fourth on the list. He copied down several names then folded his sheet and placed it in his pocket.

'Good work. You two divide the rest between you,' Os handed the papers back to Sener. 'I'll take my car and meet you in Endremit.'

'Right, sir,' Sener answered and left in search of his partner.

The traffic out of town was gridlocked. Out of habit, Os reached for his cigarettes then remembered his decision. Instead he tuned into the World News. It was something he had got into when he had first returned from the States. Before meeting Roisin, it had been a useful way of maintaining his English, as well as following politics outside the island. He tried not to be irritated by the failings of the Northern Cypriot government but at times it was difficult. They had been waiting for years for a new bypass around Girne but just as a Turkish construction company had won the contract, the government had cancelled the arrangement, citing corruption. Now it was out for tender again with the promise that the building would start next year. Os sighed as he thought about the next two months when the cars of the tourists would add to the chaos.

At last he reached the village of Karalangalou and turned left by the butcher's shop. The owner sat outside, watching the world go by, his magnificently long moustaches beautifully groomed. The Endremit road was much quieter and within a few minutes he arrived at the village car park. Plastic tables and chairs from the café filled the grass verge. Os went over and sat down recognising Hassan, the owner, standing by another occupied table.

He was a man in his early fifties, his thick dark hair greying at the temples. He was an average height and build except for a substantial paunch which hung over his trousers. Black framed glasses rested at the end of his nose and he looked over them at his customers. He crossed over to the newcomer's table.

'An Efes beer, please.' Theoretically Os was on duty but a small beer wouldn't make any difference.

Hassan went back into the bar. Os wondered whether the man knew who he was. He used this road twice a day, on his way to work and back. Although he had never stopped for a drink, he had often seen the bar owner, shirt sleeved, standing outside talking, or smoking a cigarette. But this afternoon, he had not appeared interested in talking to Os, whereas a few minutes earlier, he had been joking with the tourists at the only other occupied table. A marked police vehicle turned right into the car park, its tyres crunching the loose gravel. Os stood up and walked over to meet his two sergeants.

'You've got your names and addresses. When you've finished get yourself home.' Both men responded with a grin at the thought of an early finish. 'I'm going to start with our man here and then see the others on my list - if they're at home. Good luck!' Os watched the two men cross the road and disappear up an alley way, which provided access to the houses behind, before returning to his seat.

Hassan banged a bottle of beer and a glass on the stained, plastic surface of the table. 'Any trouble?'

'We've found remains of two people up there.' Os nodded his head in the direction of the distant hillside. 'We're questioning anyone who was around in the sixties. You're the Muhtar here now, I believe.'

The barman stood a little straighter. 'Anything I can do to help. I've lived here all my life, like most people here.'

'We're aware of that and everyone is being talked to. Since you're the elected councillor, I came to you first.'

Hassan nodded at Os' recognition of his position in the community.

'Did you ever remember anyone go missing from the village? Anything at all that could help us discover the identity of the bones?'

The man shrugged. 'It's a long time ago.' He indicated, with an open palm, the memorial stone next to Os's parked car. 'It wasn't unusual for men to go off then. Some came back, some didn't. It was a time we didn't ask questions.'

Os smiled sympathetically. He had lost relatives himself with the internal fighting with the Greeks and he had heard many stories of how difficult life had been when he was a baby. 'But might you have heard something strange that you didn't understand at the time?'

Hassan paused, as if considering the question. 'Have you thought that it could've been something to do with the Greeks in Karmi? It wouldn't surprise me if they'd murdered someone up there and then covered it up.'

'Of course. But as they're no longer here to ask…' Os pulled a face at the complexity of the situation.

Hassan stuffed his shirt into his trouser waist band then pulled them back up to the middle of his stomach. 'Anything found with the bodies?'

'Like?' Os asked, remembering that the man had asked Martha and Roisin the same question.

He shrugged again as if indifferent to the answer. 'Something that could identify the bodies?'

Os studied him for a few seconds. 'Why do you ask?'

Hassan shook his head and took a step backwards as if intimating that he had more important things to be doing. 'No reason, I'm just trying to help.'

'A cross, chain and ring were found,' Again Os waited for any reaction, some kind of recognition.

Hassan pursed his thick lips. 'Sounds like Greeks to me. Perhaps they were murdered by us Turks.' Hassan grinned and held up a thick set hand. 'But not by me.'

'One of the bodies was a woman.'

The barman sounded almost bored. 'Someone told me. But I still can't help you. I was only a kid at the time.'

'Not exactly, you were in your late teens or maybe older.' Os looked at his list again and then back at Hassan. He was obviously not going to get anything else from this man - even if he actually knew anything. 'Is it your mother or your wife, I need to speak to next?'

Hassan picked up the empty beer bottle. 'I'm not married and my mother is in hospital. They're operating on an ingrowing toenail - but I doubt if she'd know anything more than me. She's eighty and most of the time she can't remember what happened last week.'

Os finished his beer. He would carry on down the list. Then if there were no leads and his men felt the same, they would drop the case. He was already regretting his impulsiveness, and if Atak found out, he'd be in trouble. He took a two lira note out of his wallet and handed it to Hassan, along with one of his cards.

'If you think of anything, ring me.'

'Is that all?' There was relief in Hassan's voice. No Northern Cypriot liked to be questioned by the police.

'With you, yes. Now where can I find the house of Zahide Jemal?'

Os walked along the narrow passage-way in the direction Hassan had indicated. At the crunch of his footsteps a cat, sunning itself on a window ledge, jumped down and ran off. Two young children played in a heap of builder's sand, using a basin and a mug to create structures of their own. Os knocked on the door of one of the narrow terrace houses, and after introducing himself to an elderly, black clad woman, went inside.

An hour and an half later, Os leaned wearily against a white-washed wall. He had interviewed four people, varying in ages from forty-five to ninety. They had all appeared mystified by the discovery of the skeletons above the village. Several of them already knew about the unmarked grave, news travelling fast in country areas. But Os sensed that they were telling the truth, that they knew nothing about how the bodies had got there in the first place. Many, like Hassan, when told about the cross, had decided that the bodies were from the old Greek village of Karmi, a mile above their own. He was now very tired, his eyes gritty; all he wanted was to go home.

He glanced at his watch and saw that it was six o'clock. He had been here for just under four hours and was obviously wasting his time. He wondered whether the other two had done any better. Highly unlikely, he thought. He had met both Sener and Fikri at different times, as he had come out of one house on the way to the next. Both men had looked glum and Os suspected that they were thinking that their afternoon would have been better spent on other things.

He looked at the last name on his list. Should he bother or could he go home? He imagined himself diving into the pool and then resurfacing for a cold beer. He could almost taste the hops and he realised how thirsty he was. But if he didn't do this last interview he would feel obliged to come back tomorrow. And he knew that he had already spent enough time on what was turning out to be an indulgence. Pushing aside his weariness, he trudged up the slope in the direction of the final house.

Os guessed that Kutlay Uludag was in his late sixties. The man sat at a table, an empty coffee cup and full ashtray in front of him. Os introduced himself through the open doorway. Uludag nodded as if he already knew the name of his visitor. Os was not surprised, several people would have already been to tell him that police officers were in the village.

The room was dimmed by closed shutters. Os glanced around, overpowered by the smell of neglect and clutter of furniture. A faded, multi-coloured sofa and two chairs were grouped around the open fire place which still held the ashes of a winter fire. Despite the gloom, Os could see that the table, at which Uludag sat, was scratched and dull through lack of polish. Os pulled out the chair opposite him, transferring a walking stick from the wooden seat to the floor. He was surprised that the wiry man should need such an aid.

'I'm hoping that you can help me shed some light onto the findings up the hill.'

The man put a fresh cigarette in his mouth and struck a match. His hand trembled as he stared at Os over the flame. 'My neighbours tell me that they've found two bodies, a man and a woman?' Os nodded. 'Do you know how long they've been in the ground?' He spoke without removing his cigarette.

Os shook his head. 'A silver cross and ring on a chain were found by the bodies.' Does that mean anything to you?'

'I heard.' He stared back at Os, his eyes narrowed, either in thought or to protect them against the spiral of smoke. There was slyness to his unshaven, mottled face. He knocked a strip of ash into the already full ashtray. Os sighed, did the man know something or was he just wasting police time. Then Uludag pushed back his chair and stood up. He picked up his stick and, leaning heavily to one side, shuffled passed Os to the door. He stood looking out into the lane. Despite his disability, the man stood ram-rod straight, though Os noticed again that his right hand trembled with the effort.

His voice floated back into the room. 'Why are you interested? If anyone knew anything, would there be a reward?' Hope flared in Os' stomach as he stared at Uludag's back. Perhaps interpreting the Inspector's silence for acquiescence, Uludag continued, 'I'm not saying I know anything - I'm just asking.' He turned around and leered, revealing a mouth of yellow teeth and missing spaces. 'But it would have to be worth my while!'

Os shrugged. 'I'll ask my Commandant.' Then forcing his voice in tones of respect, he said, 'I heard that you were the Muhtar of this village in those days - before Hassan Katal took over. It was an important position, even more so then than now. You would have known what was going on around here.'

The man was not going to be drawn. But perhaps he had nothing of real use to divulge. Os knew his country's history. It had been a turbulent period when the Greek Cypriots had attempted to make Cyprus part of mainland Greece. The Turkish Cypriot men had defended their properties and families with equal violence. The older generation had lots of stories but would this man's be of any use to Os? He thought again of the cold beer that was waiting for him back at the house.

'If you're worried about breaking a confidence, I'll do all I can to keep your name out of it. But it'll be different if I find out that you could've helped us and you chose not to.' Os stood up. 'I'll come back tomorrow morning to see if your memory has improved.' At the door he turned back.'I'll ask about that reward.'

The man leered again and Os felt disgust, not only at the unpleasant sight of his poor dental work but at something else in the man's personality. He ducked his head so that he wouldn't bang it on the lintel of the old house and walked back down the lane.

He thought about looking for his men but then made a decision to go straight home. Most likely they had already left. The absence of their police car confirmed his suspicion. Os climbed wearily into his own, dust-covered vehicle. Out of curiosity he glanced across to the bar but Hassan was not outside, although two new people sat at a table, drinks placed in front of them. Os thought back to the man he had just interviewed and pulled a face. He probably knew nothing but Os would keep his promise to visit him on his way into work. And after that he would leave the mystery to the anthropologists and his old colleague, Derya.

Chapter Three

Os felt in a particularly good mood. It was a beautiful morning, the sun still gentle and the sky and sea a bright blue. He was still basking in the previous evening that had turned out even better than he had hoped. Roisin had bought lamb chops and sausages from their favourite butchers in Girne and they had sat outside until eleven, barbecueing and drinking Yakut. Admittedly, he now had a small headache but it had been worth it. He had indulged her macabre interest in the skeletons and described the people he had interviewed in Endremit. They had finished their meal with coffee and what now appeared to be too many brandies.

Roisin was also of the opinion that the victims had been Greeks and she hadn't argued when he had told her that there was little else that he could do. He would question Uludag on his way to work but he felt relaxed that nothing would come of it. Domestic harmony had been restored. Finally, when he couldn't bare any more theories, he had taken her to bed.

Os had left her half asleep, a mug of tea cooling on her bedside table. He had drunk several cups of black coffee and eaten some bread and cheese before finally leaving the house. Prior to giving up smoking, he used to sit outside by the pool and watch the day come to life but it wasn't the same now. But at least having arranged to see Uludag at nine o'clock had meant a relaxed start to the day.

Although the door to the bar was open, Hassan was not visible. A middle- aged woman, dressed in black, was washing down the outside tables and chairs. Os wondered whether his sergeants had interviewed her the day before. Aware of her scrutiny, he nodded back acknowledgement of her presence.

This time the children were not playing in the alley, though the evidence of their work in the sand was still intact. Os picked his way passed doorways, careful not to tread on fallen, rotting fruit or dog excreta. He sometimes wondered why he bothered spending money on expensive shoes and suits when he so rarely spent time in the comparatively, sanitised police station. Roisin had called him vain on a few occasions after having spent time ironing his numerous shirts or leaving one of his twenty suits at the cleaners.

Uludag's house was the last in the row. His door and shutters were closed. Was he still in bed or had he already gone out? Irritated, Os knocked on the door and waited. A couple of minutes later he knocked again and then stood back to stare up at the bedroom window. Was he asleep or was the man peering down at him through the slats of the shutters? Os hammered again. Frustrated, he tried the handle and, to his surprise, the heavy wooden door moved. He pushed it open further and stepped in. An overpowering smell of stale brandy made him reach for his handkerchief. A mewling cat ran out between his legs into the street and disappeared over the wall.

Besides the strong smell, there was an atmosphere that he had not felt yesterday but then yesterday, the man had both the front and back doors open. Today the windows and doors were still closed.

'Mr Uludag! Hello!' Os listened to his own voice rattle around the room. No-one answered. A wooden stairway hugged the back wall and Os moved towards it. He was going to have to wake the man up. He really needed to be back at the station by ten o'clock in case Atak decided to talk to him again. Os didn't want to have to explain why he was late for work.

The body lay at the bottom of the stairs. It reminded him of a rag doll. It was on its back staring up at the ceiling, its arms and legs splayed out away from the trunk. As he moved forward he felt the crunch of broken glass underneath his feet. Os knelt down to feel the old man's neck but he knew that there was nothing he could do. He took out his mobile and keyed in a number.

He gave the details to Sener. 'After you've rung for an ambulance, you'd better collect Fikri and which ever photographer's on duty. I'm not sure what we've got here, so bring the gloves and specimen bags.' He was about to disconnect then added, 'You better bring two constables with you as well.'

He suddenly felt claustrophobic and went to stand outside. What ever promises he had made to Roisin, he needed a cigarette. But first he had to find out who the old man's doctor was. He pulled the front door closed, locked it and slipped the key into his pocket. He was only going next door but he couldn't take any chances.

A woman he had interviewed the day before, answered. She frowned as she recognised the policeman on her step.

Not bothering with any preamble he said, 'I need the name of your neighbour's doctor.'

Her expression changed from suspicion to one of interest. 'Is he ill?'

Os shook his head. 'Do you know who it is?' he persisted.

'He uses Mustafa Hasturk, like most of us. His surgery's down in Karalangalou.'

'The telephone number please?'

She shuffled back into her house leaving him at the door. Os looked up and down the narrow lane. It was empty now but once word got out, that a villager was dead, they would have difficulty keeping people away. Adrenalin bubbled in the pit of his stomach. The woman returned and handed him a piece of paper, the doctor's name and number printed in red ink.

Os forced a smile. 'Thank you. I'm afraid your neighbour died in the night.'

Shock but no traces of sadness showed on her face. He was relieved. The last thing he needed was a hysterical woman on his hands.

'I don't suppose you have a cigarette?' he asked.

Now she grinned, revealing teeth not much better than her neighbours. Again he waited until she returned, placing an unopened packet in his hand. She shook her head when he offered to pay.

'No. Have them on me. You look as if you need them.'

He thanked her and walked the few paces back to her neighbour's house, sensing that she still stood in her doorway, watching him. He took out his phone and ripped open the cigarette packet with his teeth. The short telephone conversation over, he lit a cigarette and for a few minutes took pleasure in a habit he missed every hour of every day. Finally, stubbing out the fag end on the stone wall, he unlocked the old man's door and entered for the second time.

It took a few moments to get used to the gloom and then he crouched down over the body. Taking a pen from his pocket, he slid it under the head that now looked a great deal older than it had fifteen hours ago.

The back of the skull was matted with blood. It was impossible to examine the wound without disturbing the area. Was it caused by a weapon or had the skull been bashed by a fall down the stairs? Carefully he laid it back on the floor and wiped his pen on his handkerchief. A short distance from the body a broken brandy bottle lay against the bottom step. Os looked up the stairs, considered investigating further and then stopped himself. He knew he should wait until the others arrived. There was no point leaving his footprints everywhere until they had taken photographs. Os glanced back at the remains of the brandy bottle. Had Uludag dropped it falling down the stairs? Or had it been used as the murder weapon he wondered?

He went back to the shutters, careful that he didn't stand on anything else. Unfastening the latch, he pushed them open, allowing the morning sun to stream in. Now that there was natural light, it confirmed what he suspected yesterday, that the room needed a good clean. The tiled floor was stained and there was thick dust everywhere. Os had been in several houses like this, where an elderly man had lived on his own. Then he noticed the scuffle of footsteps by the base of the stairs.

There was a clear sign of footprints making their way in and out of the room. But around the body the dust had been disturbed to such an extent, that it was difficult to work out where one foot print started and another finished. Was this because the falling man had destroyed the demarcation lines or because there had been some kind of fight? He stared at the dead body and thought again about the strange placement of limbs. A small pool of blood had collected on the floor tiles by the head, and the eyes seemed to be staring at him. He would have liked to have closed them, as if to put them out of their misery. But he knew that job had to be left to the doctor.

He went outside again and leaned against the wall. Three people were watching the house from further down the lane. The neighbour must have already spread the word that Uludag had died and they had gathered to watch events. He turned his back, confident that they would come no nearer. They wouldn't want to be singled out and they would probably know that he was the same policeman who had been making enquiries the day before.

Os was on his third cigarette when he saw the men walking towards him. He recognised the three constables along with his two sergeants. He nodded at them all but didn't smile, focusing on the photographer.

'You go in first, Ali. We'll wait here until you've finished.' Os watched the tall man prepare his camera before he ducked his head to enter the house.

'It's not an accident then?' Fikri asked. He and Sener had joined Os, distancing themselves from the two constables.

'It probably is but I don't want to risk sending him off to the morgue and then discovering that he was murdered,' Os said. His experience of dead bodies wasn't extensive, he didn't want to make any mistakes.

Fikri grinned at the cigarette Os had clenched in his hand but didn't say anything. Instead he pulled out his own packet and after offering one to Sener, lit them both.

'Did either of you discover anything yesterday?' Os asked.

Sener shook his head. 'Most of them had heard the news but you would expect that. But as far as knowing anything else…' The sergeant pulled a face. 'What about you, sir?'

'Uludag was the only possibility. He asked about a reward. I told him I'd find out.' Os shook his head. 'And then he goes and falls down the stairs - or was pushed!'

Sener's eyes widened. 'Is there a reward?'

Os shook his head. 'I let him think there might be.'

'How old was he?' Fikri asked.

'In his late sixties, I would say. It could have been an accident. The steps are dangerously steep, especially after a few brandies. There's a smashed bottle in there.'

Above them a shutter squeaked open and the photograher stuck out his head.

'You can come in now, I've finished.'

The three men ground cigarettes under their heels and followed their colleague into the house. Fikri stopped some distance from the body.

'My God, this room's filthy! You'd have thought that a daughter or someone would have come in wouldn't you!'

The stench of stale nicotine was overpowering. Although he himself had lit another cigarette, Os could understand why Roisin was so against the habit. No doubt she would accuse him of breaking his promise when he arrived home tonight.

His thoughts were interrupted by a middle-aged stranger in a baggy suit, standing in the doorway.

'Mr Hasturk?' Os asked.

The doctor nodded.

'Come in.'

The man entered, then crouched in the same place as Os had done a short time ago. The policemen waited silently as the doctor went through the usual procedures before death could be officially announced. Finally, he stood up and rubbed the base of his spine.

'As you probably guessed, he's been dead since last night. I'd say between nine and midnight.'

'And the cause, doctor?' Os's voice belied the tension cramping his stomach.

The man glanced back at the body as if to confirm his diagnosis. 'I'm afraid I can't say for definite. I'm sending the body to the pathologist in Lefkosa. There are broken bones here but whether they were broken, before or after he died, will be up to the expert.' The doctor looked up at the stairs and pointed to dried spots of blood on several of the steps. 'He could have fallen. This would be where he could have banged his head on the way down.' He glanced back at the Inspector. 'But I want to be sure. Uludag had been drinking but how much I can't tell – the Pathologist will let us know.' His eyes narrowed. 'But I wouldn't have envisaged him dying like this.' Using a handkerchief he lifted up the dead man's head and re-examined the back of the skull before carefully placing it back on the floor. 'He was a strong individual for his age. I very rarely had cause to see him. And if he had a drink problem, I didn't know about it.'

There was a knock. Standing in the doorway were two uniformed men with a stretcher. Os listened as the doctor instructed them to take the body to the morgue. He turned back to Os.

'Who will go with the ambulance?'

Os looked up at Ali who was now standing at the top of the stairs. 'Is there anything else you need to do?'

'Give me ten more minutes and I'm ready,' the photograher answered. The policemen went back outside to give the ambulance men space. The onlookers had developed into a small crowd.

Os grimaced and turned to the constables. 'You deal with this. Push them back so that the men can get through with the body.'

Os turned his back on the gaping villagers and lit another cigarette, staring up at the trees above him. He thought about the dead man, who at this moment would be in the process of being lifted onto the canvas stretcher. A few minutes later, Fikri joined him. Os looked at his sergeant through the haze of smoke.

'This could be our first murder investigation.'

Fikri's eyebrows shot up. 'Has the doctor confirmed it?'

'Not definitely. We're waiting to see what the pathologist says.' Both men watched the photographer as he came out of the house and joined them by the wall.

'Got everything?' Os asked.

Ali nodded.

'Well, stay with the body until it gets to the morgue. But I want you to stop off at the station and get someone to develop those pictures. I doubt if the old man will be looked at today but one of us needs to be there when they cut him up. Give me a call later and let me know what's happening.' Os turned to Fikri. 'You go and help. Make sure no-one touches the body before it's in the back of the ambulance. Then come back here.'

Os watched them expertly manoeuvre the stretcher down the narrow alleyway while Fikri and the two constables managed the gawping villagers.

Then turning to Sener, Os said, 'Come on, we'd better go inside.' Leaving the group of voyeurs, they stepped once again into the gloom of the dead man's house. 'You have a look around here. I'm going upstairs.'

'What are we looking for?' the sergeant asked.

Os shrugged. 'I don't know exactly until we hear from the pathologist. If you find anything suspicious, just call me.' He put out his hand. 'Give me a couple of specimen bags before I go upstairs.'

Os climbed the wooden stairway, his eyes raking the steps for anything unusual. The top landing was stacked high with clutter. There were two bedrooms: one had been used as a storage area; boxes of various shapes and sizes were balanced haphazardly on top of each other. Two broken chairs were propped against a wall. The single bed, in the middle of the room, was covered in old clothes. The smell of unwashed cloth was strong and Os went over to the window and forced it open. This had obviously once been the room of a teenager, gauging by the posters of young men with guitars on the wall. They were faded and the edges ripped but Os recognised them as groups that had been popular over ten years ago. Either there was a son or daughter around or Uludag had bought this house in the last ten years and not bothered to do any re-decorating. The door into the bathroom was ajar. Os pushed it open further.

His first reaction was to back out as the strong smell of urine hit him. He clamped his handkerchief to his face and turned away as the bile rose up from his stomach. After a couple of minutes he gained control and forced himself back into the room. The floor and wall tiles were filthy; as with the rest of the house, no one had cleaned for a long time. Os opened a bathroom cabinet, glad of the latex gloves but it only contained shaving equipment and an out of date cough medicine bottle.

The larger of the two bedrooms was where Uludag had obviously slept. Again it needed cleaning and decorating. Ali had opened the window in this room to call down into the street so the smell had had time to dilute. Beneath the dust, Os could see that the furniture in here had once been a good quality, though neglect had removed the sheen of the wood.

Interesting, he thought. He wondered what the man had done for a living. And if all his family was dead, why hadn't he paid someone to come in and look after him? If money had been a problem he could have sold some of the things here. Os stared at the chest which matched the elaborately carved, olive wood, double bed. He flexed his sweating hands inside the latex gloves before lifting the lid. A heap of crumpled clothes were jammed inside, the smell of stale sweat making him grimace. He fought the urge to leave the room and instead pulled out the soiled garments, dropping them on the floor.

As Os lifted out the last pair of underpants, his mouth moved from an expression of disgust to a triumphant smile. Two large note books and several cheque books were stacked at the bottom of the chest. Elderly people were all the same about their money, he thought. His grandfather had hidden his in a box underneath the bed. He picked up one of the books and then moved over to the open window. The pages had been divided into sections and a neat italic hand had entered names and numbers in ordered columns. Os turned back to the front cover but it was blank, giving him no clue what the list of accounts referred to. Picking up the remaining books he went in search of Sener.

Chapter Four

Os adjusted his office chair, attempting to ease his indigestion. He regretted agreeing to a late lunch in Muharrem's café before returning to the station. The London Cypriot cook did an excellent pizza but now the dough lay heavily on his stomach. He reached into his pocket for the unfinished packet of cigarettes and then remembering Roisin, he slid it back into the top drawer of his desk. For emergencies, he thought.

He and Sener had left Fikri and the constables to interview the neighbours and to organise a twenty-four hour rota for protecting the potential murder scene. If Uludag's death had been an accident then they could lock up the building and leave it to the solicitors. What with a rota for the excavations and now the house in Endremit, he would be running up quite an overtime bill. It wouldn't be long before Atak called him in to explain himself.

Uludag's cheque books and ledgers were spread out on the desk in front of him. If Uludag's accounts were correct, he had three hundred thousand Turkish Lira sitting in his account. Os picked up a bundle of weekly pay slips, yellowed with age, weighing them in the palm of his hand. How could this man have saved so much when he had only earned eighty Turkish Lira a week?

The biggest surprise had been in discovering where Uludag had worked for ten years before he retired. His neighbour had told Fikri that he had been employed as a porter at the police station in Girne. Fikri couldn't remember him and, ten years ago, Os had been a constable in Lefkosa. He picked up the internal phone and rang the porters' room.

Five minutes later a man, in his late fifties, knocked on the open door. Os smiled, attempting to put him at his ease and indicated he should come in and take a seat.

'Thanks for coming up. I wanted to ask you about someone who worked here ten years ago'

From the porter's expression it was obvious that the news of Uludag's death had not yet reached him.

'Kutlay Uludag?'

The man rubbed his forehead as he trawled through his memory. 'Oh, yes, I remember Uludag, though I didn't have much to do with him. He always wanted to work nights, and me with my family, have always done days.' He took out a handkerchief and blew his nose. 'I haven't seen him since he left.'

'He died last night. I was at his house in Endremit this morning.'

Recep nodded as he took in the news but he didn't appear affected by the information or interested in the details.

'What was he like?'

'He was not a man I would have coffee with.'

'Why's that?'

'Nosy. He always wanted to know your business. Anything at all about yourself - people you worked with - your own family. He tried to make it sound as if he cared about other people's troubles but it was just his way of getting hold of information.'

'Did he tell you about other people's business?'

The porter shook his head. 'I didn't talk to him unless I had to. But no, he wasn't a gossip, he just liked knowing things. Some of the younger ones would confide in him but he gave me the creeps.'

'He left here before he was sixty-five. Can you remember why?'

The porter nodded. 'He was in a car crash. He wasn't driving but he damaged his leg. They started his pension early. I don't think he would normally have got it but he was given a lift home from an Inspector who'd been drinking. I think they...,' the porter looked up into the air as if that was where the authorities housed themselves, '.... wanted to keep things quiet.'

Os digested this information then asked, 'Do you think any of the men kept in contact with him after he left?'

The man shrugged and for the first time Os noticed the state of his shirt. Although it was clean and pressed, the collar and cuffs were frayed. But if the man was having to support a wife and children on his porter's salary, it wasn't surprising.

As if aware of the Inspector's gaze, he pulled down the sleeves of his overall. 'I haven't heard anyone talk about him for a long time. But I'll ask around if you want?'

Os smiled again. 'I'd appreciate that. You know where to find me if anything comes up. Spread the word that if anyone has any information on Uludag, I want to speak to them.'

The porter stood up. 'I'd better get back to sorting the post then, sir. I'll let you know if I hear anything.'

Os returned to the books in front of him. It was interesting how they were set out. Perhaps Uludag had been the Treasurer for some organisation. But if that was the case, why wasn't the official name on the front of the books? And some of the entries didn't make sense. He could see that instalments had been listed on a regular basis, over a long period, but by whom? There were people's names alongside the payments, and by others there were words he didn't understand. They weren't even in Turkish. Again for an uneducated man that was also strange. If everything was legal, Os would have expected to see the books kept more professionally. Perhaps his role of Muhtar of the village had put Uludag in a position where he had to collect money. But then he hadn't been Muhtar for many years and the last entry date was only two weeks ago.

Os looked at his watch. Ali had rung when the ambulance had arrived at Lefkosa General Hospital but he had heard nothing since. He had hoped that the presence of a policeman would have given priority to an autopsy. He wondered whether he should drive over there himself. It was four o'clock, which would make it nearer five by the time he arrived at the hospital. There was of course the risk of a wasted journey if the pathologist had left for the day but he couldn't concentrate on anything else anyway.

It was the first time he'd had to personally deal with the pathology department though he'd spent two days there as part of his specialist, homicide training. He looked down at the name and telephone number, Ali had given him - a Mrs Leigh Gok. She had done well to reach such a position. He admired successful women and, unlike some of his colleagues, he didn't have a problem working with them.

He picked up his mobile and keyed in Ali's number again. The tone sounded several times and then transferred over to the answering service. Irritated, Os left another message for him to return his call and then broke the connection. He pushed back his chair and went in search of his sergeants.

A solitary Fikri was sat at a desk in the sergeants' room. Os stood in the doorway listening to the man's conversation with his wife. He appeared to be attempting to explain why he had arrived home so late the previous night. Fikri, suddenly aware of his boss's presence, rang off.

'Are you doing anything?'

'Nothing that can't wait, sir. I can finish the report on Uludag's neighbours tomorrow.' Fikri lumbered to his feet, unhooking his jacket from the back of the chair. 'Where are we going?'

'I want to hear first hand if our man was murdered or just careless. There's no point delving into anything if he just fell down his own stairs. We've got enough work to do.'

'Is it all right if I put in for overtime? I should be finishing at five.'

Os hesitated, anticipating the reaction of the Commandant. 'All right.We'll have to hope it's murder to justify the expense.'

They cut across the heavy traffic of the ring road and then Fikri took the back roads until they joined the quieter Girne, Lefkosa - highway. Os loved the route through the mountains and down on to the Mesaoria Plain. It was now early May so the shrubland was losing its bright green of winter. They passed the huge army base on the left and Os stared at the houses for commissioned, married officers, just inside the perimeter.

'I lived six months in that camp,' Fikri nodded in the direction of the barbed- wire fence. 'Spent my time driving a Colonel around. Very nice it was too. Where did you do your National Service, sir?'

Os was surprised that he hadn't already known this about his sergeant but then they very rarely talked about their personal lives. 'I was with the military police in Ankara in the beginning and then spent the second year in a small town by the Iraq border.'

Fikri glanced across at him. 'Did you enjoy it?'

Os thought back to the last two years of his teenage life.'Some of it. I didn't like it so much in the second year. It was a dreary town and most people who lived there owned nothing. There wasn't much to do when you weren't on duty and you never knew when the Kurds would decide to blow you up. It could be interesting work though - it's why I became a policeman.'

'But you went to University in Istanbul afterwards, didn't you, sir?'

Os nodded. 'Neither of my parents wanted me to join but they said that if I hadn't changed my mind after I'd done my degree, they'd go along with it.' Os smiled as he recalled the heated conversations in the family kitchen. 'I'm sure they thought that I would grow out of the idea once I'd been to Istanbul.' He looked across at his sergeant. 'What made you join the force, Fikri?'

'They were doing a big recruitment when I came out of the army and the pay was better than anything else that was going at the time.'

Os said nothing. That was the difference between him and his sergeant. Os had felt passionate about his work from the beginning. Still, Fikri did a reasonable job if you kept an eye on him and there was always Sener if he needed someone to bounce ideas off.

Os stared out at the passing scenery. This was a journey he used to make twice a day when he had lived in Lefkosa and he still never tired of it. But if he hadn't decided to transfer to Girne Police Station he wouldn't have met Roisin. He had rung her earlier that afternoon to tell her about Uludag's death and been surprised that she was yet again with their American neighbour, Martha, arranging flowers in the Karaman church. He knew that some of the ex-pats looked after the Greek Orthodox Church, opening it up every Sunday for visitors. Perhaps now that she was beginning to mix with the people in the area she would start to feel at home.

They were now entering the suburbs of Lefkosa. Os preferred the gentleness of Girne and was glad it was Fikri who was doing the driving. The four-lane traffic that snaked its noisy way through the capital needed all your attention. He sat back listening to the honking of horns as frustrated drivers attempted to get home. He tried Ali again without success.

The State Hospital car park was full but Fikri found a place reserved for officials. He leant across his boss and fumbled in the glove pocket, pushing aside sweet papers and tapes until he found what he was looking for. He propped the police disc in the window screen and opened his car door.

They registered their names at the front desk of the pathology department and a few minutes later, a woman strode through the swing doors titled - Theatre.

'Leigh Gok. Nice to meet you, gentlemen.'

She included both Os and Fikri in her smile and firm handshake. She smelled strongly of roses and it occurred to him that perhaps it was to counteract the stench of death. Her dark hair was cut stylishly around her pale, elf-like face and although she was lined around her mouth and eyes, she was still an attractive woman. She wasn't like many of the Europeans, who spent far too much time in the harsh, Cypriot sun until their skin turned to leather. She was wearing the green gown of the operating table but Os noticed through her strappy sandals that her toenails were painted bright red. He guessed that she was in her fifties, not so different from his youngest aunt. But there the comparison stopped. With a surname of Gok she must be married to a Turk but her confidence and mannerisms were still very American.

'Can I get you coffee or something cold to drink?'

Os shook his head for both of them. He didn't want to waste time and he sensed that they had only been offered refreshment because this woman was used to the hospitable customs of Northern Cyprus.

'I'll take you in then. Gown up first please.' They followed her through the swing doors and she pointed to a collection of green gowns hanging on the wall. 'You're lucky. We're quiet at the moment and since you'd sent a police officer with the body, I decided to see to him straight away. Normally it would've taken a couple of days.' She stopped for a second to help Os into his gown, grinning at his clumsiness. Her teeth were perfect in shape and dazzling white like those of so many Americans. He found himself wondering if she visited the dentist here in Lefkosa or went back to her homeland for her twice yearly check-ups.

'By the way, your policeman is still in the rest room.'

Os found himself grinning back. Ali had obviously not enjoyed the autopsy.

A trolley stood in the centre of the operations room next to a metal table. Leigh Gok pulled back the white sheet. Uludag's eyes were closed and the grey skin now appeared both translucent and paper thin. He looked even older than when Os had found him that morning. The head wound had been cleaned and the surrounding skin, visible through the shaved head, was bruised black. The pathologist had revealed only the top of the body; Os was relieved, he had no desire to stare at the rest unless it was absolutely essential.

Os caught the pathologist's eyes and sensed that she could read his thoughts. He felt as guilty as if he had spoken some anti-ageist comment out loud. Would he have felt the same if there had been a young woman's body under the sheet? Embarrassed, he concentrated on what Leigh Gok was saying.

'We're still doing some tests on his blood. But I'm sure that despite the level of alcohol in his body, this man died from a blow to the head which then caused a cardiac arrest. I'd say that he was attacked from behind, probably by someone taller than him.'

'So he couldn't have fallen down the stairs?' Os asked.

Leigh Gok's eyebrows shot upwards. 'A possibility but he would already have been dead.'

'Are you sure about that?'

'Quite sure. Bones are broken in one leg but this happened after he died.' She pulled the sheet up from the man's feet and touched the thin, white, left leg. 'I'd say your man was murdered. He was attacked, then thrown down the stairs to make it look like an accident. Your weapon would be something round, possibly made out of wood. Metal wouldn't have made this kind of injury.' She re-covered the man's legs and smiled. 'The likelihood of him banging his head, dying and then falling down the stairs seems unlikely. Wouldn't you agree?'

Os was unsure whether it was sarcasm or humour he heard in her voice. He recalled the rooms of Uludag's house but no likely murder weapon came to mind. He hadn't seen the walking stick but then he hadn't been looking for it, his attention had been on the dead man. At that stage they hadn't been at all sure that it was murder. He had then discovered the cheque books and ledgers upstairs in the bedroom. But if his sergeant had seen anything covered in blood he would have said something. Os was sure that between them they wouldn't have missed anything so obvious. But they had the photographs at the station. He would check when he got back.

Leigh Gok snapped off her thin, protective gloves.'I'd estimate that he was killed sometime between nine and midnight last night.'

Was it just co-incidence that Uludag was killed a few hours after Os had spoken to him, he wondered? He turned back to the pathologist.

'Have you finished with the body?'

'Yes.' She indicated to her assistant that he remove the trolley. 'I'll wait for the results of the blood tests and then send my report to you tomorrow. But if nothing new comes up, we'll release the body to the relatives. A daughter is asking for custody.'

Os stared at her. 'Have you seen her?'

'My secretary took a phone call. We've agreed for an ambulance to take the body to Girne Hospital, in the morning. The daughter is intending to have the funeral tomorrow afternoon - in accordance with Muslim law. Presumably you have her number - you can ask my secretary for it on the way out otherwise.'

When they had realised there was a daughter, Os had asked the Gazi Magusa police to inform her of her loss. Nevertheless, she couldn't have had the news longer than a few hours. Os thought back to the neglected state of the house. It would be interesting to find out how close daughter and father were? He shook the pathologist's hand and thanked her for her help.

'Not at all Inspector, if there is anything else I can do, please don't hesitate to ring my office.'

Os turned back at the door. 'Could a walking stick have caused that wound?'

'If it had been brought down on the old man's head with enough force - yes. At his age his skull would have thinned considerably. Good luck!'

Fifteen minutes later Fikri was manoeuvring the car onto the dual carriage way. A subdued Ali sat in the back. Os glanced at his watch. It was seven o'clock. If they were not held up, he should be back home by eight. Not too late for a meal with Roisin. But then he thought about the photos waiting for him in the drawer of his desk.

Chapter Five

On his way to his office, Os acknowledged the greeting of the duty sergeant as he passed. He'd sent Fikri off duty despite his offers of help. It was common knowledge that the sergeant wasn't that enamoured with his home and took any opportunity to volunteer for overtime. According to station gossip, Fikri regularly spent his evenings in one of the casinos that were opening up across the country. Os just hoped that he wasn't getting into financial trouble. He himself had once accompanied a friend to such a place but then couldn't bring himself to put any coins into the machines. Bored, he had accepted the free drinks and watched people throw wads of notes at the gaming tables. In the end he had caught a taxi home leaving his friend behind.

A cleaner was swabbing the huge expanse of hall tiles. The building was a year old but Os preferred the old station that had since been knocked down to make space for a new block of apartments. It had been far more homely, whereas here, most people were expected to work in open plan offices. Trying to get work done, amid all the noise, was an impossibility. After much complaining they had eventually given him his own small office on the second floor.

He took the stairs three at a time. The doors along his corridor were either shut, or if open, revealed that the occupants had gone home. Os flicked on the light of his room and noticed that the bin had been emptied and the tiled floor washed. But the curtain still hung off the rail. He had mentioned it several times to the cleaner but it obviously wasn't high on the man's to-do-list.

A thick envelope lay on the scuffed surface of his desk. He sat down and spread the photos out in front of him. Ali had done a good job. The body and the downstairs room of Uludag's house had been photographed from several angles. Os flicked on the table lamp to add depth to the fading natural light. He examined each photo but he couldn't see a stick. He distinctly remembered Uludag using it to walk to the door but now it was no-where to be seen. If this had been the weapon, then the murderer had obviously taken it away with him or her.

Os recalled the daughter who had asked for her father's body. Although it seemed that she hadn't cared about the state of her father's house, she was now planning his funeral. What could she expect from his death? Perhaps Hassan would know the answer.

The one good thing about going home late was that the traffic was light. Fifteen minutes later he was in Endremit village. The lights were on in the bar and through the open doorway, Os could see Hassan polishing glasses. He smiled as the policeman walked up to the counter.

'A drink, Inspector?' The bar man moved across to stand in front of the beer pump.

'No, thank you. I've just called in to ask for your help.' Os looked around him. There were four people sat on the plastic banquettes by the empty fireplace. They looked like tourists judging by the two women with sun-burned shoulders.

Hassan's eyes flicked over the Inspector but he didn't respond to the intended flattery. 'What can I do for you?'

'Uludag' daughter - how close were they?'

Hassan shrugged his shoulders. 'You know how it is with families. She married early and moved to Gazi Magusa. I believe they have a business over there - selling carpets and tablecloths to tourists.' He glanced across at his customers, as if checking to see if they needed fresh drinks. 'I've not been there myself.'

'Was she the only child?'

'No. She had an older brother but he was killed in the seventies. His name's on the monument outside.'

'And Uludag's wife?'

'Died years ago. The daughter was closer to her mother. When she was buried the daughter stopped visiting.'

Os felt pangs of hunger. He dismissed the idea of eating one of the cheese rolls displayed in a glass jar and instead asked, 'How would you describe the marriage?'

Hassan pulled a face. 'Who knows? Put it this way, I wouldn't have wanted to live with him but women are different. She was quiet, kept herself to herself - except for a friend in the village she would drink tea with.' Hassan bent down and began to transfer Fanta bottles from a crate to a shelf.

Os watched him for a few moments. It was clear that he wasn't going to get any more information and indeed he had no idea what he had hoped that Hassan would tell him. It was time to go home.

'If you think of anything else, you've got my card. How's your mother by the way?'

'I'm bringing her back home tomorrow morning,' Then, as if in exchange for Os's concern, he added, 'Mrs Assim will have the daughter's number if you haven't already got it. She was the old friend of her mother's. She lives in the blue house, four doors down from Uludag's.'

Os jotted down the name next to the telephone number of the daughter he had been given that morning. He would go and talk to the old woman tomorrow. Perhaps she would give him an insight into the Uludag family. The breakdown of communication between daughter and father was unusual. Gazi Magusa was only an hour away; it would not have been difficult for her to visit her father but it appeared that she had made a conscious decision not to.

The thought of his father dying and his mother coming to live with Roisin and himself flashed across his mind and he grimaced at the prospect. It was the Cypriot way but he knew that it wouldn't work for them. Let's hope that both mother and father keep their health, he prayed.

Roisin was in her study, the door open. She saved her work and then turned off the computer. 'Do you want a drink?'

He nodded. 'I'll just change and have a shower. Is there anything to eat?'

'Some cold chicken and salads if you fancy that?' She stood up, stretched and then gave him a kiss on the way to the kitchen.

Feeling more human, he went back out onto the terrace and handed the photos to her. While he ate, she went into the sitting room and examined them under the lamp.

'There's certainly no stick there,' she said, sitting down opposite him.

For a minute he forgot the case as he looked at her. She had washed her long, red hair and it hung in waves down her back. He never tired of the colour, having spent his life surrounded by dark haired women. There were a few blondes in Northern Cyprus but red hair was so unusual. He loved the freckles sprinkled across her face and the paleness of her skin. In this light she glowed, reminding him of silkworms he had once seen in a farm outside Gazi Magusa. He reached across and took a few strands between his fingers, twisting them. She smiled back at him and he knew he loved her, more than he had loved anyone. He wanted to marry her but she'd already told him that she didn't want to marry anyone. Unlike his own childhood, she had experienced nothing but parental arguments. Perhaps one day he would convince her that it wasn't the formal vows that spoiled love. But he could wait, there was no hurry. There was his mother who constantly asked him about it but he could handle her.

She poured them both wine then sat back in her chair and grinned at him.'I've got something to tell you.'

'Go on.'

'After you rang this afternoon, Martha and I went to this woman's house in the village. We'd been arranging the flowers in the church and she offered to make us all tea. She's a German, called Maria, and she's lived here since the fifties.' Roisin paused, presumably to see how much interest she had aroused.

He smiled. 'And?'

'She used to be friendly with a Greek Cypriot woman, who had an affair with your dead man forty years ago.'

Os put down his glass. 'Tell me more.'

'Well, obviously, after you called me, I told them that you'd found Uludag dead. Maria knew him well by sight. Her friend, Antalya had an affair with him in the late sixties. He could only go up to her house at night because he was both married and a Turkish Cypriot. At the time, Maria thought that she was the only other person who had known about it. She assumed Antalya had confided in her because she was German - she didn't have the same prejudices about relationships between Turks and Greeks.'

It suddenly occurred to Os that perhaps the reason the daughter no longer visited her father was because she'd known about his affair. It was also possible that the female skeleton had once been this Antalya. Could this be why inititally, Uludag refused to say anything when he'd been questioned? Even though his wife was now dead, the remains of his mistress being discovered could have caused some difficulty for him.

'Are you listening?'

'Of course. Go on, what happened between them?'

'Apparently, Uludag always told Antalya that he would leave his wife and they would go to Britain and start up a business there. But then in 1972, the Turkish army invaded and the villagers, including Antalya, fled to the south of the island. As far as Maria knew, her friend and Uludag never saw each other again. Maria never heard anything more from Antalya.' Roisin sipped her wine. 'She occasionally saw Uludag when she called in at one of the Endremit shops but they had never been on speaking terms. Maria assumed that Antalya had told her about the relationship in confidence and anyway Maria never liked him - she always thought that he was after her friend's money.'

Os stared across the swimming pool to the hill on which the lights of Karaman glowed in the night sky. If the bones belonged to Greek Cypriots, then the likelihood of it being proved was negible. There was little co-operation between the North and the South - even for things like this. He needed DNA from a relative of Antalya if he was going to prove her identity. And that was not going to happen. But if Antalya was the female corpse, who did the male remains belong to? And why and how had they died? It didn't make sense.He realised that Roisin was waiting for him to say something.

'There was that old man – more likely than not, lonely - rattling around in a filthy house. And yet when he was younger he was carrying on with another woman even though he had a wife and child. So far I haven't found anyone who was really upset to see him die. Perhaps the funeral might throw up something.'

'Are you going to it?'

'Oh yes. Interesting things funerals!'

Roisin came and sat on his lap and he put his arms around her as they both listened to the trickle of water from the overflow swimming pool and the occasional hoot of an owl. Tramps padded out from the garden and nuzzled his head up against Os's leg. He rubbed the dog's ears, aware of a feeling of deep contentment with his lot, the stress of the day having seeped out of him. Roisin whispered in his ear. He took her wine glass from her and then picked her up and carried her into the bedroom.

Chapter Six

Mrs Assim was a small woman, with the appearance of someone in her early seventies. Her thin body was covered in a black, shapeless dress and thick black stockings that wrinkled around her ankles. A black scarf was knotted underneath her chin.

'Hassan said you might come,' she said, moving aside to let Os pass. No longer marvelling at the speed news travelled, he followed her into her house.

It was a simple cottage with tiled floors and the uncomfortable wooden seats that you so often saw in the houses of the older generation. She shuffled back to her wooden kitchen chair indicating with her hand that he could take the other seat.

'You want to know the address of Nurten?' She slipped a gnarled hand into her black apron pocket and pulled out a piece of paper. Os glanced at the spidery handwriting and thanked her. He had no need to tell her that the police had already visited the daughter's house.

'When was the last time you saw Mrs Isler?' he asked.

She shrugged her shoulders. 'Not for several years, but I talk on the telephone sometimes.' Os looked around for a landline, not able to imagine this woman using a mobile.

'Not here,' she said, 'Hassan lets me use the phone in the bar. Nurten sends me money so that I ring her every month.

She wants to know how her father is.' The old woman's jaw worked continuously. 'I talked to her yesterday morning.'

'Was it you who told my sergeant about her?' Os asked. She looked surprised. Did she think that the police didn't talk to each other? 'She didn't get on with him then?' Os continued, trying to reconcile a woman who never visited her old father but demanded monthly bulletins about his health. Had she known about his money and was waiting for him to die? If she disliked him so much, perhaps she had killed him. It would have been easy for her to slip back late at night, she probably still had the front door key.

Mrs Assim continued to move her jaw from side to side. 'They didn't get on. But he was her father.'

'What happened between them?' Os kept his tone light. Most villagers had an innate suspicion of the police and he didn't want to frighten her.

'He treated Fatima without respect. She died of cancer but it was brought on by him.' The woman stared out through the open doorway, her milky eyes seeing things that had happened years ago. 'Nurten and I were the only ones who knew what he did to Fatima. He would hit her but never where anyone could see.'

Os had witnessed enough marital violence through his job not to be surprised. In his experience few women reported the beatings, it was the neighbours who rang the police. And afterwards, the wives would refuse to press charges and history would repeat itself.

'As soon as someone asked Nurten to marry her, she was off. She's lucky- he's turned out to be a decent man.'

'And she never returned after the wedding?' Os watched her closely. He knew she would lie if she thought it would help her old friend's daughter.

'No, she would have come to visit me if she had. I'm always here.'

Os thought she was telling the truth but he had made mistakes in the past, especially with old women. They rarely looked you in the face when they were talking.

'And the funeral?'

'It's taking place this afternoon - within the time.'

Ideally, the body of a Muslim should be buried within forty-eight hours but when they were connected to a police investigation this wasn't always possible. The daughter had managed it with a few hours to spare. Had she gone to all this trouble because she was a devout Muslim or was she looking towards her inheritance? He would delve into the background of Nurten Uludag, or Isler as she now was, as soon as he got back to the station. But first he needed to have another look around Uludag's house.

Os stood up and handed her his card. 'Thank you, Mrs Assim. You've been most helpful.'

'So he didn't just fall down the stairs then?'

For a moment Os was taken aback but here he was again, taking old women at face value. He caught her eye and saw a shrewdness there he hadn't observed before. He was interested in how accurate the word on the street was.

She paused for a moment as if wondering whether to tell him anything. Then suddenly grinning, she answered, 'We'd heard he'd fallen down the stairs. But then when a policeman was on duty all night - we realised that there must be more to it.'

Os waited but she either knew nothing more or that was all she was going to tell him. She held onto his card but he suspected that, despite the fact that she had permission to use the phone in the bar, she wouldn't ring him.

Instead of turning right towards the car, he turned left in the direction of Uludag's house. A man in a police uniform sat on a kitchen chair, outside the main door, reading the paper. When he saw Os he leapt to his feet.

'Good morning, sir.'

'Morning, constable. How long have you been on duty?'

The young man folded the newspaper and put it down on the chair as if it had nothing to do with him. 'Since seven, sir. I relieved Mustafa Gokcekel.'

'Did he say how his night had been?' Os's eyes raked the small stretch of land around the house.

'Quiet, sir. I've had a few villagers asking me questions but nothing else.'

'I'm looking for a walking stick, constable, or a heavy piece of wood. You haven't seen anything like that have you since you've been on duty?' The younger man shook his head, his eyes anxious. Os smiled back at him trying to put him at his ease. 'I'm going into the house but I want you to search around out here. If you see anything likely, don't touch it, just call me. It could be our murder weapon.'

The constable's anxious look was replaced by one of eagerness. Os left the young man with his task and unlocked the door into the house. The musty smell was now stronger. He unlatched the windows then looked around him. Everything was as he remembered, except that there was no corpse at the foot of the stairs. Snapping on thin rubber gloves he lifted the cushions of the old sofa. Rubbish and fluff had collected there over the years but there was no walking stick.

After checking the other furniture, he went upstairs. The bed in the spare room was heaped with boxes and old clothes but there was no stick. He sighed. He had to get back to the station if he was going to make the funeral this afternoon. The constable could continue to search the area outside, it would give him something to do, make him feel important.

Then, as he was leaving the main bedroom, he saw an old biscuit tin on top of the wardrobe. He dragged across a chair and, stepping on it, clutched the tin with both hands and jumped down. The metal was rusty and it was difficult to open but using the pen knife he always carried, he snapped off the lid.

He hadn't known what he expected to find inside so he wasn't disappointed when he saw that the tin was full of old photos. They were probably of no use but he would take them back to the station. There might be something that would throw more light onto the life of this man. He was just about to put the lid back on when he felt something hard underneath the black and white pictures. It was a leather wallet. Inside was a police badge belonging to Kutley Uludag.

Os stared at it, suddenly oblivious to the smell and dirt around him. For a fleeting moment he thought there must have been a mistake. Why had people thought that Uludag had been a porter not a detective? Then he realised that he was looking at a forgery.

He left the constable in his search for the murder weapon. He would send men up to help him as soon as he got back to the station. No-one crossed his path on the way back to his car but he felt as if he was being watched. According to Mrs. Assim everyone in the village now knew that he was investigating murder.

The duty sergeant called across to Os as soon as he walked through the main door.

'The Boss said you had to go to his office when you came in. He's been waiting since half-eight.'

Os glanced at his watch. It was eleven-thirty and he needed to sort out a search party before getting back for the two o'clock funeral. 'Have you seen Sener or Fikri anywhere?'

'Fikri was in the canteen half an hour ago. He might be still there.'

Os was sure that he would be. He must have once been more enthusiastic to have reached the rank of sergeant but now that he was waiting for retirement, he did his best to take things easy. Os ran down the stairs to the basement. Fikri sat at a formica table reading the Volkan newspaper, an empty plate and cup in front of him.

'I've got a job for you,' Os said. Unlike the policeman in Endremit, the sergeant did not shoot out of his chair but at least he looked up from his paper. 'I need you to go through the records and see if we've got anything on the dead man's daughter. I'm going to see the Commandant so I'd appreciate it if you could start on that immediately.' Suddenly irritated by the sergeant's lack of movement, he snapped, 'You could also organise two men to give the constable in Endremit a hand. I've left him looking for the murder weapon. Uludag's walking stick is missing and according to the pathologist it's more than likely to have been the murder weapon.'

Os turned to go and Fikri picked up his newspaper paper.

'Now, Fikri. I'd like the information in an hour's time and I want that stick found this afternoon.' He waited for the sergeant to stand up and then in silence they walked side by side back up to the ground floor.

Atak's door was open as if he was waiting for him. 'Come in, Osman. Take a seat.' He watched Os for a few moments then said,

'So we've got a murder case on our hands?'

Os told him about his trip to Lefkosa and his conversation with Mrs Assim that morning. The big man took a cigarette out of a box, then lit it.

'You think his daughter killed him?'

Os sighed. 'She's a strong candidate. But I'm curious about these accounts. We need to find the people who were paying him money. He could have been stealing from them of course. That's a lot of money that he's got stashed in his bank account - people have killed for far less.' Os watched the spiraling cigarette smoke. Perhaps responding to Os's look of need, the Commandant pushed the box across the desk. Os shook his head and continued with his theory. 'Although we're looking into the daughter's motives, I'm sure the case isn't going to be that easy.'

'Most people are killed by someone close to them.' Atak's head had lowered onto his chest, creating a collar of surplus flesh above his white, starched collar. Os guessed where this might be leading.'I don't want this dragging on too long, Osman.'

'No, sir.' Os sat on his hands to stop him from clenching them. It would have been easy to snap back but instead he waited.

'It'll be all over the papers tomorrow and I don't need the politicians on my back. This country has a low crime rate - the last thing they want is a murder, even if it is a local. Thank God it's not a tourist.'

Os stared at his shoes. If he caught the Commandant's eye he couldn't trust himself to keep his feelings to himself. After a few moments he looked up and focused on the wall behind Atak's head.

'I'll get on with looking into the daughter's past then, sir. I want to be in Endremit for the funeral this afternoon.' He stood up, the chair screeching on the tiles as he pushed it back.

'Keep me informed Osman, keep me informed.' The big man picked up the phone.

As Os closed the door behind him, he wondered whether his boss was reporting back to one of the politicians he had been referring to. Certainly, the man was being far more deferential on the phone than he had been talking to Os. He fingered the false police badge in his pocket. He had intended showing it to Atak but the realisation that his Commandant might then feel that he had to become more involved had stopped him. Perhaps he was being unprofessional but at the moment it was a risk he was willing to take.

On his way back to his office he looked through the open doorway of the sergeants' room. Sener was stood talking into the phone. Os indicated that he should join him in his office and then left him to finish his call. While he waited, he ordered a sandwich and a bottle of water from the canteen. He had an hour before he had to leave. A knock on the door marked the arrival of his sergeant.

Os waved at the chair opposite his desk. 'How did you get on with the bank?'

Sener sat down, stretching his long legs out in front of him. Os noticed that his shoes needed soling.

'No-where fast. The bank hadn't taken any notice of the money in Uludag's account. He always deposited the money in cash and since he spent little, his account was of no interest to them.'

A porter entered the room.

'Do you want anything?' Os asked.

Sener shook his head. 'No, thanks, I've eaten.' He waited until the man had left then pushed a sheet of paper across the table. 'I've divided the list of payments into peoples' names and the words we don't recognise. I was going to go up to the village this afternoon to see if anyone knows any of these people.'

Os remembered what Roisin had told him the night before. He repeated the story of the affair to Sener.

Sener shook his head. 'I can't believe that it was his girlfriend lying up there.'

Os took a bite of his sandwich. 'I'm sure you're right, Sener. But I'm convinced that Uludag knew something the evening I went to see him, and I don't like coincidences. He was killed the same night.'

Sener stubbed out his cigarette. 'I've asked some of the older porters whether they kept in touch with Uludag but no one seems to have done. They all agree he was a nosy devil though, always asking about personal things. One of them said it was like he had no life of his own, so got his excitement from other people.'

Os glanced at his watch. 'Do you want to come with me to the funeral?'

Sener smiled 'What time are you going, sir?'
'In half an hour. I'll meet you in the car park.'

Chapter Seven

The traffic was solid. Os wound down the window rather than turn on the aircon. He hated the noise and it always gave him a sore throat. He had used a mosquito net and kept the bedroom windows open in his apartment in Lefkosa but Roisin had already told him she wouldn't survive without it in the heat of the summer. But at the moment it was still cool at night. He glanced in his rear mirror and checked that Sener was right behind him. The sergeant had the radio on and Os could hear the music booming through the open window. He was passing the time and waiting for the traffic to move by enjoying a smoke. Os opened the glove compartment and took out a stick of chewing gum. He had never really liked the stuff but it gave him something to do with his jaws. At last the car in front started to edge forward.

Os took the turns in the road to Endremit faster than usual. The funeral had started in the mosque in Alsancack but the body was to be buried in the Endremit cemetery. Instead of stopping in the village car park, Os continued up the hill. Five or six cars had been left by the side of the road and Os parked behind them. He waited for Sener to arrive before entering the small cemetery that Os drove passed every day, but had never had a reason to visit before now.

An abandoned Greek church stood at the far end but for years this ground had been used by Muslims. Forty people clustered around the freshly dug grave but the two policemen stood apart, out of respect and also to give them a better view.

Os scanned the crowd for Mrs Assim. If anyone would be standing by the daughter it would be her. As he suspected, she stood next to a tall, thin woman, whose hair was hidden under a black shawl. Nurten Isler's arm was linked through that of a man, presumably her husband. Hassan was there in a dark suit but the rest he didn't recognise. A huddle of women wailed in the manner that was common at funerals, then the daughter threw a handful of earth into the grave and others followed.

The mourners were an assortment of all ages. Whether they had come to pay their respects because they liked the man, or because it was a social event, it was impossible to guess. Os saw that the daughter was dry-eyed. Was this because of the Muslim directive that there should be no crying at the funeral or because she felt no sadness, he wondered? Her husband now put his arm around her shoulders and together they walked towards the gate and the two policemen.

Hassan had been one of the first of the mourners to throw his handful of earth onto the coffin before he followed the Islers out of the grave-yard. Nurten's eyes flicked over the two policemen but when she saw Os was watching her, she stared down at the ground. Her husband showed no such modesty but Os didn't sense any hostility in his stare. They walked passed without speaking.

'I'm providing coffee and tea in my bar if you'd like to join us.'

Os looked back at the middle aged man who, in his suit, cut an attractive figure. He was surprised by the offered hospitality. Hassan had not exactly been hostile but neither had he encouraged conversation. Although Os had intended following the crowd into the bar it was certainly easier if he had an invite.

As if reading his mind, Hassan explained, 'Mrs. Isler has asked to talk to you. It's easier for her here than down the station. She wants to ask you about her father – how he died. The Gazi Magusa police didn't seem to know anything – or they wouldn't tell her.' He lowered his voice. 'She knows that you've been asking questions about her.'

Os stared into the older man's brown eyes. As ususual they revealed nothing of his true thoughts. 'That's kind of you, Hassan. We'll follow in a few minutes.'

'He likes being in the centre of things, doesn't he, sir,' Sener said as they watched the Endremit Muhtar climb into his car.

'Mmmmm. He takes his role very seriously. He appears to help all sorts of people.' Both men watched the man negotiate a three point turn.

'One of the villagers told me that he wasn't married so maybe he's got the time. He's not spending hours running after his wife and children.'

Os looked at his sergeant. From what he had observed, it was Sener's wife, Fatima, who did most of the running around.

'He's been very kind to Mrs Assim, letting her use his phone to ring the daughter. And now he's using his café for the funeral. What do you make of that?'

'Perhaps he fancied the daughter once, sir. He must have known her all her life. Perhaps that's why he never married.'

Os's mobile rang. He moved out into the privacy of the road when he recognised the number. 'Yes, Fikri, what have you got for me?'

Excitement crackled in the older man's voice. 'The daughter. You wanted to know if she'd any kind of police record.'

'And?'

'It wasn't easy. The file was down in the basement, tucked away under the wrong classification. Three of us have been searching since you left.'

'Well done.' Os heard the surprise in his own voice. Occasionally Fikri came up trumps. Perhaps this case was resurrecting his enthusiasm. 'And what did you find?'

'She was up for shop lifting, here in Girne - twice as a teenager. The judge let her off on both cases. But the second time she was warned that, if she did it again, she would end up in a Young Persons' Institute. Her mother had been diagnosed with cancer at the time, so perhaps the judge felt sorry for her.'

'Was Uludag working at the station when this happened?'

'Yes. We were in the other building then, of course. These files were transferred up here with the rest. Perhaps that's why they were so difficult to find.'

Os grunted. If he had a daughter with a police record would he try to hide the paper work? He hoped not.

'Well, Fikri, after this success, perhaps you could have another look at the names we found in the ledger. Sener here, hasn't made any inroads yet and we're tied up with this funeral. You might come up with a different angle.'

Os grinned as he disconnected the call. There was nothing wrong with a bit of competition if it meant keeping Fikri on his toes. Most of the mourners had now left. As they walked towards their cars, Os told Sener the news.

'It doesn't make her a murderer though.'

Os agreed but the information was interesting nevertheless. The village car park was now full and they had to leave their car blocking two others.

'Hopefully, people won't want to get out in the next hour. If they do,' Os shrugged his shoulders, '...well they'll just have to come and find us.' He stopped by the open doorway of the bar. 'While I'm talking to the daughter, keep your eyes open for anybody who looks as if they might want to talk to us.' Os gave a wry smile. 'It's unlikely but you never know.'

Sener held the door open for his boss and the hum of conversation dipped as they walked in. The Islers stood by the unlit fire place talking to Mrs Assim. Os sensed that she saw him enter the room but she didn't acknowledge him.

'Tea, Inspector?' Hassan held out a metal tray, laden with small glasses of black tea.

Os took one, adding two sugar cubes to the hot brown liquid. The sergeant handed Hassan a sheet of paper. 'Do any of these names mean anything to you?'

Hassan took several seconds to read the list and then handed it back. 'Who are they?'

'People who might be able to help us in our enquiries.'

'I'm sorry, they mean nothing to me. Now if you'll excuse me I need to make sure everyone has what they need.' He moved away.

Os sipped his tea and looked around The people here were mainly elderly. The imams of Girne and Alsancak would have announced the funeral over the mosques microphones before the call to prayer. Funerals were popular meeting places. People gathered to pay their respects as well as taking up the chance to renew old acquaintances. Os wondered if the murderer was here, watching him grope around in the dark. The thought wasn't a good one. He watched Hassan bend over to talk to an elderly woman sitting in a corner of the room, her right foot resting on a low stool. He then moved away, leaving her with a fresh glass of tea.

'That must be Hassan's mother,' Os said. Their interest in Hassan's mother diminished with the approach of Nurten Isler and her husband.

Os smiled at the woman. Her hair was pulled tightly back from her face and hidden under a black, silk scarf. She had taken time to put on make-up. Unlike the shapeless garments of most of the elderly mourners, she wore a tailored black dress, while a heavy gold bangle hung on her wrist. This was not a woman struck down by grief. The husband appeared older than his wife, perhaps fifteen years older. He had provided refuge for a young woman running away from a difficult home, perhaps she had grown to love him.

She spoke quietly, her eyes, after meeting his fleetingly, remained cast down. 'I've been told that my father was murdered.'

'Does that surprise you, Mrs Isler?' Os asked.

'Of course! He was a difficult man but to be murdered?'

A silence hung between them. The husband, although still holding his wife's elbow, appeared to want no part in the conversation. From what Mrs. Assam had said, it was likely that he had never met his father-in-law. Os was interested in how she would answer his next question.

'When did you last see him?'

She squeezed her eyes shut momentarily as if the question gave her pain.

'Fifteen years ago but I kept in touch another way.'

'What do you mean?' Os asked.

Her voice inched louder. 'I knew that he wasn't ill and that he was managing to look after himself.'

'Through your conversations with Mrs Assim?'

She now looked up. He saw pain in her eyes before she pulled a handkerchief out of her dress pocket and blew her nose.

'Is this necessary?' The husband frowned at Os before putting his arm around his wife's shoulders.

'I'm sorry but I'm trying to understand how much your wife knew about her father's recent life. We need to get a picture of how he lived and the people he mixed with.' Os turned back to the wife. 'I appreciate this is a difficult time. We'll contact you in the next few days.'

Was she feeling guilty or was there another reason for her sudden distress? But here was not the time to interrogate her. His questions could wait. Still frowning, Mr. Isler reached into his inside suit pocket and pulled out his wallet. Os saw a flash of notes before a card was flicked out and the wallet closed.

'You can reach us there. We both work in the shop.'

Os took the business card. 'Thank you. Again, my condolences.'

They returned to the side of Mrs. Assim and Mrs. Isler bent down to whisper in the older woman's ear. Both women glanced across at the two policemen but seeing that they were being observed, they averted their gaze.

The two women seemed inordinately close if he was to believe that they had not seen each other for fifteen years. Had the relationship really only been kept alive through phone calls or were they both lying?

'We'll go now,' Os looked for somewhere to put his glass. 'There are not as many people here as I would've expected. He might have outlived some people but I wouldn't say he'd been a popular man. Would you?'

Sener shook his head. 'My grandfather died a few months ago. He was in his nineties but there were over a hundred people at his funeral and he hadn't been out of his house for the last five years.'

'Exactly! As his daughter admitted, he was a difficult man. But so are a lot of old men and they don't end up murdered.' Again Os looked across at the daughter who was now dabbing the corners of her eyes with the edge of a handkerchief.

'You didn't think it worthwhile asking her about the ledgers, sir?' Sener spoke indistinctively through a mouthful of pastry. Os was about to remind him that they were on duty then decided it wasn't a major issue.

Instead he answered, 'Tomorrow is soon enough - when she's at home, without an audience'.

'She doesn't seem desperate for money, sir. And she wouldn't have known about her father's money anyway if she hasn't talked to him for years. And even if she did know, why would she kill him if she was to inherit anyway?'

Os raised an eyebrow. 'What's enough money, Sener? Some people never have enough. We need to find out how well their business is doing. Perhaps they're not as well off as they seem. Look into that when you get back to the station. You can get me on the mobile if you need to. I'm going to check on how the search party is doing in a minute.'

'Another tea, Inspector, or something stronger?' Again Hassan was by their side and Os wondered how much the man had heard. The barman stared back innocently.

Os spoke more sharply than he intended. 'My sergeant will take a list of the names of the people here. I'm sure that all Mr Uludag's friends would want to help us find his killer!'

Hassan appeared unfased by the instruction and the manner in which it had been delivered. 'Of course. Anything I can do to help, Inspector.'

Os stared back, still unsure what to make of the man. 'Was Mr Uludag part of any organisation? He didn't collect funds for anything?'

For once, Hassan appeared genuinely surprised. 'Not that I know of. Why?'

'No reason.' Os made his farewells.

He turned left and then left again into the alleyway that ran up to Uludag's house. The lane was empty and he felt a flash of irritation that the constables had gone home but then he saw a streak of black above him in the trees. A policeman, he had before only acknowledged in the station corridors, was poking at the undergrowth with a stick.

'Have you found anything?'

The middle – aged man looked up. 'No sir. The others are up above. I'm down here so that I can keep an eye on the house.'

Although he knew that the station would have contacted him, Os still felt disappointed. It seemed increasingly likely that the stick had been destroyed. He thought again about the strange discovery of the forged police badge.

'You've been in the force for a long time, constable. Did you ever hear anything about Uludag wanting to join the force?'

The man shook his head. 'But I didn't know him to talk to, sir.'

'Well, keep searching until it goes dark and then if it doesn't turn up, we'll continue tomorrow as soon as it's light.'

Os glanced at his watch as he turned back down to the road. There was time for him to ring Fikri and have a swim before he and Roisin went out. He fingered the sheet of folded paper in his pocket. Someone must know who these people were and as soon as Os found out, it would be like pulling a loose thread from a jumper.

An Observers' Thoughts

The tea is good after standing so long over that man's grave. Call me a hypocrite if you want - I never liked him but then who did? I see his daughter is now crying. For what I wonder? She never bothered with him when he was alive. Not like my Handan. I couldn't manage without her calling in every day - and she's got a husband and my three grandchildren to look after. What's the point of having daughters if they're not going to look after you in your old age?

I wonder what that policeman wants now. I wasn't going to answer his questions about those two skeletons they found. Don't get involved, that's what I say. Greeks they'll be anyway. Nothing to do with us. I killed a few back in those days but never a woman. It didn't stop them murdering ours though - and children. I'd like to go up there and have a look but my old bones won't get up the hill. Maybe I can persuade my son–in–law to take me in that old car of his.

Chapter Eight

Os took out his mobile as he walked up the steps to the house. 'Any joy with the list of names, Fikri?'

'Sorry, sir, nothing yet.'

Again he felt disappointment although he knew that he was being unrealistic.

'Sener is on his way back to the station. I've asked him to look into the daughter's accounts. I want to know if everything about their business in Gazi Magusa is legit. I'd like you to help him.'

Fikri sounded suddenly cheerful. 'No problem. Do you want me to stay on for a few hours?'

Os grinned at the clumsy request for overtime. 'Better not. You can carry on tomorrow if necessary.'

He broke the connection and used his key to open the front door. All was quiet. He paused then walked along the corridor to the study. Roisin looked up from her desk and smiled.

'Hi. You're early!'

'I was in Endremit.'

'Lovely! Just let me finish and I'll come through and make us a drink.'

Os was sitting at the table, the photo-copied ledger sheets in front of him, when Roisin came out. She set down a tea tray.

She came to stand behind him, putting her hands on his shoulders. She kissed the top of his head and he reached up to squeeze her right hand.

'What are you looking at?'

'These payments. Look.' Os tapped the list of numbers with his pen. 'He collected over a thousand Turkish Lira every month. Not a huge fortune but strange nevertheless.' He pulled out a chair so that Roisin would sit down. 'I asked Hassan about it, but he didn't know of anything that the old man was involved in.'

Roisin slid the sheets of paper towards her. After a few minutes, she looked up at Os and smiled.

'It's obvious. This is a book of silence.'

'What do you mean?'

She grinned. 'He was taking bribes.'

Os stared at her as the reality sunk in. 'I think you're right. Because so little money was withdrawn, I assumed that the money wasn't his own. But this makes more sense. If we could only find out who these people are,' Os cupped his hands around his mug of tea, '…then we might find the killer. That's if it's not the daughter.'

Os told her about the funeral and his conversation with Mrs. Isler. Roisin looked down again at the sheets of accounts.

'I wonder if his neighbours had any idea what a complicated life he led. It doesn't sound as if the money made him happy.'

'You're right there. You'd have thought that he'd fallen on hard times if you'd seen his house. You wonder why he bothered if he wasn't interested in spending it.'

'Perhaps for power or revenge.'

'What do you mean?' Os wished he could have a cigarette. It would be the perfect moment, sitting out in the fresh air, mulling over a case with the woman he loved. But he knew that it if he was to light up, the mood would be broken.

'He used to be a porter at the police station. It's not exactly a high powered job, is it? At the beck and call of everyone.

Perhaps he resented it. How many times do you talk to the porters apart from telling them to do something for you? Do you ever ask them anything personal?'

He thought her criticism unfair. 'I haven't time to ask everyone about how they're feeling. I've got a job to do.'

'Do you ask Fikri or Sener about themselves or their family?'

'Of course! They're my sergeants.'

'There you are then. Perhaps it was to get back at people like you.'

Os flushed. 'That's ridiculous.'

Roisin smiled. 'I'm not criticizing you - I'm just trying to get you to see things from his perspective - to understand his anger.'

Os sighed. 'He must have passed himself off as a policeman when he first contacted these people. I'll get the lads to see if they can cross reference the names with our police records. It would have been easy for him to search through police files for suitable victims. Apparently, he liked to work nights which gave him the perfect opportunity.' Os picked up his watch from the table. 'It's five thirty. We're supposed to be there in an hour, you know.'

Roisin swore and fled to the bathroom. Os grinned. He knew that they would never be ready to leave in thirty minutes but there were worse things than being a little late. He peeled the paper from a stick of chewing gum and placed it in his mouth. What Roisin had said was interesting. He thought about calling Sener then decided against it. There was plenty of time tomorrow. He went into the kitchen, took a bottle of Yakut and one of Angora from the wine rack and left them by the front door. Then he went to change.

As predicted, they were quarter of an hour late but the traffic into Girne was light. They left the car near the harbour and, holding hands, walked through the narrow streets that led down to the Saris's harbour apartment. Os rang the doorbell.

Cassey opened the wide, wooden door. She was a tall, slim woman in her thirties. Tonight she was wearing her long blonde hair in a high pony tail, fastened with a bow, the colour of her dark, green dress. Her bare feet were visible under the floor length hem and a thick, silver bangle glinted above her elbow. Green beads, on the end of long silver stalks, hung from her ears.

Roisin leaned forward and kissed her on both cheeks. 'It's lovely to see you, Cassey.'

The hostess stepped aside so that her guests could enter. Os loved this apartment. It was old, with wooden beams and parquet floors. The front door opened straight into a galley type kitchen which led into a sitting room and dining area. The French windows faced out over Girne harbour. Aka stood at the dining table opening a bottle of champagne. He came towards them and kissed first Roisin, then Os, on both cheeks.

Roisin crossed the room to the French windows. 'Can we sit outside?'

'You three talk together. I've got things to do in the kitchen,' Cassey replied.

Os could see that Roisin was tempted to follow Cassey but then she changed her mind. Instead she went outside and sat down on one of the metal chairs, propping her feet up on the wooden slats of the balcony. Aka passed her a glass of champagne. He was a similar build to Cassey, tall and slim but unlike his wife, his skin and hair were dark.

Os sat next to her and looked down at the scene below. Dusk had fallen and the lights of the restaurants glowed. A trickle of tourists sauntered along the pavement while waiters called out, trying to entice them to sit down. About a quarter of the tables were occupied. Aka sat down on the third chair and began to talk about football. Os dragged his eyes away and gave his friend his full attention.

'We're ready to eat, you guys.'

The three of them stood up and went back in to the apartment. A large, orange striped, tagine bowl and a steaming mound of couscous had been placed in the middle of the table.

'From your last holiday?' Roisin asked.

'Aka moaned the whole way home about having to carry it in his hand luggage.'

Aka shrugged good naturedly and held out a chair for Roisin.'So how's the book coming on?'

'Slowly. I'm not used to all these distractions - the sun shining - a live-in lover - my own private swimming pool.' Roisin began to spoon food onto her plate. 'Has Os told you about our bit of excitement?'

Os sat back in his chair and watched her talk. She glowed tonight. She felt at ease here, unlike when she was at his parents' house. It helped of course that these friends were so similar to themselves. He wondered whether Cassey felt as, 'at home' with Aka's family as she appeared. He tuned back into the conversation.

'But if the government doesn't do something about the builders here, there won't be any scenery to admire. It's criminal. Are the politicians on backhanders or what?' Roisin's voice had become strident.

Os glared across at her. It annoyed him when she criticised his country, especially in front of other North Cypriots, even if they were friends.

Aka's voice was quiet but Os heard annoyance there. 'You're right, it's not good but don't kid yourself that greed is the prerogative of the Turkish Cypriots. We're new to the game. Britain isn't exactly blameless in that quarter. They've been taking what they wanted ever since the days of the Raj. And we won't even start on the Iraqi war.'

Roisin held up her hands in surrender. 'All right, all right. I know you've got a point. I just can't bear to see beautiful scenery destroyed.' She smiled across at Cassey. 'You're very quiet. You're not rushing to my defence?'

Cassey shrugged her narrow shoulders. 'I wouldn't dare. Americans can't complain about other countries destroying things for a quick buck. We're the experts.' She smiled at her guests. 'Now, who wants seconds?'

They ate cheese and fruit afterwards and then when Cassey had made coffee she turned to Roisin, 'Let's take ours outside. I've put out a couple of pashminas in case it's gone cold. '

Os watched the two women leave the room.

The phone rang and when Aka answered it, he mouthed across to Os, 'Sorry, it's work.'

Os picked up his glass and went to sit on one of the sofas. He closed his eyes and listened to the music that drifted from the bars below up through the open windows. He could smell the Jasmine plant that Cassey had threaded through the metal trellis of the balcony.

'Do you miss England, Roisin?'

Os strained to hear her answer.

'At the moment, not at all. Everything is so new and exciting still. What about you?'

'Sometimes. If it wasn't for Aka I'd go home - if only for a few months. I miss my family.' A pause, perhaps to drink her wine. 'But I couldn't leave Aka. He doesn't want to live in the States - I can't blame him after Iraq.'

'How do you get on with his mother?'

Os guessed where this was going.

'Fine. Her English isn't good but I'm taking Turkish lessons. In the beginning she was worried about me being American - now she's happy because Aka's happy.' A pause. 'How are things with Os's mother?'

Os wondered whether he should move and then decided that he wanted to hear her answer. He heard a mixture of sadness and annoyance in Roisin's voice.

'Not brilliant. I know some of it's my fault. I should take Turkish lessons.' A clink of glass on glass as someone filled their glass. 'She's such a controlling woman. I have a feeling that she resents me.'

'So why do you think any of this is your fault?' said Cassey.

Roisin's sigh was so loud that for a moment Os thought she had moved back inside the room.

'I suppose I've dug my heels in. I'm convinced she disapproves, so instead of trying to win her around - I have little to do with her. I know it upsets Os.'

Cassey spoke so quietly that Os had to strain to hear her.

'Do you think it would make any difference if you did a bit of crawling?'

Roisin sighed again. 'I really don't know and that's the problem. It seems a waste of time if, at the end of it all, she still thinks me not good enough for her darling boy.'

'I suppose it all depends on whether you two are going to get married. If not, then what does it matter? But you'll have to develop a strategy if you're serious about him.'

Os decided he had listened long enough and went in search of the toilet. When he returned, Aka was off the phone and was using the excuse, of the women being outside, to watch Istanbul against Frankfurt. He sat down next to his friend, glad that only conversation about football was required.

Os pushed Buddy Holly's, 'Greatest Hits' into the car CD player. Roisin sat back in the front seat, her eyes closed. Internally he re-ran the conversation he had overheard earlier. He hadn't realised that his mother affected Roisin as much as she did. He reached across to take her hand but she had fallen asleep. He turned on his mobile. There was one message from Sener. Os heard the excitement in the man's voice as he relayed the news that they had found something interesting about the Islers.

A daughter's thoughts.

If only I hadn't done it. If it was just for Massoud and me, we could have managed but the children.......

We were doing so well until the break-in. The little ones are used to their school and it's such a good one - far better than the state school they would have gone to. I can't bare the thought of those huge classes and no aircon. How can they concentrate when it's thirty degrees? They are having such a good education - perhaps Tayyip will be a doctor eventually. Mother would have been so proud.

But I'm frightened of the policeman. And what did my father know about those skeletons they found? Or was he just trying to make himself appear important- like he always did.

Chapter Nine

Os arrived at the station at seven thirty the next morning. He stopped a porter on the corridor and asked him to bring coffee to his office. Remembering what Roisin had said, he considered asking him about the health of his family but then stopped himself. He didn't even know the man.

A buff folder had been left on his desk. It was a breakdown of the bank statements of the Islers and the written reports of the people Fikri had interviewed in Endremit. One of the neighbours had seen a woman with a head scarf enter Uludag's house using her own key. Os became so engrossed that he didn't notice the porter until the coffee cup was pushed across his desk. He made an effort to look up and smile at the man before turning back to his reading.

Sener had worked hard, perhaps with Fikri's help. It appeared that the Islers were not as well off as they appeared. The sergeants had also contacted Gazi Magusa and found that the Islers had reported a robbery three months ago .The carpet shop had been broken into and according to the couple, 600,000 T.L. worth of carpets had been stolen. The business hadn't been insured.

Os shook his head though he knew through his own crime investigations that this wasn't uncommon. Because of the past low crime rate, business people still seemed to think it wasn't necessary to invest in insurance.

He stared out of his window. Unlike Atak's, the view was of the car park but he wasn't complaining - it was luxury to have an office of his own. His mind flashed back to a recent report on a series of robberies in the Gazi Magusa area, and in particular one gang, thought to be targeting lucrative businesses. The robberies were planned when a particular ship was scheduled to leave port. After a tip off last month, the customs had stopped a cargo ship destined for Syria but the search came up with nothing. Os supposed it was like looking for a needle in a haystack. The size of stolen goods was tiny compared to that of the cargo they were hidden amongst. But it was a new crime, and no doubt Gazi Magusa were under tremendous pressure to arrest the ring leaders.

Perhaps he would drive out to the Islers' this morning and have a little chat. He took their business card out of his wallet and studied it. He would surprise them, he decided. Meanwhile, Sener and Fikri could go back to the house of the old man and do another search. They might have missed some information on the identity of these people that Roisin was so sure were being blackmailed. If so, they would have something else to work on. There was also the matter of the murder weapon. He picked up the phone to contact Sener at home. When he had finished, he keyed in the number of his own house. Well, not his, he corrected himself, Roisin's. She answered after several rings.

'How do you fancy a drive over to Gazi Magusa?'

A short silence hung between them.

'All right. What's the occasion?'

'I'm going to visit the Islers. We've discovered something interesting about them, something I can't deal with over the phone. I thought we could have lunch afterwards in the café you like.' When she didn't answer, he added, 'I won't feel so guilty about working at the weekend then.'

He could hear the smile in her voice.

'What time are you going?'

He glanced at his watch. 'Can you make it down here for ten? I'll drive.' Os's smile faded as he disconnected the line. He would have to talk to the Commandant before he left.

The station was busier than when he had arrived an hour ago. He ran down the stairs to the ground floor, acknowledging colleagues on the way. This time Atak's door was closed. Os grimaced. He would have to go through the man's secretary, Miss Ure. He knocked on the adjoining office and opened the door. A woman in her fifties sat at her computer.

'Is the Chief Commandant available?' Os knew that she disapproved if her boss wasn't given his proper title and her disapproval was shown in a variety of ways; one being to successfully block an interview with the great man.

'I'll ring through and see if he has time for you,' she answered, without smiling.

Os crossed to the window and watched her surreptitiously. She was one of the few females who worked in the station and had been with Atak for as long as the man had been eligible to have his own secretary. She had never married. Os suspected that the Commandant, though happily married, appreciated her adoration and determination to protect him from the irritations of the outside world.

'He will see you now.' She gave a thin smile and returned to her computer. Os smiled back with as much charm as he was able, noticing that her hair needed re-touching at the roots. He opened the adjoining door.

As usual, Atak had piles of papers spread across his desk. He recapped his fountain pen and placed it in front of him. 'Good morning Osman, what can I do for you?'

'I've come to keep you up to date with the Uludag case sir.'

To his surprise Atak's big face creased into a smile. 'Excellent. I was just going to have a coffee. Would you like to join me?'

'Thank you, sir.' Os sat down in the offered chair. The man seemed in an ebullient mood. Atak laced his hands together over his stomach.

'Right, Osman, tell me what's been happening.'

Os continued talking when the secretary re-appeared, placing cups of black coffee in front of the two men. Atak took a sip then smacked his thick lips together.

'Well, you seem to be on top of things. I shall tell the same to the General when I meet him for lunch. Who would you put your money on? Still the daughter?'

'She's certainly got a motive. They appear to have serious money problems and she hated her father. But, if we're right about Uludag taking bribes, then the murderer could be any one of the victims.'

Atak nodded. 'Well, get on with it then, Osman, and keep me informed.'

Os was grinning as he left the room. The Commandant's over-riding interest in his lunchtime appointment had made the meeting very easy. He checked his watch then went in search of Fikri. He found him in the sergeants' room. Os told him to join Sener up at Endremit village.

'I'll be back from Gazi Magusa by three at the latest so we'll meet in my office then.' He was pleased to see that Fikri was already gathering his jacket and keys as he spoke. Os left him to it.

Roisin was waiting by the passenger door of his car. She was dressed in a light green, linen dress with her hair twisted up on her head. Long earrings hung from her ears and she'd even bothered with lipstick.

'You look lovely,' he said, flashing a smile. 'Wait for me to put on the aircon before you get in.'

'Why do you think I'm still standing out here? You never lock your car door,' she quipped.

He grinned as he turned on the engine. She was always amazed at how casual the Northern Cypriots were over security. He had locked his apartment in Lefkosa but never his car. He had once asked her where she thought thieves would take his car, the island was so small? But now, after this spate of burglaries in Gazi Magusa, perhaps he shouldn't be so complacent. He decided to mention his mother's invitation.

'What about lunch at my parents tomorrow?'

He waited a few seconds before accepting that she was going to say no, she always did. Even when she agreed to visit, it was done with bad grace. In many ways it was easier to go on his own, he acknowledged. At least he could relax - they could all talk in Turkish. Although his father was fluent, his mother's understanding of the English language was basic. But he knew his parents were hurt that Roisin preferred to stay at home and he hated leaving her when they had the opportunity to be together. He would have to go though and his mind trawled the variety of excuses he could use for her absence. The last three times he had said that she was behind with her work but that one was wearing a bit thin. She would have to be ill.

'All right.'

He took his eyes off the road to stare at her.

'Are you sure?'

'I haven't been for ages - I ought to make an effort.'

A lorry blasted him and Os realised that he had swerved into the other lane. He righted the wheel and stared ahead.

'Good! They'll be pleased to see you. My father is very fond of you' Surprisingly Roisin didn't say anything about his mother and Os decided not to chance his luck. 'If we leave the house at twelve, will that be all right with you?'

'Fine.'

He turned on the radio and the music of a sixties band filled the car. Fifty minutes after leaving the station, he parked the car in a place just outside the walls of the old town.

'Do you think you'll be able to find that café where we went last time?' he asked as they walked through the narrow streets.

'It's round the corner from the mosque.' Her mouth twitched. 'It's a pity I can't come with you. I might notice something that you don't.'

'It's unprofessional.' She pouted. He relented.

'Follow me into the shop if you want and have a look around. But nothing more. I'll meet you in the café afterwards'. She grinned at him and Os tried not to think of what Atak would say if he ever found out.

The shop faced a small square. One of the windows displayed leather, embroidered slippers, tablecloths and embroidered bed linen; while in the other, a carpet in muted browns hung from a pole. Until the break-in, it appeared as if the Islers' had done well. Os pushed open the door. A young woman folded cushion covers at the counter. Mr Isler was with a customer. He looked across at Os and recognising the policeman, flushed. He said something to the man next to him and then called the young assistant across. He had just joined Os, when the shop door opened. Os didn't turn around to look at who had followed him in.

'I'd like a few words with you and your wife.'

Irritation flashed across the older man's face. 'She's upstairs. It's very difficult for me to leave the shop. The girl is very inexperienced and I can't afford to lose any business.'

As if to emphasise how busy he was, he nodded in the direction of the newcomer. Os turned around and saw a red haired woman in a green dress sorting though some tablecloths.

'I understand,' Os purred. 'I'm sure your wife can answer my questions. Just a few details about her father. Nothing serious.' Os could see that the man was torn between being protective and losing the prospect of making some money.

'I'll ring up and see how she is,' he said and moved to the counter where a phone was attached to the wall. He spoke too quietly for Os to hear but after a couple of minutes he put the phone down.

'She says that she'll see you on her own. But please, be careful. She is far more upset than she appears.' He indicated a door at the back of the shop and when Os opened it, he saw stairs leading up to the next floor.

Nurten Isler stood at the entrance to her apartment. He was surprised that she was still wearing the black of mourning, considering what he understood her feelings for her father to be. There were newly formed black circles under her eyes and her long hair was tied back in the same unflattering style he'd seen before. Today she wore no make-up.

'Please, come in?' Her eyes fluttered to meet his and then slipped away to focus on some aspect of the furniture behind him.

The rooms of the first floor had been knocked into one, allowing a sitting, dining and kitchen area. Os supposed the bedrooms were on the floor above. He accepted the seat she offered him, noting the dirty dishes in the kitchen area and the clothes piled up on the back of chairs. Was it an indicator of her distress or a family trait? The mess wasn't so dissimilar from her father's house, though hers was far cleaner. She sat down opposite him, twisting the ring on her left hand.

He spoke gently. 'We're having difficulty understanding something. We're hoping that you would be able to help us. Your father had amassed a large amount of money over the last few years - strange considering what he earned as a porter.'

She stood up and walked into the kitchen area, opening the fridge to take out a jug. She poured water into a glass and then returned to her seat. He watched her sipping for a few seconds, her eyes fixed on the tiled floor. Os wondered how she managed with customers if she was unable to make eye contact.

'I've already told you, I haven't been in contact with my father for years. I know nothing about his finances. Mrs Assim told me that he'd taken on a few gardens, for people in the village, since he retired - but I shouldn't think that would bring in the kind of money you're talking about.'

It was interesting that she hadn't reacted to his mention of money. But he was suddenly irritated by her behaviour. He spoke more harshly that he had intended.

'We think your father could have been taking bribes and this might have been the reason he was murdered.'

This time he was sure she wasn't acting; horror filled her face before she could pull it blank again. She spoke haltingly as if she had difficulty believing him.

'I know my father had a dark side to him - I saw it enough with my mother but a blackmailer?' She shook her head as if to come to terms with such news. 'I wouldn't have thought he was capable of it.'

If she was genuinely shocked then he felt sorry for her; it could not be easy to find out that your father had been extorting money. He wondered how he would feel but then the idea of his gentle father even considering such an activity was ludicrous.

He returned to what she had just said.

'You mean not capable of extorting money or not having the ability to do it?' he asked.

'Oh, he had it in him, he was a very angry man. But I didn't think he would have had the courage to bribe people.'

'Courage?'

For the first time she looked him full in the face. 'My father always liked to be thought well of by people outside the family. He could be very charming when he wanted to.' She went quiet as if thinking over what she had just said, as if the analysis of her parent was new to her. 'I'd have thought he would have been too frightened of other people finding out. That was why he was always careful where he hit my mother.'

Os felt sympathy for the woman nearing middle age, who clearly was still affected by the horrors of her childhood. He waited while she took a hankie from the pocket of her apron and blew her nose.

'You said he was angry.'

She sighed, as if this was a story she had told many times. 'He was an unwanted child. His mother had a relationship with a married man which ended when she became pregnant.

She was training to be a nurse in Lefkosa and he was one of the consultants.' She took another sip of water. 'He wanted her to go to one of those back street abortionists where they rip your insides out but she refused. Instead she went back to her village but you can imagine the reception she got.' She looked at him. When he nodded his understanding, she continued. 'Her parents allowed her back but they never forgave her for bringing shame on the family. Once my father found out why he was different,' she sighed again, '…I think he never forgave her either. I assume that's why he had no respect for women. As I said, he could be very charming. My mother only saw the violent side of him after she married him.'

'So he didn't like women?' Os thought back to the names in the ledgers.

She stood up and began to pace the room, obviously agitated. 'I wouldn't say that. It was more that he liked to have power over them. I don't know if you've been told , but he had an affair with a woman in the village for several years when I was a child - he made sure my mother knew about that.' Her bitterness after all these years could not have been more evident.'She didn't go out much in the end. I did the shopping for her and Mrs Assim would come and visit when my father was at work. They had been friends since they were children.' She took out a handkerchief and dabbed her eyes. 'I know she died because she just didn't want to live anymore. She didn't try to fight the cancer.' Her shoulders slumped and she gulped several mouthfuls of water.

He passed her a sheet of paper. 'Does this list mean anything to you?'

She looked down at the names. He watched closely but after a few seconds she handed the sheet back, her voice dull. 'I'm sorry. They could be anyone. I can't help you.' She flushed before she added, 'I know that this will sound dreadful but if you find out who these people are, will the police give them back the money that's in my father's account?'

At last, a reference to why he was sure Uludag had been murdered.

'I can't say at this stage. It depends on the courts.'

Again she stared at him. 'You know about our robbery. If it was just myself and my husband, it wouldn't be so bad but there are my children's school fees.' Her voice broke. 'The money would solve our problems,'

The sympathy he had felt a few minutes before was replaced with distaste. However much this woman disliked her father, there were similarities between them. She was quite prepared to spend his ill-acquired money.

'When was the last time you visited your father, Mrs Isler?'

'When I was married - fifteen years ago.'

If Fikri hadn't interviewed the British, retired, school teacher, Os might have believed her.

'His neighbour saw you coming out of the house the day before he died. It was dark and you were wearing a headscarf. But the description fits you, I'm afraid.' She flushed. 'So why the lie?'

'I went to see him.' She shrugged as if accepting that it was time to now tell the truth. 'He's old. I'm his only daughter. With all these tourists buying up property, his house should be worth a lot now. I didn't want him leaving it to someone else or the state taking it.' She stared at him as if daring him to criticise her. 'I wouldn't have gone if it was just for me but he has grandchildren he's never seen. I took photos with me to show him. That was one thing he had a soft spot for, children. My father was good to me when I was a child - I just hated him for how he treated my mother.'

'So what did your father say to you?'

'He wasn't there. I still had the key - so I went inside to wait. It took me over an hour to get there and I wasn't sure if I could make myself go back.' She stood up and walked back into the kitchen area. 'I started to poke around - I suppose I wanted to see if there was anything left belonging to me or my mother. That was when I came across the bank books. I knew something was wrong when I saw them. He could never have saved that kind of money.' She took the jug of water out of the fridge. 'I was scared so I left.'

Os stared at her hunched shoulders. 'Why didn't you tell me this before?'

She turned around and glared at him. 'Would you have believed me? My father has been murdered and I'm the person who will benefit.' She stood silently for a few seconds then, as if puzzled, asked, 'Are you going to arrest me then?'

He shook his head. 'But I expect you to remain here so that I can get in touch with you.'

Tears, real or fabricated flooded her eyes. 'I didn't murder my father. I often wanted to but I didn't.'

Os stared, still unsure of his opinion of the woman. 'You've got my number. I'll leave you with the list of names. Ring me if anyone comes to mind. Obviously, it will help your case if we can find out who these people he was blackmailing were.' He left her staring at the sheet of paper.

As he expected, Roisin was no longer in the shop. The husband was now serving a group of British tourists. Os nodded his thanks and the two men's eyes locked before he opened the door and left.

He turned right and hurried along the cobbles in the direction of the café. Glancing at his watch he saw that he had been with Nurten Isler for an hour. Ahead of him he saw wicker tables and chairs on the pavement. Roisin was sat with her back to him, reading a newspaper, a cup of Nescafe in front of her. He bent down and kissed the back of her neck.

Chapter Ten

'What discoveries did you make then?' he asked, after they had both ordered.

'Not a great deal. I had a look through the rugs but there wasn't much of a selection. A few people came in and bought cheaper things - like tablecloths and wooden bowls.' Roisin rested her sandaled feet on another chair. 'The shop appears to be popular. How did your interview go?'

Os told her what had happened.

'Could she have killed her father?'

He took a bite of his sandwich. The cheese was hot and he had to wave his hand in front of his mouth to cool it down.

'There's a ruthlessness in her that I think would make her capable of anything- especially to do with protecting her children. It'll be interesting to see whether she contacts me over the list of names I left her.'

'So what are you going to do next?' Roisin asked.

'After we've finished this, we'll go back.'

'Okay, I'll get on with some work this afternoon, but we'd better stop and buy some meat on the way back to the car.'

Os caught the waiter's eye and ordered two coffees. He brought the conversation around to the book she was writing and they sat in the midday sun, happy in each others company. It was when the call for prayer drifted over from the mosque that Os got to his feet and picked up her bags.

'I don't want those two going off early because they think I'm not coming back.'

They walked back through the ancient, cobbled streets, stopping to buy steak from a butcher's shop which used refrigerated, glass cabinets to keep away the flies. An hour later in the Girne police car park, he saw her to her car and waited until she had driven away.

Fikri and Sener were in the canteen smoking. Both had empty coffee cups in front of them and Sener was laughing at something in the newspaper. Irritation slashed across his stomach.

'You two got nothing better to do?' Os derived some pleasure from the speed Sener closed the paper and stood up. 'I'd like a meeting in my office in five minutes time.'

He wasn't sure why he was so irritated. He'd had a semi-productive morning and a very pleasurable lunch with Roisin. But they had come to a dead end. He suspected that it might take some time to find the people on Uludag's list and the longer it took, the less likely they were to find the murderer. To be fair to Atak, he had left him on his own for now; but as this was his first murder case - if he didn't make some progress, they could easily replace him with someone from Lefkosa who was more experienced. He reached into the drawer and took out the packet of cigarettes. He had just lit up when his two sergeants entered the room.

'Sit down,' he said and squinted at them over the circling smoke. 'I take it you didn't find anything?' Smiles spread across the men's faces. Os suddenly forgot his need for nicotine. 'Go on. Tell me.'

Fikri leant forward and placed two typed sheets on his boss's desk. 'I think you'll find these interesting. They were under a pile of old bills in a box under the spare bed. We only got back half an hour ago - it took us that long to search the house.'

Os heard the criticism in Fikri's tone. He pulled the police reports towards him. One was ten years old and the other dated two years later. The first belonged to Sevgul Gul, who had been picked up for soliciting in the old town area of Lefkosa. It had happened twice and the courts had fined her, threatening to put her behind bars if she was seen again. Her address was in the village of Karsiyaka and she had been nineteen years old at the time. She would be twenty nine now, possibly married and moved away. But it was a start. Os began to feel his sergeants' excitement.

The second sheet was on Erim Gorus. It was a photocopy of a report made by the Istanbul police. How Uludag had got hold of it Os couldn't imagine. Eight years ago he had been taken to court in Istanbul, for supposedly interfering with a young boy. The police assumed they had a definite conviction and then the boy's family withdrew their accusation.

'He owns one of the biggest car hire companies in Northern Cyprus, sir,' Sener said in response to the puzzlement on Os's face.

Os suddenly recalled the name he'd often seen associated with highly advertised social events. The man was often pictured with a middle-aged woman, attractive still and always expensively dressed. But when he had seen Uludag's list of names three days ago, he had not imagined that they were the same person. They had now identified two names which left three still a mystery.

'You've done well - is there anything else?'

Fikri spoke and this time criticism was replaced by eagerness. 'We think we've found the murder weapon, sir. It's with forensics now.'

Adrenalin surged through his body. Os leaned forward in his seat. 'Where?'

'It had been thrown into the undergrowth in the land above the house. Most of the blood had been wiped off - fingerprints too, probably. But some of the blood had seeped into the cracks in the wood.'

'The walking stick?'

Both sergeants nodded. The three of them sat in silence for a few seconds.

Then Fikri asked, 'How did you get on with the daughter, Sir?'

Os related what had happened above the shop. 'I'm going to see Hassan on the way home – find out who the old man gardened for. I'm convinced he has his finger on the pulse as far as the village is concerned. It's just getting him to talk. Otherwise I could ask the old woman - Mrs Assim. I'm sure she knows a lot more about the Uludag family than she's letting on.' He opened his drawer and took out the police badge.

Sener picked it up. 'It's quite a good forgery. If this was shoved in someone's face - they wouldn't know any difference. I wonder where he had it made?'

'Lefkosa I should think.' Os answered. 'At least we know now how he did it. Passing himself off as a detective is a little more intimidating than a porter.'

'What about Gorus and Gul Sir?' Sener asked.

Os stood up, hoping that the movement would help his thinking process. 'Sener - you find the telephone number of this businessman and give him a call. If you get hold of him, we'll go around there straight away.' He turned to Fikri, 'And you look into whether Sergul Gul is still Gul or whether she's married. We need her address. I'll be here for another half hour, then you'll be able to reach me on my mobile.'

The two sergeants left the room. Os took out his handkerchief and mopped his brow. Was it getting warmer, or was the excitement, that they were making some progress, affecting him? He pushed the window as far open as possible and stood staring out to the patch of sea that was visible between two apartment blocks. On an ordinary Saturday afternoon he would have suggested to Roisin that they went down to the beach for a swim but there was no time for that now. He turned back to his desk. With what was unfolding, he would be lucky if he managed to get to Lefkosa at all tomorrow.

He reached into his drawer and took out the photographs of the crime scene. Pushing his other papers aside, he dealt the photographs like a pack of cards until he found the enlargements of the head wound. Could this be done by a woman, he wondered? There was no reason why not. Uludag was a man in his late sixties. As the pathologist had said, his skull had thinned considerably over the years. It wouldn't have needed a great deal of strength as long as the instrument was solid. Os touched the face. It was impossible to read any expression in the blank eyes. Did Uludag know his killer? Os was assuming that he did. It was highly unlikely the murder had been speculative. Had the old man kept money in the house? A lot of elderly people didn't trust the banks. But that wasn't the case with Uludag; he had saved far more than Os could ever imagine doing himself. A potential thief might have killed Uludag if he or she had been disturbed going through the old man's belongings. But no, it was more likely that this murder had been planned.

Uludag knew his killer but whether it was his daughter or one of the victims, Os still had to find out. And what was the connection to the bones on the hillside? A knock on the door broke his line of thought. Sener put his head around the door.

'What news?' Os asked.

'I rang Gorus's office and spoke to his secretary. Apparently he's in Istanbul until Tuesday, sir.'

'I don't suppose we can have everything going our way today. What did you say you were calling about?'

Pan faced, Sener replied, 'I didn't think you'd want me to give him prior warning, sir - so I said I was the traffic police.'

Os smiled. 'You'll come with me when I interview him. Give Fikri a hand with the Gul woman now before you finish for the day.' Os pushed back his chair and stretched. 'Since

I can't see Gorus, I'll get off to Endremit. I'll carry on home afterwards but call me if you find anything.' Os slipped on his jacket and patted Sener on the arm as they both left the office. 'I'll see you on Monday. Have a good weekend- what's left of it anyway.'

As usual the traffic was bumper to bumper along the upper ring-road of town. Music blared out of the Mercedes in front of him. The young man had the soft top down and was oblivious to the fact that other drivers might not be appreciating the hard rock that was emanating from his speakers. Os stared idly at the shops that had sprung up on either side of the road. Five years ago, shopping had been so limited that anyone with money would fly to Istanbul - otherwise they would drive to Lefkosa. But now, that was no longer necessary. The Mercedes in front and the vast variety of merchandise in the shops was a sign that there was a lot more money in the country. Os glanced in the rear mirror and realised that he was frowning. Whether the new wealth was a good thing, he wasn't sure. Certainly, five years ago traffic jams didn't exist and murder had been an extremely rare event.

Were the people happier now, he asked himself? Certainly the ex-pat community wasn't. He only had to read their newspaper, 'Cyprus Today,' to find out how they felt. They had escaped to what they had thought was a piece of Mediterranean paradise, to find that Northern Cyprus was catching up with the rest of the world. He had to agree with some of their moans. Concrete structures were going up everywhere, slashing into the countryside, destroying the natural beauty Northern Cyprus had been so famous for.

But there also wasn't the infrastructure to support such a vast programme. The builders were becoming very rich, as were probably some of the politicians but now there were several power cuts a week. Sometimes they were without electricity for hours. And the water shortage was another thing. Last week, he and Roisin had been without for three days. They had been forced to flush the toilet with water from the swimming pool and his wash in the morning had been a swim. Yes, they had run out of water as a child but there was a well in his parents' garden so it had never been a problem. But he couldn't remember such a shortage of electricity, ever.

At last the congestion ahead eased and the Mercedes moved forward. At the roundabout the car in front turned off to the right and Os relaxed now that the bass guitar wasn't pounding his ears. A few minutes later he saw the sign for Endremit and the road that wound up to Karaman and home.

Hassan was inside, talking to a man at the bar. He glanced across at Os, his expression blank. 'A drink, Inspector?'

Os went to stand at the far end. 'An Efes beer.' It was the end of the day and in a few minutes he would be going home.

Hassan placed a bottle and a glass on the counter. 'How are your investigations going?'

'We're making progress,' Os answered. 'But I need your help again.'

Hassan showed no response as he picked up a glass from a shelf and began to polish it.

'How well did you know Kutlay Uludag?'

'It's a small village. He's lived here all my life.' He flicked the towel and continued to rub the already shining glass. 'He was older than me of course.'

Os wiped the neck of the opened bottle, drank from it then rubbed the back of his hand across his mouth. 'Any idea who he gardened for?'

'He was a tough old bugger. He had more energy than a lot of these young ones.' Hassan's eyes narrowed. 'You don't think one of the people he worked for killed him, do you?'

Os shook his head. 'We're only trying to get a full picture of the man. What I don't understand is why anyone should want to kill someone his age, who had so little.'

'He did all right did Kutlay. He must have saved when he was working as a porter and of course he had those jobs on the side. He laid those new marble steps last year. I heard he paid the builders in cash.' Os wondered whether he could hear resentment or admiration in Hassan's voice. 'The first bit of extravagance I've seen with him. He was never one to throw money about.' His eyes widened. 'Perhaps he kept a hoard of money in the house and someone knew about it.'

'It hardly seems worth killing an old man for a few thousand Lira. I shouldn't think on his salary, however frugal he was, he would be able to save much.'

Hassan ran his thumb and forefinger down his greying moustache but didn't make any further comment. Os waited for further observations but there were none. Eventually he opened his notebook.

'Can you give me the names?'

Hassan shrugged as if implying that it was not information that he felt necessary to keep secret from the policeman. 'He had three houses that he'd been going to for years. Two were in Karaman village and one was that big house on the curve of the road down there. Hassan pointed in the direction that Os had come from. 'The white house with the swimming pool. Nadir, who owns the yard in Karalangalou that provides wood, paint and everything for building, lives there.' The barman winked. 'He's got a very attractive young wife.'

'What about the two in Karaman?'

'If you go to the top of the village, there's a large house with a black door and shutters. It has a garden sloping down to the metal fencing. It's owned by a retired English man. I think he was an officer in the British army.' Hassan grinned. 'No beautiful young wife there, I'm afraid.'

Os wondered why Hassan had never married since he appeared so interested in women. 'And the third?' he asked.

'Next to that house. Two sisters - German. They've been there for years. Very nice women. They come in here sometimes which is more that I can say for a lot of them.'

Hassan pursed his lips to show his disapproval, of people who didn't support businesses that were practically on their door step. Os slid his pad and pen back in his jacket pocket and finished off his beer.

'Thank you, sir, you've been very helpful.'

'The sooner you catch whoever did in old Uludag, the better. None of us feel safe in our beds at the moment, especially old women like Mrs Assim.'

'I can understand that - thanks for the drink.'

Os turned as he reached the door and saw the other customer move over to where he himself had stood a few seconds ago. Nosy bugger, he thought, but then who could blame him. Not a lot happened in these villages so when something did, it was natural that people should extract every interesting detail. Os walked back to his car wondering how he should handle the next stage. It was six o'clock. It had been a long day and all he wanted was a swim and another beer. But he knew that would have to wait. Sighing, he decided he would walk down to the house that Hassan had mentioned. If he left it until Monday he would only spend the next twenty - four hours wondering.

The road was steep, forcing him to lean back as he walked. A ragged dog ran ahead of him, barking, her distended teats brushing the dusty road. An old man sat outside his house on a wooden chair, sunning himself in the late afternoon sun. They greeted each other. Os wondered if he had been friendly with Uludag - he would have certainly known him. But he didn't stop to ask.

Already a picture of the dead man was forming. He was obviously a complex person, good to his daughter as a child but ill treating his wife. He'd an affair with a Greek woman and for the last fifteen years had had no contact with his daughter. He was very active, even though he was nearly seventy and capable of saving a great deal of money. But why had he bothered? He lived a frugal life, though he had once spent some money on the house. Hassan said that the marble steps were fairly new but nothing else had been improved - he hadn't even employed a cleaner. What was he saving his money for? If his daughter hadn't been in touch for years, would he bother to leave it to her? Perhaps there was some guilt about how he had treated his wife and he wanted to make amends to the only child he had left.

He had reached the metal gate to the Nadir home. Os pushed it open and walked along the path, looking at the garden. Uludag had obviously done a good job - the borders were neat and the bushes well trimmed. A red bougainvillea cascaded over a metal trellis that was fixed around the wooden door. He rang the bell.

Chapter Eleven

Nothing happened, no dog barked, no footsteps were heard from inside. He waited a couple more seconds then rang the bell again. The house remained silent. A wide path led around the back of the house. He followed the stone walkway, passing bushes of lavender and ones with red and yellow flowers of which he didn't know the names.

The back opened out onto a large patio with a swimming pool twice the size of the one of Roisin's. There were no towels draped over the plastic sun beds or any other sign that there was anyone around. Os sighed. He would have to come back later; turning, he left and walked back up to his car.

The steepness of the hill had made him come out in a sweat. He put on the aircon and started the engine. Instead of turning left at Treasure Restaurant, in the direction of home, he carried on up the hill towards Karaman village. Leaving the car by the church, he then walked up the narrow path that led to the row of houses hugging the top of the village. The views of the land that fell steadily away below and then to the sea in the distance, were fantastic. Os stopped for a few minutes to catch his breath and stared. He'd been here once before to investigate a reported burglary. It had turned out to be a waste of time, a tourist's attempt to make a false claim on his insurance.The village was so peaceful, unlike the clutter and noise of most other Northern Cypriot villages. This was partly because many of the houses were holiday homes, only occupied a few months of the year. He glanced at his watch. Six o'clock. With some luck, the people he wanted to talk to would be at home. He stopped outside the house with black shutters. There was no-one to be seen, so he pulled out his mobile and keyed in his own home number. It rang for a few seconds before Roisin answered.

Os sensed immediately that he had interrupted her work. 'I'll be late tonight. I'm still working.'

'No problem.'

After a few words, he pushed the mobile back into his pocket, thinking how different his relationship with Roisin was from the other women he had known. Perhaps it was because her work took up so much of her time that she was never annoyed when he was late. He was used to tantrums, especially when social plans had to be cancelled but Roisin seemed happy to potter in the garden or swim when she wasn't working.

A small white dog rushed down to meet him. Os walked up the stone steps. Again, this tiered garden was pretty, with flowering bushes and several large cacti. He hoped that if he reached the age of Uludag, he would be just as active. The climb up the hill had reminded him that he was not as fit as he should be. Certainly, at the moment, he wouldn't be able to keep up with the young recruits on the police training programme.

As Os raised his hand to knock on the black door, it was opened by a tall thin man in his eighties. He wore his thinning, grey hair long at the front so that he could wind it around the bald spot at the back. It was a strange British custom that Os had observed before and he wondered how these men coped in the wind.

'Yes?'

Again, it surprised him how people lived in Northern Cyprus and made no attempt to learn the language. This man could have been opening the door in a house in Britain for all the effort he was making. Os was tempted to blast him with a mouthful of Turkish but knew that would not help his cause. Instead, he brought out his Inspector's badge.

'I'd like to talk to you about your gardener.'

'Oh, yes?' He spoke very differently to Roisin, there was a strong nasal quality to his accent. 'What about him?'

Not for the first time Os was pleased that his English was fluent. 'Could we talk inside?'

He stepped back so that Os could enter the large, stone-flagged hall. The walls were covered in pictures of horses and dogs and men wearing bright red jackets with rifles under their arms.

'You'd better come in here,' he said.

Os followed him into a spacious, airy, sitting room, its open French windows leading out onto a back garden. He glanced out at an area of fruit trees and bushes that sloped upwards to a stone boundary wall.

'Please sit down.'

He fluttered his blue-veined hand towards one of the fading, yellow linen-covered sofas. He himself hovered for a few seconds and then perched on the edge of a chair.

'I was expecting him this morning, actually,' the elderly man gushed. 'He usually comes twice a week. Has anything happened?'

'I'm sorry, but I don't know your name,' Os answered.

'Jack Pout,' he replied. 'Colonel Jack Pout.'

Os noticed the emphasis on the rank. 'I'm afraid Mr Uludag was murdered in his home - on Wednesday night.'

The ex- colonel pushed himself on to his feet. 'I think I need a drink! Can I get you one?'

Without waiting for an answer he crossed over to a selection of decanters on the sideboard. Glass rattled against glass as he poured himself a generous measure of what looked like whisky. It occurred to Os that this man didn't need an excuse to have an alcoholic drink. Perhaps remembering his manners, Pout glanced across at the Inspector. Os shook his head. The prospect, of alcohol on an empty stomach, was unappealing. He watched the man swallow a large mouthful.

'Could you tell me where you were on Wednesday night between the hours of nine and twelve?'

The man's closely shaved jaw fell open and then he made an attempt at a laugh. 'You surely don't believe that I killed my gardener? What possible reason could I have?'

When Os didn't answer, he hurried on. 'He was in his seventies for God's sake and probably didn't have two pennies to rub together.' The glass clinked against his teeth and he took another large mouthful of whisky. 'I can't think of why anyone would want to murder him.'

'Could you answer my question, sir?' Os spoke quietly but there was an authority there that the colonel immediately responded to.

'Well, I was here, in this house.' Perhaps suddenly understanding the reason for the question, he hurried on. 'But I'm afraid I was on my own with the dog - wife died three years ago. I have a cleaner but she's only here two mornings a week.'

'You said that you couldn't imagine why anyone would want to kill Mr Uludag. Did he say anything at all to you recently that you thought strange?'

The alcohol appeared to have calmed the man. He went back to top up his glass then sat down again, nursing the glass in both hands.

'Didn't say much to each other. His English wasn't brilliant and I don't speak Turkish - apart from the odd word.' Pout forced a grin. 'Had the run of the garden - did what he thought needed doing. Didn't interfere - used to be my wife's domain.' He pointed at the decanter in case Os had changed his mind. 'Would pay him every week of course but can't say I knew anything about him.'

'How long has he worked for you?'

The man scratched between the thin strands of hair. 'Must be ten years I would think- though the wife took him on. Worked for the two dears next door and so Gwen asked him to do a few hours here.'

Os examined the Colonel's thin frame beneath the short sleeved shirt and shorts that ended at his bony knees. Having watched him pour the whisky, he doubted that the man would have the strength in his arms to kill another man. He wasn't even on Uludag's list but never-the -less it was interesting to get a fuller picture of the dead man.

'Well, thank you for your time, Colonel Pout – you've been most helpful. I'm sorry to have disturbed you.'

'Not at all - just doing your job. Quite enjoyed our little chat. Was in the military police myself you know.'

Os smiled politely. 'You said Mr Uludag worked next door?'

'For Ilka and Suzanne, yes. Gwen took the man on after they told her how good he was.' He scratched his head again. 'Keep themselves to themselves most of the time. Gwen went in occasionally for a coffee and such and then she'd invite them back here for tea.' He grinned, 'Usually sent off to do a few errands. All stopped now of course.' He followed Os out into the hall. 'Any news on that business on the hillside, Inspector? Heard they were from this village – Greeks!'

'That's just a theory, I'm afraid,' Os pulled open the front door.'Investigations are still taking place.'

He thanked the man again and picked his way down the garden steps. Exhaustion made his step heavy but he still needed to question the German women. The outcome would most probably be as unprofitable as the last interview but as with their neighbour, it was necessary to hear what they had to say.

Os rang twice before the door was opened. This time he found himself looking at a tall slim woman, whose age could have been anything between sixty and her early seventies. Her short blonde hair was sculptured around her still attractive, curiously unlined face. He wondered whether he was looking at the results of a face lift. She regarded him politely but without warmth.

Os flashed his police badge. 'I'd like to ask you about your gardener, Mr Uludag.'

She took his badge and examined it long enough to take in every detail, then she stepped back. 'Please come in Inspector Zahir.' Her English was perfect except for the guttural accent.

He was aware of her light perfume as he followed her into the living room. This was very different to the one he had been in a few minutes earlier. Again, French windows opened out onto a beautifully kept garden but there the similarities ended. This was a supremely feminine area. Two large, white, soft leather sofas were placed on either side of a white coffee table. A Chinese rug covered most of the lightly varnished parquet floor. Long cream curtains, in a heavy material were tied back with elaborate gold tassels. Instead of hunting pictures, the walls displayed pastels of Mediterranean scenes. An older, still pretty woman sat in a matching leather armchair, an open magazine on her knees.

'This is a policeman, Ilka. He has come to talk to us about our gardener.'

Ilka's magazine slipped to the floor. She bent over to retrieve it, her grey hair flopping forward, hiding her face.

'Please.' The sister, whose name must therefore be Suzanne, waved a manicured hand towards a sofa.

Os sank deep into the leather. Both women were now watching him with polite interest. He looked from one to the other.

'When did you last see Mr Uludag?'

Suzanne spoke. 'Wednesday afternoon. Is there a problem?'

Os thought he detected fear in her cold eyes.

'I'm afraid he died on Wednesday night.'

Suzannes's hands curled into fists and she closed her eyes for several seconds. Ilka pushed herself out of her chair and crossed over to the window. He hadn't known how they would respond to a dead employee but they were certainly more affected than he had imagined. Ilka was quite frail and, despite her careful grooming, looked as if she was the older by ten years. From what their neigbour had implied, these women were semi- recluses so perhaps their reaction was more to do with their lack of social contact.

'I take it you were both fond of him?'

This time Ilka turned back into the room and answered. 'Quite the opposite, officer. We no longer wished him to work for us.'

Suzanne cut in. 'But it was naturally difficult. We assumed he was desparate for the money, otherwise he wouldn't still have worked at his age.'

'Why?'

Neither women answered.

'Why were you thinking of getting rid of him?' Os repeated. 'I noticed your lovely garden - he was obviously doing an excellent job.'

After a few seconds Susanne sighed. 'A few things went missing. We couldn't prove it was him of course but we don't employ anyone else.'

'What sort of things?' Os attempted to lean forward but the softness of the sofa stopped him.

'A silver picture frame, a small, silver casket and some money that we left here, on the table.' Susanne's bony shoulders twitched under her yellow silk blouse. 'The doors to the garden are always open during the day - it would have been easy for him to come in.' Again she sighed. 'But we couldn't be sure and we didn't want the fuss of the police.'

Suzanne played with the gold ring on her right hand. Ilka had returned to her seat and her fingers were now worrying the pages of her magazine. At last, Ilka asked the question Os had been waiting for.

'How did he die? He seemed in good health when he was here on Wednesday.'

'He was murdered.'

They were either very good actresses or this was the first time they had heard the news. They both stared at him. Susanne was the first to recover.

'Do you know who did it?'

He ignored the question but instead asked, 'I must ask you where you were between the hours of nine and twelve on Wednesday night?'

Susanne frowned. 'Here of course. Occasionally we go out for a meal but most nights, we are here.'

'On your own?'

'You mean can anyone vouch for us?' She shook her head. 'But this is too ridiculous. We would hardly kill him because he stole a few of our things.'

Susanne crossed to her sister's chair and rested her hands on the frailer woman's shoulders. Os watched, appreciating their closeness. He understood and respected family loyalty. There was nothing more he needed to ask them this evening.

'Thank you for being so candid.' He hoped that he had used the right word, he would check with Roisin when he got home. He placed one of his cards on the table.

'My number if anything occurs to you.'

Suzanne followed him outside and waited as he made his way down the steps. When he turned around at the gate she was still there but when he looked a few seconds later, he saw that the green door had closed. He wondered what they were saying to each other now that they were alone. What secrets did they have?

He rolled his stiff shoulders back as he walked then glanced at his watch. Eight o'clock. Not surprising he was so tired. The thought of sitting down with Roisin, drinking a cold beer, gave him a spurt of energy. He was in the process of keying in his home number when the phone rang.

A German woman's thoughts.

What does he suspect? He was very polite for a policeman but his questions – what does he know? Is he just playing with our minds like those policemen in Germany? Then they would return with more questions.

I'm worried about Ilka – she's not so strong. If our secret is discovered what will we do? Will we have to leave here or will they make allowances for two old women? I feel that same sickness in my stomach again.

Chapter Twelve

He walked back through the village, the mobile clamped to his ear.

'So she's living in Karalangalou?'

'She's been married eight years - done well for herself,' Sener spoke quickly. 'She married someone called Mandrez. He's management with Cyprus Turkish Airlines.'

Os grunted. 'Well, it's not surprising she was paying Uludag. Unless her husband was one of her clients, she wouldn't want him finding out.' Os opened the car door and climbed in. 'But we've got to handle this carefully. If we want the truth then we need to see her when she's on her own. I'll meet you first thing on Monday morning in Karalangalou - by the London Butcher's.' A Sunday without having to work was now appearing a possiblity. 'We can leave one car there and go together,' Os continued. 'Make it nine thirty - the husband should have gone by then.'

'Right sir - have a good weekend.'

In a much better mood, Os started the engine. He would be home in a few minutes so there now seemed little point in ringing ahead.

Tramps sat sentinel - like at the top of the steps and ran down to meet him. The dog's barking gave him an inordinate satisfaction that he was home. He ruffled the animal's ears and went in search of Roisin.

She was curled up on the sofa watching the World News. He sank down beside her, stretched his feet out and closed his eyes. He felt the sofa cushions move and then she kissed him on the cheek.

'Shall I fetch you a beer?'

He reached out to take her hand and gave it a squeeze. His eyes were still closed when he heard her return, her bare feet slapping on the tiles. He held out his hand to accept the ice cold, can.

'Have you eaten yet?'

'No, I said I'd wait for you.'

He listened to her return to the kitchen, open the fridge and then the cupboard doors. The smell of frying steak hung in the air. He had finished his first beer when she called him outside.

'So what have you done since I left you this afternoon?'

Os told her about the visit to Hassan and then the talk with the ex – military policeman and the two German women.

'So you think the Englishman has nothing to do with all this?' she asked.

Os leaned over and with his thumb, wiped a grease mark off her face. 'Highly unlikely - nor the women either. But I found the way they reacted odd and they're not in Uludag's book.'

Roisin grinned at him. 'You mean The Book of Silence?'

He pulled a face at her joke. 'If that's what the ledgers really are, yes. Of course we don't yet know for definite that he was a blackmailer.'

'I can't think what else those payments could be.' Her eyes narrowed. 'But how did the German women react?'

'They seemed far more affected by his death than I would've expected.' Os sighed. 'Considering he was so well organised, it's strange he didn't keep a record of the money he earned as a gardener.'

'Since they weren't on the list, what made you go up there?'

Os pulled a face. 'It's like prodding a snake nest with a stick. If I rattle it enough then something will come out.'

'As long as you don't get bitten in the process,' she answered without smiling.

This wasn't a subject he chose to continue with, instead he said, 'A most intriguing visit.'

'Why?'

'Their house was beautiful but the sisters interest me.' He smiled as he recalled the visit. 'They were in control of the situation not me - it was as if they were intuitively plugged into each other.' He helped himself to more potato salad. 'I think one of them was a widow.'

'What makes you think they're sisters?'

Os sensed what she was going to say. He found himself answering defensively. 'Hassan told me - as well as the old colonel. They've lived here for years.'

Roisin sat back, the same look of satisfaction on her face as when she had told him that she thought that Uludag had taken bribes.'If they're not really sisters but gay and this Uludag knew, then they would be the perfect people to blackmail.'

It had been obvious that there was a close bond between them but women were different to men, they were more physical towards each other. And it was common knowledge in the community that the German women were sisters. But he couldn't help but feel that Roisin was right and the fact annoyed him.

He stood up and walked over to the kitchen, returning with two beers.When they had both snapped their cans open and poured the cold liquid into glasses, she continued.

'I once asked our neighbour, Martha, why she hadn't been tempted to buy one of the lovely old cottages in the village. Apparently,' Roisin said, warming to her theme, '...if you buy up there, you have to go through a kind of vetting system. It's run by a local committee and one of the many things they don't approve of is gay relationships.'

Roisin swung up her legs so that they rested on his knees. Os started to knead her feet as he thought about what she had just said.

'If he was visiting their house every week, he probably saw something.Uludag was obviously practised at extorting money, and those women would have been very vulnerable.' Roisin wiggled her toes. 'If Karaman has been their home for years, they'd be terrified that people would find out. It would have been very difficult for them to cope with the gossip - much easier to pay him to keep quiet.'

'Or would you kill him to keep such a secret?' Os asked.

'I wouldn't,' Roisin answered, 'But they both had a lot to lose. Maybe he was asking for too much?'

Os walked over to the garden wall and stared across at the distant lights of Girne. Even if he hadn't realised that they were gay, he had been aware that they had lied to him. They had successfully hidden their secret for years and why shouldn't they! It was outrageous that they had been forced to invent the deceit in the first place. It was the twenty-first century and yet in many ways society hadn't developed at all.

Os shook his head in disgust. 'And it's the people in the village that make these rules, the British and the Germans? I don't understand them.'

Roisin stood behind him, her arms around his waist. Os leaned back into her, aware of her perfume that was not dissimilar to that of the flowers that covered the wall. He would have to go back and talk to the women again but only after he had made some more enquiries. But if their names were not in Uludag's book, was there any point in carrying this any further? Why not let the old women live in peace? But instinct told him that Uludag did know the women's secret and that they had paid him to keep his silence.

He sighed. Despite his years in the police force, he was still disgusted and shocked by the evil he uncovered. He felt Roisin move away. He turned around and watched her as she started to pile the supper dishes onto a tray.

'Do you want another beer? You look as if you could do with one.'

He nodded. 'But I think I'll get in the pool. Do you fancy a swim?'

She grinned. 'Give me two minutes.'

He was floating on his back, staring at the stars when he heard her wade into the water.

'It's not as warm as I thought,' she said.

He smiled to himself but didn't answer. Relaxation was seeping through his body and he didn't want anything to disturb the process. He felt Roisin's hands on his feet and then she was pushing him through the water until his head went under. He broke free, spluttering. She turned and swam away from him but he was too quick and grabbing her ankles pulled her down. Like two porpoises they played until Roisin said she was cold and that she was going to bed. As she walked up the pool steps, she turned around and looked at him. He pulled himself out of the water and reached for a towel.

He woke up at seven o'clock even though he hadn't set the alarm. Closing his eyes again, he hoped that he would get back to sleep but eventually he knew that it was useless. Slipping out of bed so that he wouldn't wake Roisin, he pulled on his swimming trunks and went out to the pool. It was one thing swimming nude at night but he had no intention of being caught en-flagrente in daylight.

He knew why he had woken. The thought of the visit to his parents was affecting him more than he admitted. If only there wasn't this problem with Roisin and his mother. Despite her overbearing ways, she was his mother and she had always done her best for him. It bothered him that Roisin didn't make more of an effort; his mother would be less dogmatic if she saw more of her son's partner. But when Roisin did choose to visit she was not herself. He knew there was a language problem but most of the conversation was carried out in English for Roisin's sake, even if it then meant that his mother couldn't contribute a great deal. Os dived into the water and then turned on his back, enjoying the sun on his face. To be fair to Roisin, she made an effort with his father but it only emphasised the lack of any warmth between the two women.

His train of thought was interrupted by the dog, who hearing movement had risen from his outside kennel and come to the side of the pool for a stroke. Os pulled himself out of the water and towelled himself dry. He would take him for a walk now so that there wouldn't be an excuse for them to be late for lunch.

The animal, as if reading his thoughts, barked. Os put his hand on its muzzle and calmed him with a few words. A few minutes later he was walking down the steps, the dog running ahead. It was still early and he appeared to be the only person out. He couldn't decide whether to walk up to the village or turn right, in the direction of the hills. But Tramps was already heading down to the excavation tent.

A pile of cigarette butts marked the spot where the duty policemen had sat. It was difficult to believe that the graves had been disturbed only four days ago, so much had happened since. And within those four days they had uncovered deceit that stretched its thin fingers into all levels of the community. If this land had not been disturbed by the construction company then the bones would have been left in peace and probably Uludag would still be alive. Not that he was a man that Os found a least bit attractive but there was no excuse for murder.

Despite it being Sunday and early, two of the team were already at work. For a few minutes they were unaware of him and then both acknowledged him with a nod but continued as before. He watched them carry buckets of earth to a large wooden frame with some kind of netting stretched across. As the earth sieved through, one of the women picked up something that had been caught in the net and showed it to her colleague. Os thought it looked like a piece of bone. She slipped it inside a white envelope and wrote a list of numbers on the packet, placing it, as if it was some priceless object, into a plastic box that was already full of similar envelopes. Since the anthropologist he had had dealings with was not there, he decided to walk on.

The duty policeman fell in along side him. Os decided not to ask where he had appeared from. Perhaps he had been to the toilet or for a little walk - it was boring work sitting out here, the man needed some kind of a break.

Instead he said, 'I bet you're glad this is their last day.'

The policeman shrugged. 'I've had a lot worse jobs. The others went back to Lefkosa last night - those two are just finishing up.' He pulled a sour expression. 'Will the builders start again now, sir?'

Os shook his head. 'They've put a court order on the land, just in case they need to come back. Nothing will happen here for at least a month.' He had heard that the locals had been delighted with the decision but Os knew that it was just putting off the inevitable. This hillside, with its shrubland and olive trees, would be transformed into concrete boxes - the process was just being delayed.

A wave of irritation flooded over him. Although he disliked it when Roisin criticized his country, privately he was outraged by the destruction that was going on. There were bulldozers everywhere - tearing up the landscape, destroying the hundreds of olive trees that he understood were under a protection order. It was tragic but not surprising, since money was the God in any country, especially one that had been poor for so long. He sighed and decided to go home. Perhaps the day would turn out better than he thought.

Roisin was sitting outside, a pot of coffee in front of her. He bent down to kiss her, smelling the freshness of her newly washed hair.

'Did I wake you?'

'The dog did. How was your walk?'

'We went down to the site. They're finishing up there now.'

Roisin pushed a mug of coffee towards him. 'I was wondering whether there a pattern in the way Uludag worked or was he just an opportunist?'

Os recalled the list of victims which was now imprinted on his memory.'There are people's names, as well as titles that could be organisations. Gorus and the ex- prostitute, Gul, are listed.' Os thought for a moment before adding, 'So he picked on both men and women – young and old. The common denominator will either be sex or money.'

Roisin poured out more coffee for herself. 'Have you dealt with anything like this before?'

He shook his head, 'But I read about it when I did my training.'

'What do you know about this man's past? What happened to him that made him turn to extortion or did he just see an opportunity to make a lot of money?'

Os was silent for a few minutes and then he began to talk, raising a finger on his right hand for every point he made. 'I know that he worked for years as a porter in the police station. The men had a mixed opinion of him. They found him too willing to please and extremely nosy. He was retired early after a road accident which was the fault of the driver- a drunken police officer. He was a good gardener even though he was nearly seventy and he used a walking stick.'

'Go on,' Roisin persisted.

Os raised the thumb of his left hand. 'His daughter had nothing to do with him because he beat her mother and had an affair with a Greek Cypriot.'

Roisin's eyes widened. 'You don't think he saw himself as a vigilante, do you?'

'He wouldn't be the first hypocrite that I've come across in this job. It couldn't have been easy for him being from a one parent family, growing up in a village just after the war. Plenty of reasons there for resentment.'

'Does that make him anti men or women?' Roisin asked. 'Did his father have nothing to do with him? Not even financially?'

Os shook his head. 'Apparently not.'

' Did the daughter know who her grandfather was?'

'Just that he'd been a doctor at the hospital.'

She sighed then glanced at her watch. 'We'd better get ready if we're not going to be late for your mother's lunch.'

Their conversation kept drifting back into Os's head as he took the road through the mountains. It certainly made sense that Uludag had taken to blackmailing as a way of getting his own back on his difficult childhood. But he needed to put the case aside for a few hours and try to enjoy the afternoon. He slipped in a Buddy Holly tape and glanced across at Roisin who was staring out at the wall of craggy mountains towering above them.

'Are you happy?'

She smiled and reached out to squeeze his leg.

'What do you miss?'

'About Liverpool?'

He nodded.

'The weather,' she grinned.

'No seriously,' he persisted. 'You must miss something.'

'Not worrying about the cost when I ring my friends or my sister.'

'What else?'

He didn't want her to spoil it with anything negative but he couldn't help prodding. Despite the difficulty with his mother, he worried that she would tire of their life together and decide to go back to Liverpool. She was the most independent woman he had ever known and yet there was a vulnerability about her that she occasionally allowed him to glimpse. And she made him think. He wasn't used to that in a woman. But it always came back to the same thing - without being married would their relationship last?

She smiled at him and he felt himself relax.

They had reached the outskirts of Lefkosa. There was less traffic because it was Sunday and they were soon in the area that Os had grown up in - an area of detached houses with well-established gardens. He parked the car outside a stone-built bungalow with the Cypriot arches Roisin loved, marking the edge of the covered veranda. Geraniums cascaded over the front of the house, their red and orange petals bright in the June sunshine. Two large palm trees gave further shade.

A man in his sixties stood at the top of the steps. Like his son he was chunkily built and had the same thick hair - except that his was streaked with grey. He wore a brown cardigan over a checked shirt and thick, corduroy trousers.

'Hi, Dad,' Os called. 'I see it's not hot enough for you yet.'

His father smiled and came down to hug his son. He then turned to Roisin and kissed her on both cheeks. 'Lovely to see you, my dear. Come in, come in.'

They followed him into the shade of the covered veranda just as Os's mother appeared from inside the house. She wore a blue printed silk dress covered by an apron. Her thick, brown hair, clear of grey, was twisted up in a bun. She was still a beauty. It was obvious why Os's father had been so captivated by her and perhaps still was. She greeted the two young people with equal enthusiasm and Os breathed a sigh of relief. Perhaps it really was going to be a good afternoon. They sat down on old arm chairs that had been relegated from the sitting room to the veranda. His mother went back into the house to reappear again with glasses of orange juice.

'How's work, Father? When are you going to retire?' Os knew the answer - the subject had become the usual banter between them.

The older man smiled and took a glass from his wife. 'It might be sooner than you think. These students are the laziest we've ever had. The worst are those with rich parents - they think their money will buy them their degree.'

'You say that every year,' his wife chided. 'What would you do if you weren't working? You would be even more bad tempered under my feet all day.'

Her husband looked offended but Os knew this was their game. 'I have my books - I would read and perhaps write another fascinating text book.'

She ruffled his head. 'Do it then if it will make you happy.' She went back into the house.

The older man shrugged his shoulders. 'She's right.' Roisin put down her glass and followed Os's mother into the kitchen.

His father settled back into his chair. 'How are you son? How is work?'

They were called in for a dinner of Meze, roast lamb and tiny roast potatoes. The conversation led onto Os's brother in the States and his new wife, a Turkish American.

'It shouldn't be long before you're an uncle,' his mother said, having made certain everyone had what they needed.

Os glanced across at Roisin but she was talking to his father and wouldn't have understood his mother's Turkish anyway. She only used her broken English when she was speaking directly to Roisin. Despite this, Os found himself changing the subject of grandchildren to that of her friends and their children, many of whom Os had grown up with and still kept in tentative contact. There was sudden laughter between his father and Roisin and then the four of them talked about relatives in England. Two of Os's uncles had moved to

London in the seventies and his parents were planning to visit. At last his mother stood up.

'You two men go outside. Roisin and I will clear away and make the coffee.'

They all did as they were told. Feeling mellow, Os followed his father back out to the veranda. The older man lit a cigarette and leaned back in his chair.

'She's a nice girl? Do you think you'll end up marrying her?'

Os's sudden glare made him hold up his hands. 'Hey, I'm not your mother, I'm just interested.'

'Sorry, Dad. But you know what Mum is like. She can't wait to see me married with babies.'

His father put his head on one side as if trying to understand his son's reaction.

'Well, we were married at nineteen, you're thirty-four, what do you expect? I know it's the modern way but you can't blame her for being worried about you. She just wants you to be happy.'

'It's been less than six months.'

'But you're living with her, son. If she's good enough to live with, surely she's good enough to marry.' The older man sighed. 'It's difficult for your mother. All her friends' children are either married or still living at home.'

Os saw the concern in his father's eyes and felt guilty. 'I haven't asked her to marry me but I know she wouldn't anyway. She doesn't want to marry anyone.'

'Do you love each other?'

Os didn't have to think this time. 'Her not wanting marriage has nothing to do with me. She just doesn't believe in it.' Os attempted to smile. 'You have to remember, Dad, that marriage isn't such a big deal in Britain.'

'But it is here, son.' His father leaned over and patted Os's knee. 'I hope it works out for you, I like her and your mother does too.'

Os didn't contradict him. Although she hadn't said anything to him, he sensed his mother would prefer to see him married to a Turkish-Cypriot girl. It was a pity that he couldn't exchange places with his brother in Chicago. She could then introduce all her friends to her established daughter-in-law and spoil the inevitable grandchildren.

His mother brought out their coffee and some time later Roisin appeared. Os and his father were in the middle of a conversation about University politics but when he did turn to include Roisin, he saw immediately that she was angry. She sat sipping a Nescafe and flicking through an old magazine.

'Are you tired?' He asked. Roisin's mouth formed into the thin pretence of a smile. Os glanced at his watch. It was four o'clock. He stood up and stretched. 'We'd better get off, Dad. I've a long day tomorrow. I'll go in and tell mum.'

They had driven though the suburbs of Lefkosa and were on the straight, flat road that cut across the Mesaoria Plain before either of them spoke.

'So what's the problem then?'

Her voice slashed through any remaining feelings of contentment he still held on to. 'Your mother! She can't leave the subject of marriage and babies alone. As soon as we were in the kitchen, she started. It wasn't easy for her - you know how bad her English is - but she did her best.' Roisin stared straight ahead. 'It's every time we go there.'

He sighed, the afternoon ruined. A nugget of anger formed in his stomach.

'You can't blame her. Most people here would think it was strange that you didn't want to get married or have children.' He regretted the words as soon as he had spoken them. She shifted in her seat so that her back was between them. He suddenly felt tired.

'I'm sorry but that's how it is here. This is a traditional country compared to Britain or The States.' He rubbed her leg but she didn't respond. Sighing, he put both hands on the wheel and concentrated on the road.

The rest of the evening wasn't much better. Roisin said that she had to work so Os left her to it. Annoyed, he slumped on the sofa in the sitting room watching the football but his mind on the events of the afternoon. His parents had tried to make her welcome. His father would have to have been totally insensitive not to have noticed her moodiness when they left. In future, he would visit on his own. They were an important part of his life and although he loved Roisin, he would not allow anything to affect his relationship with his parents. Besides, with his brother out of the country, it was his duty to visit them regularly and make sure they were all right. He put his feet on the coffee table and poured himself a large glass of brandy.

Chapter Thirteen

Sener was waiting by the side of the road.

'Leave your car there and we'll collect it afterwards,' Os called through the window. 'Good weekend?' He asked, as his sergeant climbed into the passenger seat.

Sener nodded. 'We had my family over – had a barbeque. What about you?'

He waited for Sener to fasten his seat belt then edged the car forward, waiting for a car to let him onto the main road. His sergeant lit a cigarette.

'Fine!' Os answered, 'Nothing special. Do you know where this house is?'

'I looked it up on my way home on Saturday. Turn left here and go passed the supermarket. It's on the road that leads down to Karalangalou beach.'

Os moved out into a space in the heavy traffic, glad that he was not on the opposite side where the cars were bumper to bumper on their way into town. With some luck, the traffic would have eased by the time they had finished with this woman. He turned off onto a narrow, pot-holed road, passing signs advertising various restaurants. On the right were several detached houses that were separated by generous gardens.

'This is it.'

Os stopped the car in front of a large, white, multi-balconied house. This woman had obviously done well for herself. He hoped that the absence of a car in the drive meant that she was alone.

A woman in her late twenties answered the door. Dark, shiny hair hung sleekly to her shoulders and despite the earliness of the hour, Os noticed that she wore makeup. Her white dress, though not too short or too low, still showed off her excellent figure. A baby sat astride her hip.

'Mrs Mandrez?' Os asked.

She nodded, her eyes puzzled by two strangers at the door.

Os flashed his police badge. 'We'd like to ask you a few questions - about Mr. Uludag.'

Her eyes widened then settled into a frown. 'I'm not sure I can help you.'

'Oh, I think you can,' Os said. 'Shall we talk inside?'

She hesitated and then, knowing she had no option, stepped back to allow the two men into her home. The tiled hallway opened into a large sitting room which, despite the presence of the baby, had the appearance of a show house.

'One minute,' she said. 'I'll put the baby in his cot.'

The two men remained standing. Os looked out of the open, patio doors to where a circular pool was surrounded by fancy paving. He had just begun to examine a large painting, when she returned. She appeared more composed.

'I'm really not sure how I can help you officer.'

With the disappointment of the previous day and because he had slept badly, Os snapped at her. 'We haven't got time for games, Mrs Mandrez. Mr. Uludag is dead - murdered - and we know that he was taking money from you.'

The woman's head jerked back. She put her hand on the back of a chair as if to give herself some support and then her eyes filled with tears

Os softened his tone. 'We already know about your police record. It would save time if you could just be honest with us.'

'Are you going to tell my husband?' Her eyes darted around the room as if looking for an escape route.

'We need only to understand your relationship with Mr Uludag. If you co-operate,' Os shrugged, '...then hopefully we can leave you in peace.'

She pulled a lace handkerchief out of her dress pocket and started to twist it between both hands. Both men waited. Then just as Os thought he would have to try another tactic, a tear rolled down her face. He wondered whether it was genuine or, as he had often found with female suspects, an attempt to gain sympathy. The sudden passion in her voice took him by surprise.

'I'm glad he's dead. I would've killed him myself if I'd known how.'

She dabbed her eyes and then abandoned the now, rag-like handkerchief. There was more silence. She watched him from underneath her thick, black eyelashes, then her pretty face twisted in bitterness.

'I've been paying the dirty old man two hundred lira every month for over five years. Can you imagine how hard it's been to keep it hidden from my husband? Money that should have been spent on the children and,' she sniffed, '...my self.'

'Did he come to the house?'

'He called soon after I was married. He said he was from the police and that he had something of mine. He showed me the copy of my old court order. I was just married – I wasn't going to risk losing this.' She indicated with a manicured hand, the expensive Italian suite and marble table lamps. 'Anyway, I love him.'

'So your husband was not one of your clients?' Sener asked.

She scowled across at the sergeant. 'Of course not! He has no idea what I used to do.' She turned back to Os, the higher-ranking policeman, her voice taking on a more plaintive tone. 'I had to work in Lefkosa. My father died of a heart attack and my mother was left to bring up seven children. What else could I do?' She paused as if waiting for Os to agree or disagree.When he remained silent she shrugged, 'My mother was trained for nothing - my father left no money- and there were the young children to look after. I told her I worked in an expensive restaurant and was given good tips. ' She tossed her head. 'I kept the family for three years before I met Aydin.'

'And now,' Sener asked, '…do you still support your family?'

She nodded. 'Aydin is very generous. But,' she spat, '…it will be a lot easier now that that snake is dead.'

'How did he get his money?' Os asked.

'He came here. I've no idea where he lived, I never asked him.' She curled her lip as if remembering the scene. 'He would come to the door and I would hand it to him in an envelope.'

'And where were you on Wednesday night between eight and midnight?' Os asked.

Triumph, then panic flitted across her face. 'I was here with Aydin and the baby. But you can't ask him to confirm it - he would want to know why the police were asking questions.'

Os stared at the pretty young woman. He felt some sympathy for her predicament but if she had murdered the man, it was a different matter. He reached into the inside of his jacket and handed her one of his cards.

'If you think of anything that will help us in our investigations, please ring me, day or night.'

She took the card but he suspected that she would rip it up and throw it in the bin as soon as they left.

She sounded suddenly very tired.'I've told you everything I know. I just want to be left alone.' They held eye contact as he attempted to see behind her glossy mask.

'I hope so,' he said at last. 'We don't want to waste our time coming back and we can't promise that it would be during the day. We're busy people.'

He felt a twinge of self disgust. He hated this side of the job. This woman was probably innocent of anything but poor judgement. He glanced at Sener. The sergeant stood up and led the way out of the house. At the front door, Os turned back but now her face showed no emotion at all.

He joined Sener in the car. 'Do you fancy a coffee before we go back?'

The sergeant nodded as he fastened his seat belt. 'I feel quite depressed after that.'

Os grinned, grateful for a grain of humour. 'Perhaps now you'll think differently about policeman's pay? At least you know Fatima married you for love.'

Sener grunted and stared out of the window. 'I wonder sometimes, the amount of moaning she does.'

'Maybe a coffee will cheer you up,' Os said as he turned on the engine.

There was still a space next to where Sener had left his old Honda. Both men got out and slamming the doors shut, walked back down the lane to the main road. The traffic had eased and a few seconds later they were both sat on hard wooden chairs, outside the village coffee shop. At the next table, two old men played backgammon, the scratched wooden board between them. Os ordered two coffees and then stared across the road at a carpenter's shop. Three carved Cypriot chests were displayed outside, next to a row of elaborately carved mirror surrounds. Under an awning a man sand-papered a table, a cigarette hanging out of his mouth.

'How do you fancy a job like that?' Os asked. 'No stress, just having pleasant conversations with customers - instead of always having to think the worst of people.'

Sener scowled. 'I'll go across and see if they've got any vacancies.'

He was prevented from doing so by the arrival of their coffees. Os took a tentative sip to check that the thick, black mixture was sweet enough.

They sat in silence with their own thoughts for a few seconds before Sener asked, 'What do you think then?'

Os stretched out his legs and leaned back against the hard chair. 'She's probably innocent - if not, she's a practised liar. But I do think she was telling the truth that she didn't know where he lived. What do you think?'

Sener gave the same grunt that he had made earlier. 'It was a lot of money for her to find every month and she'd dug herself in pretty deep. If her husband found out that, one, she'd been a prostitute when he met her instead of a young innocent and, two, that she'd been giving away the money he thought she was spending on their children,' Sener shrugged. 'I know what I'd do if I'd been duped by Fatima in the same way.'

Os looked at his sergeant but resisted from asking him to explain. He wondered what the man's marriage was really like. Sener certainly gave the impression that he made all the decisions. He went to work and Fatima stayed at home, looking after their four children - all under the age of six. Os didn't envy him but Sener seemed happy enough if not overwrought at times. Os drained his coffee, careful to leave the brown sludge of sediment at the bottom of his cup.

'She certainly has a lot to lose. Apart from the children and that fine house - think of all those free flights she must get. Mandrez is one of the top people in Cyprus –Turkish Airlines.'

'I couldn't imagine my Fatima ever wearing a dress like that - never mind when she was just at home, looking after the kids.'

Os didn't comment, instead he said, 'We'd better get back. I want to have another look at that list.' His thoughts returned to the two German women. Nothing would please him more if there was no further connection between them and the old man.

He placed a two Lira note under his cup and then both men crossed back over the road to their cars. He pushed in one of his favourite CDs. For a few minutes he wanted to forget the sordid aspects of life that all led back to one man.

As both he and Sener entered the police station, the duty sergeant called across to the Inspector. 'The Commandant wants to see you in his office now, sir.'

Os frowned. He could do without this. The man obviously had little to occupy him. Irritated by the sudden grin on Sener's face, he snapped, 'I'll catch you later.'

Atak's secretary was dressed in her usual funereal black. She peered at Os over her heavy framed, glasses. 'The Commandant's been waiting for you, Inspector.'

He had no intention of making excuses for his tardiness. Instead he asked, 'Shall I go straight in?'

She shook her head which made the surplus skin around her chin wobble.

'No, I'll ring him first to make sure it's convenient.'

He turned away to stare out of the window. He knew her first name was Handan but even though they had both worked in the same station for as long as he could remember, she would have been outraged if he had attempted to be so familiar. He wondered whether she was more relaxed with Atak?

'You can go in now, Inspector.'

Os pushed open the door not bothering to thank the woman, knowing that he would pay later for his lack of respect. Atak sat at his large desk, a cup of coffee in front of him.

'Can I get you something, Osman?'

'No thank you, sir.'

He was obviously in a good mood so perhaps this wouldn't take too long. Os took the chair on the other side of the Commandant's desk. It was much lower than that of his boss. The first time he had felt uncomfortable and wondered whether the positioning was intentional but now he was certain. Ironically, since he had come to that conclusion, it no longer bothered him.

The Commandant looked pointedly at his watch. 'We've been waiting for you all morning, Osman.'

Os wondered if this was what Roisin called the 'Royal We, before telling Atak about the interview with Mrs Mandrez - he omitted mentioning the coffee afterwards.

'Excellent. It looks as if the case is developing nicely - just right for bringing in another Inspector.' The large man sat back in his chair beaming.

Indignation flared up inside him. 'What do you mean, sir? I don't think that's necessary. I've got Sener and Fikri working with me. If you want to put anyone else on the case, we could do with another constable. But that's all.'

Atak continued to smile, seemingly unaffected by his subordinant's outburst. 'I know I've been saying we're short of staff but I want you to do me a favour.'

'What kind of favour, sir?' Os felt a sense of foreboding.

'A friend in Istanbul has asked that we give some experience to one of his recently, promoted Inspectors. The intention was to transfer her to Ankara but at the last minute there were difficulties.' Atak smiled so broadly that Os could see his gold fillings. 'He helped me out when I was having a problem with my son - so naturally I couldn't say no.'

Os thought he must have misheard. 'Did you say she, sir?'

Atak nodded. 'It will certainly be unusual for us to have a female Inspector on our force. Very modern! In fact,' he said, as if the thought had just occurred to him. '...I think we'll bring in the press and take some photos. Neither of the stations in Gazi Magusa or Lefkosa have any women in such a high rank. We should make the most of the good publicity.'

'But why have you allocated her to me sir. I'm sure there are other Inspectors who would love to work with her.' Os couldn't think of one of his colleagues who would like to be on an equal footing with a female, though several of them would be very keen to have her on their team as a sergeant.

'You're the only Homicide Inspector we have at the moment and,' here Atak shrugged his well padded shoulders, '...you have an office to yourself. It wouldn't have been fair to ask her to work with five other men when she could so easily share with you. The porter put a desk in there this morning.'

'This morning?' Os had difficulty keeping his voice from rising.

'Oh, yes. She arrived last night. My friend rang me two days ago. I didn't mention it earlier as I knew you were busy and it was not definite that it would go ahead anyway.' Atak bulldozed on before Os could interrupt. 'I'm sure you'll find a woman's perspective very useful - there appear to be so many women involved in this case.' Atak placed his two, large hands together, his wide, gold wedding ring glinting on a thick finger. 'For instance these two German women in Karaman village - it would be useful to have a woman questioning them on such a sensitive subject as their sexuality. Don't you agree?'

Os couldn't reasonably dispute this argument and not for the first time he admired Atak's ability to manipulate situations.

'You're still in charge, Osman but I want her to do the interviews with the women. We don't want any report of harassment coming in.'

'How long do you envisage her working with me, sir?' Os knew that the decision had been made and nothing he said was going to make any difference.

The Commandant screwed up his face so that the heavy flesh drooped into jowls on either side of his mouth. Os suddenly saw facial similarities with his secretary and for a second he wondered if they were related.

'Six months, perhaps,' Atak answered. 'At this stage I've really no idea.'

Os sighed. 'Is that all then, sir?'

'Yes, yes. I won't keep you. An early closure on this murder would be excellent.' As Os walked to the door, Atak added, 'Now that you've got extra help.'

'Don't push it,' Os muttered to himself as he closed the door behind him. He thought about going to find Fikri and Sener but then curiosity got the better of him. He ran up the two flights of stairs and strode down the tiled corridor to his office.

He hadn't had time to have any preconceived ideas about his new room mate, so he wasn't prepared for the dark haired beauty who sat at a new desk, nudged up opposite his own. She looked up and he found himself staring into the large, brown eyes of a woman in her early thirties. Her shiny black hair hung straight to her shoulders and diamond earrings, the size of pearls, glinted in her ears. She was wearing a sleeveless black top which displayed her arms, brown and slender. Smiling, she stood up and came around to the front of her desk to shake his hand.

'Hi, I'm Zelfa Urfa. Pleased to meet you.'

The black top was actually a shift dress that ended just above her knees. She wore stockings that made her slim legs gleam and she smelled of roses. It took Os a few seconds to reply.

'Osman Zahir.'

She waved towards her desk. 'I've been reading the reports of your murder case. The Commandant gave me photocopies.'

Os' half-hearted attempt at friendliness dissipated in the light of Atak's high handedness. He scowled. She smiled, ignoring his response.

'I'm looking forward to starting work.'

Suddenly, not knowing what else to say, Os forced himself to smile back. He'd shared cases with other Inspectors before but now he was the only homicide specialist in Girne, he wasn't keen to relinquish superiority to someone else -especially, he hated to admit - to a woman. What qualifications did she have? The dark thought that she might have more experience than him was very unsettling.

'I thought you only arrived last night. Don't you need time to settle in?' The words slipped out and Os cursed himself. He hoped that she didn't notice how insecure he was feeling. But again she smiled back at him, totally relaxed and in control.

'The Istanbul police have put me up in a small hotel in town until I find an apartment. I'm all unpacked and ready to go.'

Os knew he was being rude and that he had to pull himself together. She was handling the situation far better than him but she would be used to men's negativity in the police force. It seemed she dealt with it by being charming. He cleared his throat.

'Well, if you're sure you're ready to start work - I'll fill you in on what's happened so far.'

As Os talked, he watched her take notes. Occasionally she interrupted him to ask questions and, by the time he had finished, he realised that she not only was very attractive but that she also had a very sharp mind.

'So we're interviewing these two women this afternoon and then, tomorrow, there's a visit to Erim Gorus?'

'Well, yes,' Os hesitated, aware of his prior agreement with Sener. He reached into his drawer and pulled out photocopied sheets of Uludag's accounts, positioning them so that they could both read the names. To his embarrassment, Zelfa sat down on the edge of his desk and picked up a sheet. Os couldn't help but notice that her skirt had risen a few inches. Her forehead creased in concentration.

'Just go through this again with me. There are five different sources of money here. Your sergeants were able to trace the prostitute through her maiden name. You interviewed her this morning and at this stage, there's no need to go back for further questioning?' She pushed back some loose strands of hair and looked up at him for confirmation. Os nodded. 'Then we have the surname Gorus. He's the businessman you and I are going to see tomorrow - the one who was accused in Istanbul of paedophilia.' Again, she looked at Os for agreement. 'And then we've got two anomalies; 'Die Bergen' and 'Cartref hapus a chyfeillgar.'

This time Os shrugged in response to her raised eyebrows. 'I don't know what they mean. And before you ask, I have no idea about the fifth list of figures. Who ever the person was, he didn't give the old man any money for the last two months. Or if he did, it wasn't entered in the book.'

Os stood up and went into the corridor to find a porter. He desperately needed a coffee. He called across to a man mopping the corridor tiles before turning back to ask her what she wanted. The job done, he leaned against the door, hoping that she would realise that her close proximity was making him uncomfortable.

'And since he was always thorough in keeping his accounts, I think it likely that Uludag didn't get the money,' she said, as if there had been no interruption.

'Perhaps the person decided not to pay any more - his circumstances could have changed. By the way, we're waiting for Immigration to tell us whether the German women's residency permits list them as sisters.' Zelfa's eyes narrowed. Os wondered what this Istanbul Inspector's slant was on gay women. 'If they are sisters, then I think we can cross them off our list of suspects.'

Zelfa tapped her pen against his desk. "'Die Bergen' means mountains in German. Where do these German women live?'

Although Os was fluent in English now, he was always impressed in the skill in others. 'Where did you learn German?'

'In Munich. I lived there as a child. My father was in the police.'

So that was the reason she joined the force, he thought.

'He was killed in a bombing in Istanbul six years ago.'

'I'm sorry.' He was aware of how inadequate the words sounded.

There was an awkward pause. Eventually she said, 'You didn't answer my question.'

Relieved that they were back on safe ground, he answered, 'In the village near where I live. Up in the mountains.' He stared at her as the realisation dawned on him. 'It's the name of their house isn't it? I forgot these foreigners like to give their homes names.'

'I think it could be. It seems we'll be confronting them with their relationship after all. Don't worry,' she said, when he pulled a face, '... I'll question them if you want?'

Os didn't repeat Atak's instructions that she should interview all the female suspects. The sudden arrival of the porter with their coffees spared him from answering. She sat down behind her desk. With the new filing cabinet, there was now no room for the two chairs that Os always had ready for visitors. From now on, if he wanted to call a meeting, he would have to book a room.

He manoeuvred himself behind his own desk and sipped his coffee, staring at the list he now knew by heart. 'That leaves us with the other two victims.' He made an attempt to pronounce the strange words, 'Cartref hapus a chyfeillgar' He glanced at Zelpha. 'It's no language you recognise then?' When she shook her head, he continued, 'And then we've got a number, but the person hasn't paid for two months.'

Os stood up. 'I'll go and talk to my sergeants - it's something they can be working on this afternoon. We'll go to Karaman at two o'clock if that suits you. There's a canteen down stairs in the basement if you want to get anything to eat beforehand. I'll meet you back here.' Os pulled his face into what he hoped was an expression of friendliness and left the room.

Chapter Fourteen

Hassan was sitting, smoking a cigarette, outside his café door. Os held up his hand in acknowledgement and then pulled into, what now was becoming, his regular spot.

As he and Zelfa walked back down the hill, he was aware that they were being watched. They had been on their way to re-interview the German women when they had seen the car in Nadir's driveway. It was too good an opportunity to miss.

Even though Os had been here before, he was struck again by the beauty of the garden. In between the plants, he could see sections of the automatic, watering system that snaked across the parched earth. Zelfa, uninterested in her surroundings, strode ahead. After ringing the bell, she stood staring at the sign hanging to the left of the lintel. The pale wood was highly varnished and the words, 'Cartref hapus a Chyfeillgar' were stencilled in contrasting black ink.Os pulled out a creased sheet of paper. The words were exactly the same. He watched Zelfa push the bell again.

A female in her late twenties, in shorts and a cut - off T shirt, opened the door. She had long, blonde hair tied back in a high pony tail. Her bright, red mouth formed a tight smile. Zelfa held up her police badge.

'Inspector Urfa and this is Inspector Zahir. We need to talk to you about your gardener, a Mr. Uludag.' Mrs Nadir stood with her legs slightly apart, her hands resting on her bare waist. 'We'd like to come in?' Zelfa's tone implied that refusing her request was not an option.

Os recognised irritation and some other emotion flicker across the young woman's face before she turned with a flick of her pony tail and led them along the wide, marble corridor into a large lounge. An enormous Turkish rug covered three quarters of the room. Mrs Nadir flopped onto one of the three cream, leather sofas.

She managed to pout as she spoke. 'What's he been up to?'

Zelfa, possibly irritated by the young woman's dismissive attitude, spoke sharply. 'We have to warn you that this is a murder enquiry and your answers will be treated seriously. We'd like to know where you were last Wednesday evening, between the hours of nine and midnight?' Mrs Nadir's beautifully, manicured hand flew to her painted mouth as Zelfa continued. 'We know that someone in this house was paying him money on a regular basis - beyond that of the work he was doing for you in the garden, of course. Until we have information to the contrary, we're linking these payments to his murder.'

Os sat down, intrigued by how this young wife would respond. Although Mrs Nadir gave the appearance of being able to handle herself, he doubted that she would be any match for Inspector Urfa. The young woman was now giving the appearance of being shocked by the news.

'Of course, we could have made a mistake. Perhaps your husband has been paying the money himself?' Zelfa gave an exaggerated performance of looking around the room for Mr Nadir. In finding him missing, she added, 'In that case we can only apologise and come back this evening.'

Now that Zelfa knew that the occupants of this house were connected to the dead man, it seemed that she felt no need to handle the situation sensitively. Her cheeks now bright pink, Mrs Nadir stood up and crossed over to the French windows. Os found himself hoping that they had not made a mistake in talking to the wife first; it could have easily been the husband with a secret. His colleague did not appear to have the same concerns. Mrs Nadir stood with her back to them for a few seconds. Then she turned around and glared at them. 'I don't expect you to tell my husband.'

Zelfa smiled sympathetically and indicated that Mrs Nadir sit down again.

The young wife hesitated, then rested herself on the arm of a sofa as far away from the two police officers as possible.

'I paid him two hundred Turkish Lira a month. I'm glad he's dead.' She glanced from Os to Zelfa as if waiting to see how they would respond to her statement.

'Why?' Zelfa's voice was gentler now. When Mrs. Nadir looked puzzled, Zelfa repeated her question. 'Why did you pay him?'

The young wife spoke like a little girl, explaining away a minor demeanour. 'He caught me with my friend in the pool one afternoon. It wasn't his usual day for gardening and my husband never comes home during the day.'

'How long ago was this?' Os asked.

'Three years.' She tossed her blonde, pony tail.

'And do you still see,' Os hesitated over the word, and then deciding its meaning was clear, added, '….this man?'

She nodded. 'But we're more careful now.'

'We'd like his name. We'll need to talk to him as well,' Zelfa said.

Anxiety clouded the young woman's eyes. 'I thought you promised that it was just me that you wanted to talk to.'

'We said that we wouldn't tell your husband unless it was absolutely necessary.' Zelfa's eyes were cold as she met those of the young wife. 'Your friend is different. His reasons for getting rid of Uludag are just as strong as yours. You say it was worth paying him but I find it impossible to believe that it wasn't a great worry to both of you. The old man couldn't be trusted.'

Mrs Nadir began to play with her wedding ring, her voice displaying the same agitation. 'His name is Ali Alnar. I work with him.' Zelfa took a note book and pen out of her bag, flicked it open and started to write.

'Married?' Os asked. Mrs Nadir shook her head. 'Does he know about the payments?'

She shook her head again. 'And I don't want him bothered.' She glared at him, as if daring him to disobey her.

Os was puzzled. Why carry the burden of being blackmailed on your own? Who was she protecting, him or herself? Zelfa's voice slashed across his thoughts. Mrs Nadir's head jerked in a nervous response.

'I don't believe that you wouldn't discuss it with him.'

Again she spoke in her little-girl voice. 'I thought he might find someone else if there was any trouble.'

Zelfa glanced scornfully at Os then back at the woman. 'An attractive woman like yourself. I can't see a little blackmailing making any difference to him. It's not as if he'd anything to lose by it.' Zelfa paused, as if inviting a confession from the woman. When it was not forth coming, she continued. 'I'm not convinced that you're telling us the whole truth but we'll leave it at that for now. But I'm sure we'll be back.' She nodded at Os, picked up her bag and left the room.

Embarrassed by the abruptness of her departure, Os stood up and handed the young wife his card. 'Thank you for your honesty, Mrs Nadir. Obviously, we expect you to tell us if you intend leaving this area.' He smiled, sympathetically. 'If you remember anything that will help us with our enquiries, please contact us.'

Her eyes seemed unable to focus on him. He wondered what aspect of her predicament she was really anxious about. Was it the possibility of divorce and losing her very comfortable lifestyle, losing her boyfriend or being charged with murder? Or was the whole performance an act?

As he reached the door he asked, 'What does the sign outside mean?'

She stared at him, then her eyes widened in understanding. 'Home Sweet Home.' She pulled a face as if in mockery of the translation. 'My husband bought the house from a Welsh couple. Why?'

Os dismissed her question with a shake of his head. 'You didn't say where you were last Wednesday?'

Sullenness returned to her eyes. 'I was at Ali's flat. My husband was working so I ate with him.'

They stared at each other, he assessing whether she was telling the truth, she attempting a look of defiance. Then he walked down the corridor to the open front door, closing it quietly behind him. Zelfa was waiting on the path; she started to walk off as soon as he joined her.

As soon as they reached the road, Os asked, 'What if it had been the husband? She might not have known a thing about it.'

Zelfa pulled a face and tapped her nose. 'I knew as soon as she opened the door.'

'That's the second woman in this case who's married for money,' Os remarked. 'At least I won't need to worry about that happening to me - not on my pay.'

'I know a few women like that - people I went to school with.'

'What? Married for money?' Zelfa nodded.

'And does it work out for them?' Os asked, genuinely interested.

'Sometimes. If the woman is clever, the man gets what he wants out of the arrangement.' She tossed her head back in the direction of the house they had just come from. 'I think that one is probably keeping both men happy at the moment - though for how long is anyone's guess.'

Zelfa offered Os a cigarette. He hesitated, then declined. He noticed that she could walk up the hill and talk without it affecting her breathing; he made an effort to regulate his own.

'If a man in his fifties is stupid enough to think that a beautiful young woman is interested in him for anything but his money, then he can only blame himself if the arrangement backfires.' She pulled a face, 'You can see that I'm not very sympathetic.'

Os wondered if she had personal experience of such an arrangement. He brought the conversation back to the case. 'So do you think our Mrs Nadir is capable of murder?'

'The old man was a big threat to her. You saw the house. I doubt that she experienced such luxury before she married Nadir. The gold she was wearing would have paid for a police constable and his family to eat for several months.' Her sleek, dark hair swished as she shook her head. 'No, she won't easily give up what she has there. Besides,' she said looking across at him, '...she's a tough one under all that make-up - don't be misled by the little girl look.'

Os said nothing. He hadn't misjudged Mrs Nadir as Zelfa assumed, though he was interested in his colleague's analysis. He wondered whether she had a man waiting for her in Istanbul; Inspector Urfa, under her striking good looks was possibly tougher than the woman they had just left behind. No female could reach the level of Inspector if she hadn't already developed a hard, protective barrier around herself. Although the force was rife with chauvinism, Inspector Urfa could obviously handle herself. He had to admire her for that. If she used her obvious skills to help her succeed in a male dominated police force, then could he really blame her? He reached into his pocket for his car keys.

'It will be interesting to see what the boyfriend is like.'

'Young and good looking but without much money,' Zelfa answered. She looked across at the plastic chairs and tables of the café. 'Does this belong to the man you mentioned?'

Os nodded. 'I sometimes wonder how he makes a living. It's not a particularly busy place.'

'Do you fancy a drink?'

He would have preferred to carry on but he nodded. 'But I don't want to leave it too late before we go up to see the German women. Are you still happy to do the next interview?'

Zelfa threw him a lascivious smile as she sat down on one of the metal chairs.

'Of course! Aziz is keen that I talk to them and besides, I'm enjoying myself.' Os noted her use of the Commandant's first name as she held up her hand to attract Hassan's attention. The bar man's eyes ran appreciatively over Zelfa's body as he took out his pad and pen to take their order. Os took pleasure in introducing her as Inspector Urfa and watched surprise replace that of sexual predator.

When he returned with their drinks, he asked, 'Any news on the identity of the bones, Inspector?' Os dragged his attention back to a subject that had now taken second place in his investigations.

'We're still waiting for the full lab report, Hassan. These things take time. Lefkosa will be dealing with it from now on. How are the villagers bearing up?'

'Locking their doors, most of them, and there's an atmosphere that didn't exist before.' Hassan made an attempt at a laugh. 'Perhaps we're all wondering whether our neighbour is the one who killed old Kutlay and whether we'll be next.'

Os smiled sympathetically. 'It must be very difficult. Sometimes things like this pulls communities together and at other times…'

When the man moved away, Zelfa asked, 'What do you think of our Hassan?'

'I'm not sure yet. He's the local Muhtar so he's got to be seen to be supporting the villagers - but he knows more than he's admitting. And, of course he's aware that I could make things difficult for his business if he doesn't answer our questions.' Os swallowed a mouthful of beer. 'But whether he's protecting anyone, I don't know.' Zelfa seemed to consider his answer but didn't make any further comment.

At last Os said, 'Why don't I drop you off at an estate agent's on the way back? I'm happy to write up the reports. The sooner you get settled into your own place, the better.' He hoped he was not being too obvious about wanting some time on his own. Although he had accepted, if not unwillingly, that he had to share his office, he would be glad when Atak gave her, her own case.

She flashed perfect white teeth. 'All right.' Feeling a sense of relief, he drained his glass and stood up.

There was plenty of car space in the Karaman village square. The white washed cottages were at their best with an abundance of brightly coloured flowers cascading down from balconies and flat roofs. As usual, it was quiet except for an old man brushing up the leaves. For the first time that day, Zelfa appeared to notice her surroundings. She exclaimed her delight at the well-kept, stone houses with their painted shutters and wrought iron-work. The lane was clear of the usual rubbish found in Cypriot villages and the trees and bushes were neatly pruned. Os knew that the gardener was paid by the villagers to keep their idyll; the most beautiful village in Northern Cyprus.

This time he saw the sign immediately. The words, 'Die Bergen' were fashioned in wrought-iron on the gate. Again, he chastised himself for not noticing before. Zelfa ran a pale pink, finger tip over the metal letters.

'Strange how he listed some payments under house names and others under the actual person he was blackmailing. Why would he do that?'

'Who knows?' Os answered. 'It might be for no other reason than he felt linked to the house because he did the garden. We could be making this man more complex than he actually was.'

He followed Zelfa up the narrow, stone steps, making an effort not to stare at her shapely legs. Now that they had proof that the inhabitants had been blackmailed, he felt less uncomfortable about the interview that was about to take place. He hoped this time Zelfa would be a little less arrogant with these foreigners than she had been with the Turkish Cypriot woman but he didn't feel that he knew her well enough to say anything.

Os raised his hand to the brass knocker. Suzanne opened the door. She showed no surprise at the presence of a police inspector accompanied by a strange woman on her door step.

In response to the woman's silence, Os said, 'This is Inspector Urfa. I'm afraid there are some further issues that we'd like to discuss, concerning the murder of Mr. Uludag.' The older woman stood staring at them, as if deciding whether to bar their entrance. Then, without a word, she turned and led the way into the sitting room.

'Is your sister at home?' He spoke to her back, uncomfortable with the title, now he knew it to be a lie.

She indicated, with a wave of her hand, that her visitors should sit down. Os did so, but when it was obvious that his colleague preferred to stand, the elderly woman shrugged and sat down herself, crossing a long, thin leg over the other. As before, she was dressed elegantly, this time in a cream pair of trousers and hand painted, T shirt.

'Ilka's in bed. She gets terrible migraines.'

Zelfa appeared in no mood for chit chat. 'Can I see your passports please?'

Os winced at her tone. He frowned up at her but she continued to stare at the German woman.

'Is there a problem?' She remained in her seat making no effort to oblige the policewoman.

Again Os glimpsed the inner strength of the elderly woman. She must have realised that Os would come back but she was not going to make things easy for them.

'Now please,' Zelfa ordered. She was stood, in front of the empty fireplace, with her legs slightly apart and her hands linked behind her back.

Susanne ignored her but when Os nodded encouragement, she stood up and walked to the sideboard. Pulling out the left drawer, she rifled through some papers then turned back and handed the documents to him.

Os flipped open both passports and read what he already knew. One passport belonged to Susanne Weiss and the other to Ilka Schmidt; both maiden names, there being no mention of a previous marriage. He passed them across to Zelfa. She looked down at the woman who had resumed her seat.

'There seems to be some misunderstanding, Ms. Weiss. You've given everybody in the community the impression that the two of you were sisters. Could you explain why?'

Again, she ignored the policewoman, directing her answers to Os. She spoke quietly and he couldn't help but be aware of the unflattering contrast between his colleague and the more genteel, German woman.

'Is there a reason for this intrusion? Am I supposed to have committed some crime?'

Os saw that her right hand was shaking. He would have liked to take over but Atak had made his instructions very clear. He had no doubt that Zelfa would complain to the Commandant if he interfered. He wondered whether his distaste for her methods was because he felt that this elderly woman didn't deserve such treatment or, as he had questioned her initially, he thought he should be in charge.

'That's what we're trying to ascertain,' Zelfa snapped. 'As you're aware, Mr. Uludag was murdered. We've since discovered that he'd built up a lucrative blackmailing business - of which you were one of the victims! It's a pity you couldn't have mentioned this before to Inspector Zahir, instead of wasting valuable, police time.'

Ms. Weiss' licked her lips then leaned back against her chair and smoothed out the material of her trousers. The back of her hands were age spotted and lined though her face showed someone much younger. Could these two women really have committed murder, Os wondered? Set against this beautifully, elegant backdrop, the concept seemed bizarre. But they certainly had some kind of a motive; their life here could become most awkard if their lie became public knowledge.

'No, we're not sisters, we're friends. That's all I wish to say, as it's obviously none of your business. Now, if I can help you in any other way, please tell me, otherwise there's no reason for you to stay.' For the first time, Susanne Weiss glanced at Zelfa, who straightened her back and glared back at the older woman.

'I'm afraid we've every reason to stay. We found a list of names amongst Mr Uludag's belongings. It appears you've been paying a sum of money to Mr Uludag for some time.'

Miss Weiss raised her eyebrows. 'Naturally. He's been doing our garden for many years.'

Zelfa sighed as if to emphasise that time was being wasted. 'Yes, we know. But it's far more than you would pay a gardener. The amount was two hundred and fifty Turkish Lira a month.'

Susanne shook her head, emphasizing how ridiculous she found the accusations. 'I wouldn't dream of paying that man so much. You must have made a mistake. We paid him thirty Lira each time he came, with a little extra at New Year.'

She stood up and went to the same drawer from which she had taken the passports. When she turned around again, she had a thin cigar in her hand. It took her a couple of attempts before she was able to strike a match. Os fought back the need to cross the room to help her.

'Mr Uludag kept records of all the payments he received. The other people have admitted to paying him - I don't believe that he could have made a mistake with you.'

Susanne leaned back against the solid piece of furniture as if needing it's support. 'We always paid him in cash. Unfortunately, he's now dead, so it's impossible to sort out this misunderstanding.' Os could hear a new weariness in the German woman's voice as if she knew herself that her protestations were a waste of time.

Zelfa tutted. 'I think we both know why you thought it necessary to pay, Ms Weiss. It's quite obvious that you and Ms Schmidt are more than friends - not that, in normal circumstances, it would be of any interest to me.' Zelfa waved her hand extravagantly as if to show how broadminded she was. 'But in this village, you had a lot to lose if they found out that the two of you had been lying all of these years.'

'And you think we would kill him for this?'

Os wondered whether Inspector Urfa was typical of the Istanbul police. There was no sense of subtlety, just an ability to bully. However, Ms Weiss was not to be cowed by a young slip of a girl, even if she was an Inspector of Police. Indignation intensified her clipped, German accent.

'Your accusations are outrageous. Your only proof appears to be some doodlings belonging to a dead man. I assume that the courts would require something a little more substantial. Now it would be better if you left.' The hand that held onto the sideboard shook but she gave herself a small push and walked stiffly towards the door.

Os stood up and, without looking at Zelfa, followed Susanne Weiss out of the room. She stood waiting for them by the front door, staring fixedly at a painting on the opposite wall.

Os attempted to make eye contact. 'Thank you for your time, Ms. Weiss.' She behaved as if he hadn't spoken so Os walked down the path and waited for Zelfa on the road.

They made their way down the hill, the only sound coming from Zelfa's heels, clacking against the tarmac. This time, Zelfa made no reference to her surroundings.

'How do you think that went?' he asked.'

'What a hard-faced, lying cow.'

His casual shrug hid his irritation. 'What else could she say? She's right. We don't have any proof.'

Zelfa did not reply but the tension bounced like static between them. He pulled open the car door and climbed in, leaving her standing outside, drumming her long nails on the roof. She bent down to talk through the open window.

'I think we should go back - make her admit to paying Uludag that money.'

Os made an effort to keep his tone neutral. 'Let's leave it for now. She's not going to say anything more unless we put a great deal of pressure on her and at the moment, I'm not willing to do that. She's part of the European community - we don't want them to turn against us without it being absolutely necessary. She's an elderly woman - we could easily be accused of bullying her.'

Again, her long nails drummed the roof above him. Finally, she made what was obviously a reluctant decision. 'If that's what you want, I'll go with it.'

Os started the engine and completed a three point turn. Silence returned as they drove down the hill. Taking a corner, just below the village of Endremit, he had to break to allow a line of goats to scuttle across the road. A dog hurried them along , nipping at slow legs, continuously circling. A young boy, no more than eight years old, stood in the middle of the road, his eyes intent on his protégées. Os slipped in a CD.

A few minutes later they joined the coastal road. Turning right, the sign for 'Ian Smith Estates,' appeared ahead on the left. Os pulled into the parking area and kept the engine running. He nodded towards the glass and marble frontage of the shop, the large window busy with property details.

Os turned to Zelfa, 'Ask for Mehmet and mention my name. They'll drop you off at your hotel afterwards. Good luck.' He forced a smile. 'I'll see you tomorrow.'

Os drove off before she had reached the office door. A tight band of tension squeezed his eyes. Should he have cut in during that last interview? But Atak didn't appreciate disobedience and the insecurity of this being his first case wasn't helping. And perhaps he was being overly sensitive? There was a possibility that Atak would prefer Zelfa's interviewing skills to his own. He overtook a row of cars, dismissive of the horns that shrieked after him.

As he walked into the station, the duty sergeant called across that Commandant Atak had instructed that he was to report to him when he got back.

Zelfa's thoughts

What a good looking man but so easily put out! I know I upset him with my questioning today - I could feel him getting all edgy. I wouldn't have thought he was tough enough for homicide - they'd make mincemeat of him in Istanbul! He's more bothered about what the European community think of him than in finding out the truth. That German woman knew more than she was admitting. I could tell she was hiding something.

He's obviously angry about sharing this murder case as well as his office. But he's doing his best to be polite. After all the lechers I've met in the job, I think he's going to be a pleasure to work with.

And there's no getting away from the fact that he's rather good looking – perhaps not like Mehmet, but I have to forget about him. He dresses well, which is pretty unique in the police force - most men are such geeks. I wonder if he's single. I might ask him. It is the twenty first century after all.

Chapter Fifteen

Atak's secretary was not in her office so Os didn't have to go through the sycophantic behaviour that was usually necessary to see the great God. Os found him working through a document, a fountain pen in his right hand. When he saw his Inspector he grunted and, pushing the cap back on the pen, lounged back in his chair. He didn't smile. Something was not making the big man happy, so Os sat down and waited, observing the bloated face for any indication of what was to come next.

'How is Inspector Urfa? Are you looking after her?'

Os kept his face bland. 'Of course. She's finding somewhere to live at the moment. I thought she should sort out her personal arrangements as soon as possible.'

The Commandant nodded. 'How do you feel she's going to work out?'

Os didn't think Atak would appreciate hearing his slant on the afternoon's interviews. Instead he answered, 'She's very capable. More than capable of taking on her own work, sir. I know she feels that way herself.'

The big man stared at Os without blinking. 'Does she indeed? And how do you feel about that? I'd have thought that it would have been a great opportunity to have someone so experienced working with you.'

Os attempted to sound more enthusiastic. 'There's nothing to stop me discussing anything with Inspector Urfa, now that we share the same office. But I thought with the department's work load, her experience would be better used elsewhere. She might have some fresh ideas on tackling the burglaries that the politicians are so concerned about.' The Commandant continued to stare at his most junior Inspector, reminding Os of a large toad.

Os was about to suggest that he should get back to his office when Atak said, 'Where are you up to in the Uludag case, Osman?'

He gave his boss a brief description of the two interviews and his plans to see the businessman, Erim Gorus, the next day. Atak asked him a few questions and then continued to stare. Os attempted to appear relaxed.

'If Inspector Urfa is keen to have her own case then we must oblige - I don't want her to have any reason to complain.'

Os felt a jab of jealousy. His boss had never shown the same protective feelings towards him. Was it because of his colleague's obvious charms, or his fear of offending his friend in Istanbul, that was making Atak so attentive towards one of his officers? Hopefully, he would not find it necessary to question Zelfa about her wish to take on her own case. Since Os hadn't actually mentioned it to her, he didn't know quite what she really felt.

Atak's chest rattled as he spoke. 'I think she should do one more day with you. Both of you interview Gorus tomorrow. The gentler, female touch might encourage him to talk.'

'I doubt it, sir, if he's got a penchant for young boys.' Os kept his face in neutral as he recalled Zelfa's method in handling Susanne Weiss.

Atak picked up his pen again. 'And after that I'll call her in and give her work of her own. That's all then, Osman, keep me informed.'

Os waited until he was back in the corridor before he allowed himself to smile. He was still grinning when he passed the sergeants' room and met Sener on his way out.

'Is it good news then from the Missing Persons Department, sir?' Os stared at him.

'The envelope on your desk.' Seemingly in response to the blankness on his boss's face, Sener added, 'You haven't seen it then?'

Os shook his head. He hadn't given the skeletons much thought over the last few hours.

'The porter handed me the envelope downstairs. I was tempted to open it.' Sener grinned. 'Shall I come up with you now sir?'

'Why not? Get us both a coffee on the way will you? I need some caffeine.'

The sight of his cramped office brought on fresh irritation. Even when Zelfa was working independently she would still be using his room. Not that he didn't like her; apart from the way she had handled Susanne Weiss, he thought she would be a good addition to the Girne Police Force. He just preferred his own space. He ripped open the large, brown envelope and scanned the contents. None of the information surprised him. The male had been shot through the head, whereas the female had been killed by a blow to the head.

The door opened and Sener entered, balancing two small cups on the back of a file. He pulled a chair across and sat down opposite his boss. Os slid over the report and then sipped his coffee.

'What do you make of it?' He asked at last.

Sener picked up his cup and swallowed the thick liquid in two mouthfuls. 'I don't really know. Do you still think that they're linked to Uludag's murder?'

'We're taught not to believe in coincidences!'

The sergeant lit a cigarette. Os ignored the temptation to join him despite the continual longing he felt whenever he smelled burning tobacco. There was obvious doubt in Sener's voice.

'Could Uludag have killed the two people we found in the ground, sir?'

Os shook his head. 'But he knew who did – I'm sure of it.'

'Perhaps he was bribing the couple and then something happened and they couldn't pay.'

'So he killed them to send a message to others?' Os asked, thinking that Sener had been watching too many Mafia films.

'Uludag would have been much younger in those days - more threatening.' Sener spoke defensively, obviously hurt by Os's response.

'Except for how he treated his wife, we've not been given the impression that he was a violent man,' Os explained.

The sergeant tipped his chair back against Zelfa's desk. 'What's your theory then, sir?'

Os spread out his hands in defeat. 'I haven't got one. I've no proof that the two cases are linked. But I can't believe that it was co-incidental that Uludag was murdered within a few hours after I questioned him? Uludag knew something - but whether he was involved in the killing, over thirty years ago, and someone decided that he couldn't now be trusted - I don't know? If we could only identify the bones…….' Irritation flooded up inside him. 'If we were in America, the dental records would tell us who they were. But here, patients take their records home with them.'

Os leaned over and pulled up the Venetian blind that hung over the open window. He felt the breeze immediately. The small office still felt stagnant but whether it was the room or their minds, Os wasn't sure.

'So what's the new woman like then, sir?'

Os had wondered how long it would take Sener to ask what the whole building must be thinking. 'Inspector Urfa?'

Sener grinned. 'She's working on the case with you isn't she?' He patted the new desk behind him. 'And she's sharing a room with you. A few of the men are jealous?'

'Are they indeed!' He knew what his colleagues were like. For a moment he was tempted to play devils advocate but then he didn't need the hassle; he had enough complications in his life with Roisin. 'Well, they had better not waste their time ogling her. She's sharp and she's used to handling herself.' Os didn't add that from what he had observed, she would make light of any man who tried to proposition her. He would leave that discovery to the unfortunate person who was cocky enough to attempt it. He lifted his jacket from the back of his seat. 'I'm going home now, I've had enough.'

'Am I still coming with you tomorrow, sir?' Sener asked.

Os pulled a face. 'I'm sorry, Sener. I'm to take Inspector Urfa.' He saw his sergeant's disappointment but felt it unprofessional to make a comment. Instead, he said, 'Could you have another look at our unidentified victim? Whoever it is hasn't paid for the last two months.' Os pulled the crumpled sheets out of his pocket and stared again at the list of names. 'Why did he stop when every one else continued to pay?' He glanced at his sergeant to see if he had any ideas but if he did, he was now keeping them to himself. 'It could be that he's the murderer - he didn't have the money so Uludag threatened to reveal his secret. Who knows,' Os sighed, '...it might have been a strong enough reason to kill!'

'Or her, sir. There are more women than men in this case.' Sener pushed his chair back against the wall. 'I think I'll go home myself, sir. My wife wasn't very well this morning.'

Os felt immediate concern. 'No problems with the pregnancy are there, Sener?'

'No, sir. She's just not coping with the heat this time.'

'Well, send her my regards.'

Both men fell in step as they walked down the corridor. Os found himself thinking again about Sener's home life.

No, he didn't envy the hoard of kids who seemed to scream their heads off whenever Os had the occasion to call. But he himself wanted marriage and perhaps one or two children; but Roisin had already told him that it wasn't what she wanted, so numbers of offspring were not going to be an issue for them. He was surprised by the weight of sadness that settled on him. The excitement of being with Roisin had initially been enough but now he was beginning to question their future. What had changed? He wondered if it was just this murder case and he would feel more settled afterwards.

'See you tomorrow, Sener,' he called as the sergeant walked towards his battered car.

'Night, sir,' Sener answered.

Roisin was in the kitchen, her hands in a bowl of mincemeat and herbs. She held her face up for him to kiss. 'How was today?'

'So, so,' he answered, loosening his tie.

'Have a shower and then tell me about it,' she said. He nodded then went into their bedroom to change.

Sometime later she came out onto the patio holding two bottles of beer. He was sat in his usual chair, a towel tied around his middle. She handed him his drink then stood behind him. He felt her hands in his hair and he closed his eyes as her strong fingers began to ease out the tension.

'I've got a new room mate.'

Her fingers stilled for a moment. 'How come? I thought you'd arranged to have your office to yourself - it's not even that big.'

Os took a long slug of beer. 'An Inspector is on secondment from Istanbul. Atak called me in this morning to tell me that it wasn't fair to make her share with several men - so I've got her.'

There was a few seconds silence before Roisin asked, 'What's she like?'

He glanced up to gauge her reaction but he could see only curiosity in her face. Since she would probably meet the woman one day, he decided to be honest.

'Very good looking.'

'And her ability as a police officer?'

Os smiled at her dry tone. 'I'm not sure. I've seen her interview two women so far.' He took another gulp of his beer as he analysed Zelfa's behaviour. 'The first was in a house in Endremit. You know, the one with the large swimming pool that you can just see through the bushes when you take the sharp corner.'

Roisin nodded.

'The wife's been paying Uludag money for three years. Zelfa got her to talk in minutes. She's pretty tough.'

'Who, Zelfa or the wife?'

Os grinned. 'Both I think. It's just that Zelfa has the law on her side.'

'Well, isn't that what you want, your suspects to talk?'

'She obviously married him for his money.' Os wondered why he had suddenly focused in on an issue that was irrelevant to the case. He was becoming fixated with marriage.

'It's not exactly a new phenomenon, is it?' Roisin answered.

Something in her tone made him ask, 'Have you ever been attracted to money?' She continued to massage his head and he thought she wasn't going to answer. Then she stopped and sat down opposite him.

'I wouldn't do what that woman did, marry for it, but I've stayed in a relationship longer than I would've normally - because of the lifestyle his money offered.'

Os felt uncomfortable but couldn't help himself from questioning her further. 'Did you live with this man?'

'No. It was fun for a while, going away for weekends and being spoiled. But we were very different - and there's always some kind of payback.'

Os stared ahead at the pool and the mass of bright, red flowers on the bush behind. There was a lot he didn't know about Roisin and he felt the twist of jealousy about her life before him.

'So money means a lot to you.'

Her eyes narrowed. 'I thought we were talking about this woman. But since you're asking, no it doesn't. I don't want to be poor but big wealth doesn't particularly attract me.' A sharpness had crept into her voice. 'What's all this about?'

'Why don't we get married?'

Os was as surprised by his question as she obviously was. They stared at each other.

'What's brought this on?' She reached out to take his hand but Os heard the caginess in her voice and tried to pull it away. She held onto it. 'You know what I think about marriage.'

'Not every one has the same kind of relationship as your parents?' Now that he had brought the subject up, he felt he had to press his point.

'I've seen the affect our upbringing had on my sister. She's tried it twice and now she's living on her own.' She squeezed his captured hand. 'I don't want that to happen to us.'

'You're not your sister. We love each other don't we?' Os found himself waiting for confirmation before he could continue. 'We've lived together and that works very well.'

'This is different from marriage.'

He stood up and went into the kitchen. He was taken aback that a conversation over the contents of his day should have ended in this. What had brought it on? Had it been the obvious flirtation of the new, very attractive Inspector that had unsettled him or the constant nagging of his mother to get married and have children. Marriage, in its various forms, had been on his mind since he had started this investigation. Yesterday, he had questioned whether Sergul Mandrez had married her husband for love and then today he had felt nothing but distaste for Safiye Nadir, whose primary concern was that her husband shouldn't find out that she was having an affair. His relationship with Roisin suddenly seemed idyllic alongside such deceit. But he knew she was going to reject his offer. She had always made it quite clear that she wasn't interested in committing herself to anything more than living together.

He stood up and walked over to the garden wall. The distant lights of Girne glowed in the falling dusk. He felt her arms encircle his waist from behind, her breath stirring his hair.

'Why don't we wait until this murder case is over,' she said. 'We can talk about it properly then.'

He turned around and looked into her green eyes. She had assumed the anxious expression he had seen before. 'You're right, this isn't the best time.' He pulled her towards him and kissed her, relieved that the awkward moment had passed. 'When are we eating?'

For the rest of the evening they consciously talked about other things but when they went to bed, Os couldn't dispel the sadness that clung to him. He felt that their relationship had now entered a new phase and he regretted his impetuousness. What had made him ask such a question? Was this case getting to him? Perhaps Inspector Urfa was having a more unsettling effect than he had thought?

The next morning, he left the house at eight o'clock. Uncharacteristically, Roisin had got up with him and made coffee. The night had dissipated the atmosphere of the previous evening but Os still felt an unease he couldn't shake off.

Zelfa was already in their office, wearing a similar dress to the previous day but in white. The Volkan newspaper was laid out in front of her.

He responded to her welcoming smile. 'You look cheerful.'

'I am. I've now got a car and a lovely new apartment by the sea. Thank you for dropping me off yesterday. They really looked after me.'

'What's the place like?' Os picked up the phone and rang the Porter's office. 'Coffee?' He looked across at Zelfa, who he realised, suited white even more than she did black.

She nodded. 'It's one bed-roomed and has a balcony that looks out to the sea. The furniture's lovely.'

'How long did you take it on for?' he asked, interested to hear if her answer would tie in with what Atak had told him.

'Six months for the moment. I hired the car from Gorus's company. I thought I would see what kind of an operation he ran.' Os raised his eyebrows. 'Very professional! I was given a good deal because of the six month lease. I couldn't fault them.'

'I don't suppose the man himself was around, was he?' Os asked.

She shook her head. 'Just the office staff. I didn't get there until seven o'clock. A girl called Gill, who took me to see the apartment, dropped me off.'

Zelfa stopped talking as a porter, balancing two small cups of coffee on a metal tray, came into the room. Os, remembering Roisin's criticism, thanked him and smiled.

'The results of the skeleton tests came yesterday.' He passed the envelope across to her. 'While you're reading that, I'll go down and see my sergeants. They've been checking out the last person on Uludag's list. Number five.' Os drained his coffee in one and pushed back his chair. 'See you in a few minutes.'

Sener was also reading the paper but stood up when he saw his boss standing in the doorway.

'Any news?'

Sener shook his head. 'Fikri and I went back up to the house again yesterday but we couldn't find anything that would give us a lead. I then called in at Uludag's bank and spent an hour with the manager. There was absolutely nothing in their files that would give us any clue about our mystery person. All the victims paid in cash.' Sener chewed his lip. 'You don't think he could be dead, do you? '

'Or it could be the murderer! Go through the list of people in this area over the age of twenty who've died in the last two months and see if they had a police record of any kind. You never know, something might come up.' Os looked at his watch, 'Where is Fikri anyway? It's gone nine o'clock?'

The sergeant's eyes didn't quite meet those of his boss. 'He's had a lot of trouble with his car, sir. I'm sure he won't be long.'

Os clicked his tongue in annoyance. It was more likely that his other sergeant had been out late the night before at one of Northern Cyprus's many casinos. Or had he had another argument with his long-suffering wife? If it happened again he would have to speak to Fikri; his life seemed a mess but then a lot of it was his own fault. Gambling was an addiction that had affected several men in the force. Why the government was allowing the growth in casinos was beyond his comprehension. Perhaps they saw it as a way of bringing in money into the country but most of the profits would end up in the pockets of a few criminals. Again, Os wondered which politicians were being financially rewarded by the Casino Mafia. The continued political isolation of Northern Cyprus had such a negative effect on the economy that such money spinners, as gambling and the construction industry, seemed to be able to do whatever they wanted. Os thrust the unjustness of the embargo out of his mind before his usual anger over the situation got a grip on him.

Instead he asked, 'Are you all right with that? I should be back around lunch time so we can discuss then what inroads you've made. I'm off to visit Gorus now with Inspector Urfa.' Os wasn't sure whether he detected something in Sener's expression and then decided that he was being paranoid.

But he spoke more abruptly than he intended. 'I'll leave you to it. I'll be in my office for a while if you need me.' Our office, he reminded himself.

Zelfa was making notes on a pad, the report still open on her desk. He resisted the temptation to ask what she was doing.

'Are you ready?'

She stood up and smoothed the skirt of her dress. He noticed that she had replaced her lipstick and wondered whether this was usual or whether she was preparing herself for the interview. Roisin was very different to this excessively groomed woman. She wore make-up in the evenings if they were going out but other wise she didn't bother. He wondered whether Zelfa made as much effort when she was off duty. Somehow, he thought she probably did.

'We'll take my car,' she said, picking up her keys.

Os accepted. He was curious to discover how she drove. He suspected that it would be with the same aggression as she conducted her interviews.

The black, soft-top Mercedes in the car park confirmed that this woman did not rely on her Inspector's pay. Without comment, he directed her down back streets and into a space a few minutes walk from Gorus's office.

'Dokum Construction and Car Hire' was based in a two storey, modern block. The Inspectors were taken upstairs by one of the several attractive, female assistants who worked in the ground floor office. Waiting for them was Erim Gorus's personal assistant.

'Mr Gorus won't be long,' she said, her perfect teeth flashing white against her flawless tanned skin.

Both Inspectors declined refreshment but accepted the offer of a seat. Os found it interesting, considering the nature of their investigation, that Gorus surrounded himself with beautiful women. Was it to enhance his corporate image or to deflect any suggestion that he might be interested in young boys? Zelfa picked up one of the glossy magazines from the coffee table and flicked through the pages.

The man had obviously done well for himself. Several framed posters of Istanbul lined the cream walls. Os wondered whether the man was homesick for the city he had grown up in. Was there a reason besides money that he remained in Northern Cyprus? Os glanced impatiently at his watch and at that moment he heard a door open. He looked up to see the owner of 'Dokum Construction and Car Hire', watching them.

Chapter Sixteen

Gorus was in his fifties and looked good on it. If he had any physical defects, his pearl grey, silk suit hid them well. His hair was thick and black. For a fleeting moment, Os questioned whether he would start to die his own hair when the grey arrived. He dismissed the idea as ridiculous. He knew of men who went through some process where hair was attached to their thinning skulls and he wondered whether Gorus needed such help to look so young.

'Thank you for making time for us, Mr Gorus,' Os said as he crossed the room to shake the man's smooth hand.

'I think your sergeant said that it was something to do with the car hire side of my company?' Gorus answered. 'I hope I'm not in any trouble.' His smile made a mockery of such a suggestion. He stood aside to allow the two visitors entrance into his office.

If Os had no prior knowledge about the man's success, Gorus's working environment would have soon educated him. The room was twice the size of his secretary's next door and here, large windows looked out onto the back drop of the mountains. His desk was a slab of beautifully varnished wood, clear except for a slim computer system. Again, large, framed, colour photos of Istanbul hung on the pastel- green walls.

Gorus indicated the two leather sofas in the corner of the room.

Os waited until they were all settled, before saying, 'I see that you have an affinity with Istanbul, Mr Gorus.'

The man gave a practised smile. 'I was born there. This is the extension of the company my family built up in Istanbul. I came over ten years ago to set up a subsidiary and then I met my wife.'

He indicated a large, framed photo on his desk. From Os's angle he could see the smiling faces of two children and an attractive, dark-haired woman. 'I added the construction side a few years ago when I saw how the country was going.' The man wore a smug, self satisfied expression which was beginning to irritate.

Os decided to dispel it. 'Inspector Urfa and myself are investigating a murder.'

The smug expression faltered. Os smiled. 'I believe that you knew a man called Kutlay Uludag.' Apart from a quick movement of the irises, Gorus didn't react. Os was impressed.

Instead the businessman answered, 'You said knew?'

Os wondered whether he was a good listener or whether the death of the old man was already news to this entrepreneur. He had been out of the country for a few days and the death, although reported in the local paper, would not have been of interest to the Turkish media. Os decided that he wouldn't allow the man to prevaricate.

'Could you tell us where you were last Wednesday night?'

Gorus picked up his Blackberry and pressed the buttons until he found his diary. After a few seconds he looked up but this time his smile was not so confident.

'With my kind of schedule it's impossible to remember without help. My wife and children went to dinner with my in-laws so I stayed here and did some work.'

'What time did you leave?' Zelfa asked.

She had taken out a pad and pen and was making notes. Os preferred to use his memory but it wouldn't do any harm for Gorus to be aware that they were recording his answers.

The businessman looked up at the ceiling as he considered the question. 'About eight, eight thirty. I get a lot of work done when people have gone home.'

'So no-one saw you leave?' Zelfa asked

'I shouldn't think so. Sumer, my personal assistant, leaves here at six and I use a different entrance to the people I employ in the office below us.' He put his head on one side in an elaborate display of thinking. 'I might have looked in to say good night but I can't be sure. I like them to think I'm still in the building - it keeps them on their toes. The office is open until nine o'clock.'

'And then what did you do?' Os asked.

'I went home, had a swim and then heated up the meal that my wife had left for me. The family arrived back at about eleven.'

'And, of course, nobody can verify this?' Os asked, already sensing the answer.

'I'm afraid not, Inspector. We have a reasonable amount of land so we can't see our neighbours and they can't see us.'

How very useful, Os thought. Gorus seemed to be in complete control of the situation but then someone as rich as him was probably used to manipulating conversations.

'We know that you paid Uludag, five hundred Turkish Lira every month for nine years.' Os held up his hand to stop the businessman from denying the charge. 'We also know why.'

Erim Gorus pushed his hands into his pockets and uncrossed his legs, placing them both firmly on the ground. His eyes had assumed a blank expression, as if he was bored with the conversation. Os waited to see if he would deny knowledge of the allegation. But the businessman had more sense.

'That case was never proved. The boy's family withdrew the charge.'

'The father worked for your family business didn't he?' Os interrupted.

Gorus slid a cigarette out of the packet that was on the table. He then picked up a silver, table lighter and snapped on the flame. When he had inhaled deeply he answered to no - one in particular, 'He managed the warehouse.'

'So he could have lost his job?' Zelfa asked.

Gorus stared at the female detective. His voice, when he spoke, now had a cold edge to it. 'My family have a reputation for being good to their employees. There was never any question of the man losing his job - he'd worked for my father for years. Our two families socialised together.'

Zelfa raised eyebrows was comment enough. Gorus's eyes narrowed but he didn't respond to the unspoken insinuation.

'So the friendship you developed with the fourteen year old son was purely platonic?' Os continued.

'Yes, until I found him stealing from the warehouse. He was removing cans of paint one evening when everyone had gone home. He had his father's keys. Throwing accusations at me was his way of getting out of the situation.'

'I'm surprised you let the matter drop,' Zelfa said. 'The boy caused a lot of trouble – after all, the incident forced you to leave Istanbul.'

Gorus rubbed an imaginary speck of dirt on his trouser leg. 'My family wanted to expand the business. The Turkish government was offering incentives to businesses willing to set up in Northern Cyprus.' He shrugged his shoulders under the silk covering of his jacket. 'I was the son who wasn't married - I had no formal ties in Istanbul so I was the obvious choice. And then, as I said, I met my wife.'

'She's the daughter of the Shadow Minister for Education isn't she?' Os asked. Gorus nodded. Os felt a reluctant respect that Gorus hadn't brought up this connection himself. He was used to people hiding behind the protection of their influential relatives.

'I'm sorry, but I find it difficult to believe that you didn't sue the boy when a charge of paedophilia was being held against you?' Zelfa persisted.

Gorus's voice remained void of emotion. 'He would have gone to a Young Offenders' Institution. I couldn't have done that to the family. At least, at the time I thought that. I've regretted my leniency since.'

'Then please help us understand why it was necessary to pay Uludag?' Os asked. 'Every month, you handed over what many families here would consider a great deal of money.'

Gorus clasped his manicured hands together. 'But not for me, Inspector. I'm a very wealthy man. Uludag approached me outside this office here when I arrived for work one morning. He showed me the police report. I can't imagine why Istanbul thought it necessary to send it across to Northern Cyprus, considering how decently I'd behaved. I'd no idea that there was a copy in the Police files here.' He stood up and moved over to the window with a view of the mountains. 'Security in the station must be very lax.'

Gorus appeared in total control. Such a trait would be useful if you wanted to murder someone, Os thought. He focused back on what the man was saying.

'The incident had been extremely embarrassing at the time. The last thing I wanted was for it to be made public here. I hadn't told my wife and I couldn't see any point in upsetting her now. It was easier to pay the man.' Gorus took out a laundered white handkerchief and blew his nose. 'Five hundred Lira is not a great deal to me. If only he had known, he could have asked for more.' He slipped his hands inside his trouser pockets and forced a smile. 'I looked on it as a necessary evil for having been too lenient on the boy in the first place.'

'You were proved to be innocent, surely your wife would have understood?' Zelfa asked.

Gorus's smile hovered on his handsome features, then disappeared. 'I'm sure she would, Inspector but her father has not such a nature. And perhaps,' he glanced at her hand, '…you might know how important it is to keep in with your in-laws?'

That was the key to his behaviour, Os thought. He's frightened Nesil Eray will find out. But would he kill to ensure Uludag's silence and why now, after all these years? Os stared at the businessman wondering what Gorus's father-in-law thought of him. Gorus was still attractive with an easy smile and he was obviously good at making money. He had also managed to sire two children. Os glanced again at the family photo. Was his wife still happy with the marriage? How often did Gorus go to Istanbul on business and was this when he indulged himself with boys? Of course, the incident with the child could have been a one off. But instinct told him that wasn't the case. Os's head buzzed with questions that he couldn't answer. That Gorus was guilty of the crime that had never reached the Istanbul courts, Os was certain. But whether he was capable of committing murder was another thing.

'Did you go to Uludag's house to pay the money?' Os asked.

Even if Gorus denied this, it would be easy for a man like him to find out where the old man lived. Uludag would have let him in without any trouble. The businessman had been paying him regularly for nine years.

'No. I used to meet him at a café by the bus station. I would have a coffee and then, when he arrived, I would go. I'd leave behind an envelope inside a newspaper on the table.

'You'll be glad he's dead.' Zelfa stated it as fact.

Gorus rattled the coins in his trouser pocket. Os smiled at his discomfiture.

'Of course. Wouldn't you be? Whoever killed him did me a favour.' He paused, then added bitterly, 'Presumably he blackmailed other people? The man seems to have had free access to the entire filing system in the station.'

'I'm afraid I can't say,' Os answered. It suddenly occurred to him that this was the second of Uludag's victims that he felt no sympathy at all for.

'There are other suspects besides myself then?' Gorus made an attempt at a smile, as if implying it ridiculous that he should be considered a murderer.

Os looked across at Zelfa. Simultaneously, they both stood up. 'Thank you for your time, Mr Gorus. If you are intending to make any more trips to Istanbul in the near future, could you let me know?' Os placed one of his cards on the highly polished surface of the desk. 'Call me if you think of anything. I'm sure you can appreciate the necessity to find the murderer as quickly as possible.'

Gorus shoved back his shoulders and there was now a hint of aggression in his voice. 'So I am a suspect!'

Os turned back from the door. 'I'm afraid so.'

The personal assistant looked up from her computer and smiled at the two Inspectors as they crossed her office to the staircase. Os wondered whether the staff were taken on because of the quality of their teeth.

'I could do with a coffee,' Zelfa said, as soon as they were outside. 'Is there a decent café around here?'

Os considered the new cafes that had sprung up over the last two years. He didn't think she would appreciate stopping off in one of the places he frequented with his sergeants.

He nodded. 'There's one on the way back to the station.'

They sat out of the sun under the café's striped awning. Os stuck with his sade but Zelfa ordered a latte. What a change this country had gone through in the last four years, Os thought. Then, there had been only one café in the whole of Girne that had sold anything other than Nescafe or Turkish coffee but now you were spoilt for choice. Of course, coming from

Istanbul, she would be used to a level of sophistication that Girne was only just touching on, not that everyone considered that a good thing.

The other tables around them were empty. It was a bad year for tourists. The papers blamed the construction industry. The lorries transporting cement and workmen living on site, working all hours, wasn't conducive to a peaceful holiday. The long-standing problems with the South weren't helping either. Personally, he preferred it like this but the economy was suffering.

'Are you married?'

The question, coming from no-where, surprised him but he shook his head.

He nearly mentioned Roisin and then stopped. He didn't want to discuss her and he would be mortified if Zelfa asked him if he was going to get married. He had enough interference in his relationship with his mother and the recent conversation he had with Roisin was still raw in his memory.

He wondered again about Zelfa Urfa's personal life. She was a very attractive woman but he knew it wasn't easy for policewomen to find someone outside the force. She could be having a relationship with a colleague, of course but that usually didn't work. The hours were too erratic and it was like living in a gold fish bowl with everyone watching and speculating. And she must experience a lot of jealousy - being such an attractive woman who already had done so well in the profession. If her partner was a police officer, it wouldn't be easy for him either. But Os certainly wasn't going to ask her whether she had a boyfriend, even though he guessed that she would eventually tell him anyway. It was rather nice sitting out here on the pavement in the shade. Zelfa appeared to be enjoying herself and had put on large sunglasses that had little gems stuck to the sides.

'What made you want to come to Northern Cyprus? It must seem like a back water after Istanbul?'

She shrugged, as if to give the impression that what she was about to tell him, meant nothing to her. 'I needed a change. I've just split up with my fiancé and as he was my immediate boss, I thought it would be better that I left for a while.' She thanked the waiter who had placed the two coffees on their table. 'My family used to come here on holiday when I was younger. Istanbul is beautiful but I love the quietness here.' She spooned some of the coffee froth into her mouth. 'I appreciate how kind you've been to me. I should imagine you preferred your office to yourself.'

Os grinned. 'Was it that obvious?'

She shook her head. 'I would have felt the same if I'd been in your place. I'll try not to be a nuisance.' She took a sip of her coffee, watching him over the brim. 'So! Have you a theory of who murdered the old man?'

Os leaned back in his chair and sighed. 'No. They could all have done it. They've all got reasons. Though I think perhaps, Gorus is the most likely at the moment.'

Zelfa put down her cup and took out her pad and pen from her handbag.

'Let's go through each person individually - it'll help me sort things out in my mind. The first person you interviewed had done what?'

For a moment Os was taken aback by the suggestion. Then he answered, 'Mandrez, nee Gul, had been a prostitute in Lefkosa when she was much younger. The police brought her in a couple of times during that period – hence her record which Uludag found in the files.' Os's mouth tightened as he thought how easy it had been for Uludag, a porter, to obtain this information. At least one good thing about the new station was the tightened security.

'And what were her reasons for paying him?' Zelfa had divided the sheet of paper into two sections and was now writing down the information.

'She'd married a wealthy man who had no idea about her past. If he'd found out that she'd once been a prostitute, instead of the innocent, village girl he imagined, he might have divorced her.'

'Children?' Zelfa asked.

Os nodded. 'Both under the age of five. Presumably, the worst case scenario would be to get rid of her and keep the kids. I would think that a court would prefer the children to be brought up by, what they would see as, the duped husband. And he's certainly wealthy enough to pay for someone to look after them and keep house.'

Zelfa drew another line down the page. 'So why do you think she didn't kill the old man?'

Os took a gulp of his coffee before answering. 'Gut feeling I'm afraid, nothing more. Although this didn't have anything to do with my decision, I feel some sympathy for her. She'd become a prostitute to support her family. She kept it a secret from her mother who thought she had a good job somewhere.'

Zelfa looked up. 'Rather naive I would have thought. The girl left school at fourteen with basic qualifications - what on earth did her mother think she was doing?'

'Perhaps it suited her to believe it. If it hadn't been for the girl's financial input, I doubt that the family would have survived as a unit.' Os scanned Zelfa's face but the Inspector appeared to be concentrating on the facts. Os continued, 'And it worked out for the best. The girl managed to hook herself a very successful husband so she's still able to support them. Her husband knew nothing about her past so all was well.'

'Until Uludag appeared on the scene!' Zelfa interrupted. 'Mandrez said that she was able to afford the payments without her husband becoming suspicious but it couldn't have been easy. And while Uludag was alive she must have worried that her husband would find out. Quite a motive I'd say.'

'But was she capable of killing the old man?' Os said.

He thought back to the slim, attractive woman he had interviewed a short time ago. Although the Northern Cypriot courts dealt with a few female murderers, it was not usual.

'Have you considered that one of her family could have done it? They also had a lot to lose if the husband found out about what she'd done before he met her.'

It was a good point. He should have thought of that himself. He put on his sunglasses. 'I'll get Sener and Fikri onto it.'

Zelfa raised her hand to the waiter then turned to Os. 'Another coffee?' He nodded and watched her order; the young man grinned at her before hurrying back to the kitchen. Os wondered if she was aware that she was flirting or whether it was how she behaved with all men. He remembered the way she had sat on his desk the first morning and thought that it probably was. How she managed to work without incident, in a predominantly male environment, he couldn't imagine.

'I think checking the family's a good idea,' Zelfa continued. 'But don't dismiss the fact that she could be capable of murder, even though I'm sure she came across as a helpless, pretty woman. I would imagine she's very skilled at manipulating men.'

'I'm not dismissing anything.'

'I'm sorry.' She seemed surprised by the coldness in his voice.

Os acknowledged her apology with a curt nod. This woman was a strange mixture of feminine wiles and extreme bossiness. It wasn't surprising that she'd risen to the position of Inspector so quickly. But, grudgingly he had to admit she was helping him to focus on the case.

She smiled as if nothing had taken place between them. 'The next person was Safiye Nadir who we interviewed together, wasn't it?'

Os took off his sunglasses, polished them on his hanky and then put them back on. He hoped that a passing policeman didn't see them sitting here, enjoying a drink –it would be difficult to persuade anyone, not party to their conversation, that they were working. He was glad of the anonymity of the dark, plastic lenses.

'Uludag saw her having sex with her boyfriend by the pool. If her husband had found out, she'd risk losing the fine house and flashy lifestyle.'

'Yes. Her part-time salary would give her a very different standard of living. And I'd imagine that they've a very influential social life. Her husband's extremely successful.' Zelfa wrote rapidly stopping to ask, 'So why do you think she wouldn't kill Uludag?'

Os had to admit that again it was only instinct. 'But we're obviously going to interview the boyfriend. He might have been the one who decided to get rid of the old man himself. I'm sure they could use the money she paid every month for other things.' His attention was suddenly drawn to a tiny bird pecking at some crumbs underneath the next table. He admired the colours of the creature for a few seconds before saying, 'What do you think?'

'Like you, I would be interested in meeting... Ali Alnar, I think his name is.' She flipped back through her notes as if to check her information. 'I'd want to know what his intentions towards Mrs Nadir are. Is he just playing or is he in love? He's single so he might want to marry her himself.'

He was interested to hear how she would answer his next question. 'And the two German women - could they have done it?' Ms. Weiss had responded to Zelfa's brusque manner admirably. In reality, the two of them had been dismissed and told not to come back until they had proof that would stand up in court. As he'd expected, Zelfa's beautiful face settled into hard lines.

'Mmmm, that woman would be capable of anything.'

He nodded at her pad, indicating that she should write down what he was about to say. 'They're probably very anxious that the community will discover that they're not sisters, so they pay Uludag money to keep quiet. Bur they're certainly not physically strong characters, as we saw yesterday.'

'There are two of them,' Zelfa argued. 'They're both intelligent women - they could come up with something.'

Os was tempted to tell her that she shouldn't let her own prejudices get in the way of her professional judgement but knew he was being petty. Instead he said, 'Out of all the victims, I would imagine those two were the least likely to be able to find a killer. From what their neighbour said, they live a very quiet life.'

'We'll see,' was Zelfa's response. 'I'm going to look into their backgrounds. What kind of life did they lead in Germany or wherever they were living, before they came to Northern Cyprus? Do we know anything about them?'

Zelfa had a point. He was accusing her of prejudice but was he also guilty of feeling sorry for the women. Whoever had killed Uludag was doing society a favour but it was his job to find the murderer, whatever he thought.

'We'll do the same search on their neighbour, the retired Colonel. But I doubt that we'll find anything untoward there.' Os suddenly realised that he had not mentioned the visit. He related how they had been given his name by Hassan.

'So you're saying that because the man's own name or that of his house wasn't in the book, he's innocent?'

For a moment, Os thought she was criticizing him but then he realised she was unsure whether to add the information to her list. 'He could be our mystery person or he could be much closer to his neighbours than he admitted. He even might have helped them to get rid of their problem,' He shrugged. 'He does have a military background so he would certainly have the right contacts. But again I can't see it.'

Zelfa smiled down at her notes before continuing to write. Os wondered what she was thinking. Perhaps she was laughing at him because he hadn't come up with anything more concrete to back up his theories. He certainly wasn't about to explain that his intuition was a tool he had learned to rely on. His grandmother had read the tarot cards for neighbours, right up until she had died five years ago and his mother had always said that he took after the old woman. It was something he wasn't fully at ease with himself. Or perhaps she saw him as too willing to accept that people were innocent.

Suspecting that he was being oversensitive he added, 'Don't forget the daughter.'

'Tell me about her again,' Zelfa said.

'She left home as soon as her mother died - married a small businessman in Gazi Magusa. She has two children who go to private school.' Os drained his coffee. 'The shop was broken into recently and most of their carpet stock was stolen. They weren't insured.' Zelfa raised her eyebrows. Os found himself defending the action.

'It's not like Istanbul. A lot of people here think that insurance isn't necessary.'

'Your crime rate is rising though, isn't it? Do you wish life was like it was five years ago?' She looked at him quizzically. ' I can't believe the changes in the last ten years since I was last here.'

He sighed. 'In some ways it had to happen - but if we're not careful we'll lose the good things about the country.'

Like most Northern Cypriots, Os could have sat for hours talking politics but he resisted the temptation. He returned to the case.

'Nurten Isler hated her father because of the way he treated her mother, so she got married as soon as she could and left home - supposedly never to return. She kept an eye on him through her mother's friend, Mrs Assim, but she was seen by an English neighbour the evening he was killed, coming out of Uludag's house. The woman had only moved in two years before so she didn't know the daughter but later recognised her from a photo.' Os paused to allow Zelfa to sip her coffee.

'Mrs Isler didn't admit being there at first and then she said that she had been attempting to rebuild relationships between herself and her father. But Uludag was out when she arrived. She says she had a look around the house, found evidence of an accumulation of huge amounts of money, panicked and left.'

'How did you have a photo of the daughter?'

Os smiled, proud of this particular piece of police work. 'When Sener was looking into the Islers' financial background, he came across an article about them in the archives of the Volkan. It was a piece about the break in.'

Os drank the water that had been provided with his coffee. It was very pleasant sitting here working, much better than the stuffy office. He would make a request for a fan; he had asked before but, perhaps, now that his circumstances has changed, he would be successful. On second thoughts it might be better if Zelfa asked Atak. His mind played with other possibilities. Perhaps he could even manage a computer and printer. The other Inspectors had one but then they shared a room. Atak might agree to a request in case she told her colleagues, back in Istanbul, that working in Northern Cyprus was like being in the Dark Ages. He grinned at the prospect.

'So, her motive?'

For a second he wondered what she was talking about then he remembered they were discussing the daughter. 'She was desperate for cash. She needed to pay for her children's schooling. Perhaps seeing all that money in her father's bank account gave her the idea.' Os shrugged, 'If she killed him she would have got her hands on the money immediately - instead of having to beg from someone she hadn't had contact with for years. Big motive! She was a desperate woman and she didn't exactly like her father.' Os suddenly sighed. 'That's the trouble with this job,' he said. 'We deal with damaged people all the time. It gives you a very jaundiced view of humanity.'

Zelfa didn't respond. He wondered if the same thing bothered her. He supposed he would find out soon enough if she was going to be here for six months. Was she really as tough as she made out? He continued with the case diagnosis.

'So now we're back to our friend, Gorus. What did you think of him?'

Zelfa put her pad and pen on the table and stretched back in her chair. 'Interesting character! Good-looking man and certainly I would never have put him as gay. He surrounds himself with attractive women. His wife is well groomed and his secretary is a stunner. He's certainly giving the allusion of a very heterosexual man.' She sighed. 'But I believe he was guilty of interfering with the boy. He was just lucky his family could pay his way out of it.'

Os nodded and looked around for the waiter. He knew he would later regret three coffees in a row but now it was helping him think. 'But if he did kill Uludag, why now? He's been paying for years and as he said, it was an amount that meant nothing to him.'

'Perhaps the old man was beginning to irritate him.'

'Maybe - but why now?' Os persisted. 'It would have made more sense to do it when Uludag first approached him nine years ago.'

The waiter placed two more coffees in front of them. He smiled suggestively at Zelfa but this time she didn't notice.

'I think I'll go and see Atak when we get back.' Os said. 'It might be a good idea to get in contact with Istanbul and find out what really went on with that boy. I'd also like to know how often Gorus goes back himself.' He made another mental note to add that job to the list of activities detailed for Sener and Fikri. There wouldn't be much time for newspaper reading in the next few days, he thought grimly.

'I think we should both go over there,' Zelfa answered. 'At least, if they say that Gorus is squeaky clean and that it was all a fabrication of the boy's mind, he can be removed from the prime suspect list.' She took a sip of her fresh coffee. 'If we get the first flight in the morning we can be back by the evening.'

Os slopped coffee onto the table top. He replaced his cup in the saucer and stared at her.

She smiled at him. 'It would make sense me coming with you. It's my city and I know the right people.'

He looked at his watch. 'We'd better get back. Are you ready?'

She pushed her half-drunk, coffee cup aside and stood up, smoothing down her dress that had creased in the heat. Thereced in the heat. There was no point being annoyed with her. No way was Atak going to pay for two flights. She was right, it would be more useful to go in person but he was the one in charge. Or was he? He had to admit that, at times, he wasn't sure.

Chapter Seventeen

They split up when they arrived back at the station, Os to find his sergeants, and Zelfa to return to their joint office. Os ignored the grin exchanged between the two policemen standing at the duty sergeant's desk. Gossip was inevitable; he would just have to put up with it.

He could hear the laughter before he reached the sergeants' room. It was several moments before they saw him standing in the doorway. The room went quiet and the five men made efforts to look busy. Os wondered what they were laughing about.

'We'll go to interview room four.' The sharpness in his voice cut through the cigarette smog as he glared at his two men.

'Shall I get a porter to bring us coffee?' Fikri asked, still seemingly bouyant.

Os shook his head. 'No time for that, I'll fill you in on this morning and then I've got a few jobs for you.' He turned on his heel and strode down the corridor. He could hear the footsteps of the two men behind him, though no-one spoke. Os pushed open the door into a room which stank of stale tobacco and sweat. His irritation increasing, he threaded through the table and chairs to open the window. There was little point trying to find somewhere else, they would all be like this. One day the station would get aircon but until that happened they had to put up with the unpleasantness of sweating bodies. He chose not to dig too deeply into the reason he hadn't invited Inspector Urfa to this meeting; they could then have used his office as usual even it it was a tight fit. He pulled out a metal chair and sat down, making sure that he didn't put his elbow on what looked like coffee. The now subdued sergeants sat opposite him, placing their pads and pens on the plastic, table top.

Fikri handed over a newspaper. 'I think you'll find this interesting, sir.'

Os noticed that Fikri still looked unusually smug. He glanced at the newsprint and suddenly his irritation dissipated. The double page was divided up into photos and background details of contestants for the new mayor of Girne. Gorus's handsome face smiled at the camera. Had Uludag prior knowledge of this, or was Gorus afraid that, once he did know, the blackmailer might jeopardize his chances of success? As the business man was obviously intending to follow his father-in-law into politics, he might have decided that it was now time to get rid of the old man.

Suddenly embarrassed by his moodiness, he congratulated his sergeant. He then told them about his morning's meeting with the businessman, now turned local politician. Afterwards, he divided the work between them. Fikri was to interview the boyfriend of Mrs Nadir but if he had any suspicions at all, Os would accompany him second time around. Sener was instructed to investigate Mrs Mandrez's family to see if there was anyone capable of getting rid of Uludag. The backgrounds of the two German women were also to be looked into.

'So everybody's still in the frame, sir?' Sener asked.

'So it would seem at the moment,' Os answered.

'Will Inspector Urfa be going with you to Istanbul if the Commandant gives the visit the go ahead?' Fikri asked.

Os looked for any sign of a leer across Fikri's heavy features but the sergeant appeared all innocence. 'I don't think that's likely. I'm sure he'll only pay for one person.'

Sener changed the subject. 'Where will you be this afternoon if we find anything out, sir?'

'I'm going up to Karaman to talk to someone who was around when those bodies were buried. It's a long shot but she might remember something that she thought odd at the time. If we could discover the identity of the human remains, we might get somewhere.' Os picked up his jacket. 'I'll call in on Atak before I go - I'll be on my mobile if you need me.'

He was glad to get out into the fresh air of the corridor. No doubt the three of them had added to the combined odour of sweat and nicotine that the next occupants would be forced to endure. As he turned the corner, he saw Atak coming down the stairs.

'Can I have a quick word, sir?'

'It will have to be quick, Osman. I'm on my way to a meeting in Lefkosa. If it's important, you can come out to my car.' The man was wheezing with the effort of talking while walking. 'If it's to keep me up to date, Inspector Urfa has already done that.'

'Has she sir?'

'Yes,' Atak seemed unaware of the offence he had just caused. 'She told me that you're both wanting to go to Istanbul. I suppose it's necessary, especially since Erim Gorus is putting his cap into the ring for Mayor.' He smiled at Os's expression. 'I read the papers you know. But for godsake tread carefully. We're lucky that Inspector Urfa's contacts will open a few doors.' The man laughed. 'I'm not convinced that you'd get the same response on your own.'

Os wondered whether Atak was referring to Zelfa's physical affect on men or Os's perceived ability to liaise with another police force. The day was certainly not helping his self esteem.

'I can see you're not happy, Osman but we're not paying her wages. I'm sure the office can get good deals on the tickets - and Inspector Urfa says she can arrange for the Istanbul police to pay for a night's accommodation. It will be interesting for you.' When Os didn't reply he continued, 'I've sent Inspector Urfa off to contact the appropriate people. You'll need to talk to anyone who was involved in the discharged case. There's bound to be someone still in the force - it was only ten years ago.' The heavy man paused to catch his breath. 'I've discussed with Inspector Urfa what you need to make the accusation of murder stick.'

Os didn't bother to hide the sarcasm in his voice. 'When have you and Inspector Urfa decided that we should go?'

Atak either didn't notice or chose to ignore the tone. 'The day after tomorrow. That will give the Istanbul police time to find the old paperwork. Anything else, Osman?'

Perversely, Os decided not to tell the Commandant about his intended visit to Karaman that afternoon; not that the man would be interested at the moment anyway. He glanced at his watch. It was either an early lunch or Atak was meeting someone important - he was surprised that a name had not been mentioned. Annoyed with how the control of the case seemed to be spiralling out of his grasp, Os felt in his pocket for his car keys.

Roisin was sitting on the edge of the pool dangling her feet into the water. Her face lit up as she turned to the sound of the squeaking gate. Tramps, who was lying in the shade of the table, thumped his tail, too lazy to respond in any other way. The heat shimmered across the blueness of the water and Os suddenly wished that he could take the afternoon off.

Roisin stood up and walked towards him. She held his face in her cool wet hands and kissed him briefly on the mouth. 'Have you had any lunch?'

'What are you offering me?' His eyes ran over her slim body in the red bikini.

She grinned back at him. 'I thought you were working.'

'I am, but it's a nice thought.'

'I'll make a chicken sandwich. Do you want a cold beer?'

He nodded and, taking off his jacket, he pulled a chair against the wall of the house where the midday sun had not yet reached. There was a slight breeze and he closed his eyes, waiting for the tension of the morning to seep out. She woke him, shaking him gently on the shoulder.

'I'd like you to come with me on my next visit if you've got the time.' He bit into the thick chicken and tomato sandwich that she had placed in front of him.

Her eyes widened with interest. 'Where are we going?'

'To your old lady in the village - the one who told you about her friend who was having an affair with Uludag. She's never met me but it would look less official if you were there.'

Roisin picked up a towel. 'I better go and change then, I don't want to frighten her.' Os grinned at her departing back and then continued to eat.

Fortuitously, Maria was in when Roisin knocked on the cottage door. Os examined the old German woman while Roisin talked to her. What was it about Northern Cyprus that attracted these eccentric characters? If she was living in Germany, would she continue to wear the long skirt and solid, walking shoes that she had on this afternoon. Not that he was complaining, the ex-pat community added considerably to Northern Cyprus. It eased their political isolation a little and they spent money, though glancing through the doorway into the kitchen beyond, Os doubted that the economy gained a great deal from this individual.

Os held out his hand. 'I do appreciate your time, Frau Heinemann.'

She didn't smile or show that she appreciated his charm in any way but she did move back and allow her visitors to step down into the kitchen.

'Take your friend into the sitting room, Roisin,' she ordered, as she shut the heavy, wooden, front door behind them.

Os looked around and found himself comparing the room to that of the German women who lived further up the hill. Here was clutter and pokiness compared to space and style. He lifted a white cat off a chair and sat, aware that he would now be covered in hairs. Frau Heinemann levered herself onto the sofa opposite, lifting a tabby cat onto her knees, her puffy, white skin, florescent above her black ankle socks. Os spoke in English his American accent barely audible.

'I'm sure you're aware that I'm investigating the murder of Kutlay Uludag.'

She nodded, the fleshy jowls quivering. Interest and intelligence gleamed in her cataract-disfigured eyes. She lifted some strands of grey hair that hung limply around her lined face and stuffed them back into her thin bun.

'A few days ago, two skeletons were discovered on the hillside along from the Treasure Restaurant. We now know that they were buried there during the time of the troubles. We also found a silver cross and chain which suggests that one or both of the bodies were Greek.'

The white cat leapt onto the arm of the chair and Os wondered whether to try and ingratiate himself by allowing it to sit on his knee. Then it began to knead the linen arm covers, its claws tearing at the already snared, faded fabric. As gently as he could, he picked up the animal and replaced it on the rug. The woman stared back at him, neither reproaching, nor thanking him for rescuing the remains of her upholstery.

He continued. 'I know it was a traumatic time for everyone but can you remember one or perhaps two young people disappearing without explanation. A woman or a man, probably in their late teens? Before the Turkish invasion, I mean.'

Maria Heinemann stared at him for what seemed several minutes. She blinked occasionally but apart from the regular stroking of the cat, now lying stretched out on her knee, Os wondered if she was aware of anything else that was going on around her. Perhaps he was wasting his time. He glanced across at Roisin but she appeared to be avoiding his eyes. He was just about to repeat the question, when she spoke.

'You are quite correct - people disappeared and no-one talked about it. This village was a stronghold for Greek Cypriot activists. There were comings and goings.'

'But can you remember anything different, something unusual,' Os persisted.

She made a hissing noise. 'It was the men who disappeared. They went off to fight but came back, maybe once a week for a decent meal, or a night in the bed of their wives. But there was one incident that I remember thinking was strange. I mentioned it to my friend and,' Maria narrowed her eyes at the memory, '...she either didn't know the answer or she wasn't able to tell me.'

Os's stomach muscles tensed and he realised that he was holding his breath. Maria had a distant look in her eyes as if she was back in the cobbled streets of the early 1970's village. She pointed at the wall behind Os.

'Across the square, there's a lane that leads out to the hills. At the edge of the village it passes a large house with a small veranda above the front door. My friend used to live nearby so I passed it most days.' She seemed sad by the memory. 'It was owned by a builder and his family. The man had done well for himself but I didn't like him. A bit of a bully and a trouble maker. He was very big in local politics - whipping up the young men to fight for an island governed by Greece.' Suddenly remembering her manners, she said, 'Would you like something to drink?'

Os held up his hand in alarm. 'No - no thank you. Please carry on.'

'He had a daughter in her late teens. She just disappeared. I asked my friend about it and she said that she'd been sent to Greece, to marry a doctor there.' Maria turned her broad, calloused hands palms upwards. 'Probably that was what had really happened but I remember she refused to say anything more about it. I thought maybe she disapproved of arranged marriages but didn't want her opinion getting back to her neighbour. It was different from the norm though, even then. Girls here get married in their own villages.'

'And nothing more was said?' Os asked.

'The country was in the middle of a civil war - there were far more important things to talk and think about.'

The old woman's breathing became more audible. Os saw Roisin open her mouth and he shook his head; he sensed that if she wasn't interrupted the old woman would continue with her memories.

'I thought that Dovish already had a boyfriend at the time. But perhaps her parents didn't think he was good enough and that was why they sent her away to be married to someone more suitable.'

'Did you have any idea who the boy was?' Os interrupted.

He was on his feet, staring down at the woman whose answer could make all the difference to solving his case. The tabby cat, perhaps sensing the change in atmosphere, or just not liking the close proximity of the strange man, jumped off her knee and stalked into the kitchen. Maria smoothed down her ruffled skirt and then looked up into the face of the young Inspector.

'I'm sorry, no. I was in my fifties then. Hardly of the age when a young girl would confide in me. I'd known her for several years of course and we would say hello to each other when we met. But no, she never told me anything that was important to her.'

Os sat down under the weight of disappointment. 'So what made you think that she already had a boyfriend?'

Maria shrugged. 'She looked happy but in her own world, as young people do when they are in love. I started to see her more on her own, walking through the village or out in the hills when I was with my dog.' Maria nodded towards a framed photo of a brown and white mongrel, its mouth open in what looked like a sloppy grin. 'Before that she always went around in a gang of girls, always giggling.'

'And there wasn't any other strange happening that you can think of?' Os asked.

'As I've said, the time was full of strange events, Inspector. Several young men left the village and then the Turkish invaded. The majority of the people who lived in these houses were Greek, so they escaped to the south of the island. Now whether your dead body was one of these men, I don't know.'

Os sighed. 'Thank you for your time, Mrs Heinemann. You've been very helpful.' He stood up and leaned over to shake her hand. The skin felt papery thin but her grip was firm. A woman not to be misjudged, he thought.

She struggled to her feet. 'I'll see you out,' she said.

Os reached into his top jacket pocket and took out one of his cards. 'Just in case you remember anything else.'

She took it and placed it in a bowl on the coffee table that was already filled with an assortment of what looked like junk. 'I won't remember anything else, Inspector, my memory is as good as ever and I've told you everything I know.'

Os smiled. 'Well, thank you again, anyway.' He waited outside for Roisin. The two cats were now sitting on the front wall staring at him. It was a strange thing that these foreigners were all obsessed with animals. The Turkish Cypriots had dogs to guard their possessions or cats to keep the rats and mice away but the Germans and English had the same relationship with them as they did with children. He had become used to Tramps around the house but he had told Roisin that the animal wasn't to go into the bedroom. He suspected that, when he was at work, this rule was relaxed because he had found dog hairs on the bed.

It wasn't until they were back in the car that Roisin spoke. 'You think that the girl is one of the skeletons?'

Os nodded. 'I don't believe that story about her being shipped off to Greece. I'm sure the community thought it strange that she wasn't married in the local church but as she said,' he indicated with his head in the direction of the cottage, '…a lot of strange things were going on at the time. People would have been more interested in what was happening politically and to their own men, to care too much about anything else.' Os drew into the side of the road to allow a car, coming from the opposite direction, to pass. 'Do you want to go for a walk when we get back?'

Roisin looked across at him. 'Don't you have to go back to work?'

'No, I think I would get more sorted out in my head up here. There are too many people to distract me in the station and now I haven't got my own office, it's not the same.'

She grinned at him. 'Poor you.'

As he went into the bedroom to change out of his suit, his mobile rang. 'Yes, Sener, what is it?' Os could hear the excitement in his sergeant's voice.

'We've found out that Mandrez's brother was done for GBH two years ago. He did three months in prison.'

'So he was out when Uludag was attacked?' Os asked.

'Yes, sir. He's single, still living with his mother in Karsiyaka.'

'You and Fikri had better bring him in then. See if he's an alibi for the night of the murder. Let me know how you get on. Any progress on the two German women?'

'I've been on to immigration, sir. Their residency forms state that they worked for the German Civil Service before they retired and came out here.'

'Doing what?' Os asked.

'That's all the information they had, sir.'

'All right, Sener, you get on with interviewing the brother.' Os disconnected the call and stood for a few minutes, staring out of the bedroom window at the sea beyond. He scrolled down the numbers programmed into his phone until he found the one he wanted. 'It's me, Os.'

'I was going to call you,' Zelfa answered. 'I've booked two seats on the six am flight to Istanbul the day after tomorrow. I've also rung a colleague in my old station and he's going to put together the paper work of Gorus's arrest for when we get there.'

Os detected a hint of either gleefulness or self-satisfaction which he chose to ignore. She either had no remorse about going behind his back or she had no concept about her own behaviour. He brushed his irritation aside.

'Fine. If you've got nothing else pressing, I'd like you to do something for me.'

'Anything, Os.'

Again he wondered how she managed working around so many men when she talked in that breathy way of hers. But then he had seen the other side of her when she had interviewed the German woman, Ms. Weiss. Presumably she handled unwanted admirers in the same way.

'I'd appreciate it if you could get back to your contact in Istanbul and see if he's able to delve into the background of Ms. Weiss and Schmidt. I'd like to find out what they did in the Civil Service. Perhaps it was just clerical work but somehow I doubt it. I know that you have better facilities than us for such things.' He rolled his eyes at himself. He had never had any dealings with the German police force before, so the time he would be saving by passing this job on would be immeasurable.

'I'll get onto it now. Are you coming back in?'

'Not until the morning. I've got a few things to sort up here in Karaman but I'll be on line if you need to discuss anything.' Os threw his mobile on the bed and stripped off his work clothes. He felt a mixture of excitement and frustration. There were so many leads, he felt as if he was in a maze, not sure which way to turn. He pulled on jeans and T shirt and went in search of Roisin.

'Is there any way you can find out whether it was the Greek girl, Dovish, that was buried there?' Roisin asked, as they followed Tramps down the lane.

'I doubt it. We can get DNA from the bones but then we'd have to find a match to a close relative. We've no idea where her family went - they might not even be living in the South anymore. And even if we did find them we'd have to get their permission. If they've got something to hide then they're not likely to co-operate.' Os sighed. 'If we overcame all those obstacles the whole thing would take weeks anyway.'

Roisin reached for his hand. 'So what are you going to do?'

'About the bones? Nothing much at the moment, though I'll ring Ahmet and see how far they've got with their investigations.' Os breathed in a lungful of fresh mountain air. 'I'm going to Istanbul the day after tomorrow - we're looking more closely into the background of Gorus.'

'Can I come? I could have a look around and meet you afterwards.'

He experienced a series of conflicting emotions before he answered, 'It would be a bit difficult. Atak has said that Zelfa has to go.'

Hurt settled in her eyes. 'Zelfa? Oh your new woman.'

Os hoped that she was joking. 'Do you mind?' he asked.

'It's your job. I'll occupy myself here.'

'It's only an overnight stay.' Os felt her hand go limp in his. He decided to ignore it. 'We still haven't discovered the identity of the last victim. I've told Sener and Fikri to go through our records and cross reference them with anyone who has died in the last two months.'

'But Uludag removed papers from the station of everyone he blackmailed, didn't he? I would have thought he did the same for the mystery person.'

Os sighed. 'I can't think of what else to do. We've turned his house upside down - searched the garden.' He smiled at her. 'Anyway, there weren't so many crimes ten years ago so it won't take them more than a day to check. Here's not like Liverpool you know.'

She pulled a face and he felt that good humour was restored. They had now reached the derelict, Greek church. Attracted by the potent smells, Tramps disappeared inside. The view from up here was something Os would never tire of. The remains of St Hillarion Castle, resting on its craggy peninsular, towered above them. In front, in the far distance, was the sea. Roisin admired the view, using the excuse to get back her breath.

'Could Uludag's death have been a mistake?'

'What do you mean?' Os asked.

'Well, you're looking for someone you assume had planned the murder. Couldn't it have been an accident?'

Os stared down at the three houses, in the dip of the hills, that were in the process of being built. 'It's a possibility that whoever killed Uludag didn't intend to - but if it's not murder, it's definitely manslaughter.'

'Who do you think did it?'

Os didn't even have to consider his answer. 'Gorus. He had a lot to lose and more so now that he's put himself up for Mayor of Girne. He's wealthy - his family in Istanbul would probably still think it worth their while to back him and I sense underneath the charm that he's totally ruthless.'

'You say that this mystery person hasn't paid any money for the last two months?' Roisin asked.

'Yes, which means one of two things. Either he or she for some reason couldn't pay the money anymore, or the person's dead.' He bent down to take a stick out of Tramps' mouth and then threw it along the path. The dog barked and ran after it. 'Instead of ringing Ahmet, I think I'll go to Lefkosa tomorrow and call in at the MPT laboratory.' Os could hear the uncertainty in his own voice. If he didn't get a break soon, the Commandant couldn't be blamed in thinking that the case was beyond him.

Roisin hadn't mentioned their conversation of the previous evening and he certainly wasn't going to ask her if she'd changed her mind. He understood her reluctance to a point. In his line of work he knew family backgrounds had a huge effect on behaviour. But just because her parents and sister couldn't cope with the commitment, it didn't mean that it wouldn't work for him and her. Living together was all right for a while, in fact he was enjoying it, but it wasn't what he wanted long term.

'Shall we turn back?'

'Are you tired?' He was surprised by her question but saw that they had reached the split in the track where they could either continue around the mountain or snake back in the direction they had come.

She didn't quite meet his eyes. 'I need to get on with my work - do you mind?'

Os shook his head. He would have liked to carry on, if she had been more communicative, but if they were going to walk in semi-silence then there was little point. He wondered how his sergeants were getting on.

Roisin disappeared into her study as soon as they reached the house. Os fetched a beer from the fridge and then, taking a pad and pen, he went to sit outside. For over an hour he became absorbed in lists, details of suspects and their links with the murdered man. Then he threw his pen down, desperate for a cigarette. If he had been in the office he would have cadged one from someone. He picked up his mobile and keyed in Sener's number. It took several rings before the sergeant answered.

'Have you made any progress?'

'We've got the brother in now, sir. He says he was at home all that night with his mother and she's confirmed it of course. But then she would, wouldn't she.'

'Where was he when you picked him up?'

'At home. He works for a farmer out Lapta way, so he cycles to work at five in the morning and comes back late afternoon. He says that he rarely goes out at night expect for Saturday.' Os could hear voices in the background. 'Again, the old woman confirmed it. He's a bit simple actually, sir, though he's obviously a physically strong man. He certainly has the strength to kill someone.' There was the click of a lighter and then silence as Sener pulled on a cigarette. Os felt a twinge of jealousy. 'We brought him into the station to see if it would make him talk. His mother was hovering around him in the house - answering the questions for him.' Sener paused before adding, 'But I don't think he's your man, sir, and we've got nothing to detain him on. We're just about to let him go if that's all right with you?'

'No, go ahead.' The gloom that had settled on him earlier, increased. 'Has Fikri been to see the boyfriend of the Nadir woman yet?' Os asked.

'No. This has taken longer than we thought. I think he's intending to go first thing in the morning.'

'Do you fancy some overtime?'

'What are you suggesting, sir?' Sener asked.

'I might as well question him this evening and I'd appreciate your company. I'll meet you outside the station in half an hour?' With renewed enthusiasm, Os strode into the bedroom. He changed out of his shorts and then put his head around Roisin's study door. 'I'm going down to Girne,

Roisin. I want to do an interview before I go to Istanbul.' She looked pale and he suddenly felt guilty that he was so keen to go out when in reality he could have left it until the following morning.

She made an attempt to smile at him. 'Are you all right to pick something up for yourself? I think I've got a headache coming on. I'll probably only have something light.'

He went over and kissed her. 'I'll see you later then. Don't you think you should stop work if you're not feeling well?'

'I'll finish what I'm doing, then I'll call it a day.' She was already staring back at the screen when he closed the door behind him.

Sener was waiting in the police car park. 'He lives out in Karakum,' he said, as Os climbed in the car.

Os felt much better now that he was doing something. Even if this interview led to nothing, at least it was someone he could remove from his list of suspects. 'What do we know about him?'

'He's single and lives on his own. He's been employed for eight years, at the same advertising agency where the Nadir woman works. He probably earns a reasonable wage but not in the same league as the husband.' Sener looked across at his boss. 'He's younger than the Nadir woman by the way.'

'That's interesting,' Os said, '…a much older husband and a younger boyfriend.'

'She probably thinks it's the ideal situation,' Sener said sarcastically.

Os didn't answer, instead he took the ring road out of Girne, noticing yet another two new shops along the way. The village of Karakum had also experienced a transformation. On the left side of the main road, identical houses with their own swimming pools were being constructed in neat rows. They were near completion, the windows in and the patios laid. A huge sign, advertising the complex, dominated the horizon.

Although he would never admit it to Roisin, this change in architecture annoyed him. One of the charms of Northern Cyprus was that someone bought a plot of land and then built a house. Every house had its own uniqueness but now it was becoming like Britain with its streets of identical homes.

Sener pointed ahead at a row of modern shops with apartments above. Os pulled in, alongside a red, sports car, wondering if it belonged to the young boyfriend, Ali Alnar. Although his own car was constantly covered in a thin layer of dust, this red vehicle gleamed. Alnar must wash it every day, he thought. It was impossible to keep anything clean with the dust from the building sites and unmade roads. He went across to peer in through the driver's window. The leather seats shone and there was no sign of any personal possessions. The owner's pride and joy, he thought.

The steps leading to the first floor apartments were at the back of the oblong building. A narrow, covered passageway gave access to the four, front entrances. One door was open and the blasting of a TV drew his glance inside. A small child, surrounded by toys, played on a rug. Os smelt the strong aroma of frying onions and garlic. He passed another closed door and joined Sener outside the one rented by Mrs Nadir's boyfriend. The front door opened in response to the second knock.

A handsome man, of medium height, with wet hair and wearing nothing but a towel draped around his trim waist, stood in the doorway. He frowned at the two strangers and Os wondered whether he had been expecting someone else.

'Yes?'

Os held out his police shield. The man glanced at it and then looked back at Os. Was it fear that flashed quickly in and then out of the man's eyes? If so what did it signify?

'Mr Alnar, we'd like to talk to you about your friend, Mrs Nadir.'

The frown deepened. Alnar stepped aside and nodded to the two policemen to enter.

He lived in a very different establishment to Safiye Nadir. Os wondered if the furniture came with the apartment. The walls were bare except for one cheap, framed print of Girne harbour. In the corner, near the kitchen area, two shot guns were stacked against the wall. Os sat down in the armchair and watched Alnar perch himself on the edge of the plastic sofa, crossing his arms over his flat stomach. His eyes shifted nervously back and forth between his two visitors. Os wondered whether the absence of girly photos was because of the regular visits from his lover.

'I'm sure you know that Mrs. Nadir's gardener was murdered last Wednesday.'

Ali Alnar nodded, his hands realigning the towel. It was obvious that he had been warned of their visit and he wasn't so stupid as to attempt ignorance of the situation.

Sener spoke. 'Where were you last Wednesday between the hours of nine and midnight.'

Again the young man was ready for this question. 'Here. I brought some work back from the office.' He pointed to the white, plastic table and chairs next to the open plan kitchen area. 'I often work there on my computer. I'm a designer.'

Surprised that the man had chosen to live in an environment that showed nothing of his creative awareness, Os asked, 'What is it you design?'

'Advertisements for magazines and newspapers. That's what our company does, though I'm the only artist. Sometimes I get overloaded.' He shrugged his muscled shoulders and Os wondered if this man kept his torso toned by attending one of the new gyms that were springing up around the Girne area. He found it interesting that he hadn't bothered to put on a dressing gown. Did that mean that he was supremely confident or that his extreme nervousness had made him forget that he was in a state of undress?

Sener had taken out his pad and pen and placed them on the arm of the chair. 'No-one can verify that I suppose?'

'I live on my own.' His voice took on the tone of increduality. 'You can't be thinking that I murdered him?'

'You had good reason to. I'm sure you both had better use for the money. It could perhaps have gone towards a nest egg for when she leaves her husband?'

Instead of frightening him, the Inspector's words had the opposite affect. Alnar stood up and waved his right hand around the small room that quadrupled up as a kitchen, dining area, study and sitting room.

'Do you think she would leave her husband for this?' he asked, bitterness clipping his words. 'If I had thought that killing her blackmailer would get her to leave, believe me, I might have considered it. But I am not so naive, I'm afraid.'

Os stared at the young handsome face that had folded into a mixture of anger and bitterness. His fingers twisted the thick gold chain around his neck.

'What about Mrs Nadir?' Os continued. 'She must be worried that her husband will find out about the two of you?'

He gazed for a few seconds at the blank wall as if deciding how to answer. He then turned back to Os. 'She's not a murderer, Inspector. She might be breaking the code of Allah by being unfaithful to her husband but that's all she's doing.' He sighed. 'I know she loves me, she just loves the lifestyle her husband can give her, more. I accepted that from the beginning.'

'And you're happy to put up with it?' Sener's tone revealed the sergeant's disgust and amazement. Os watched the man attempt to cover his vulnerability.

'For now,' was all he replied.

Os stood up. 'That will be all but let us know if you intend going anywhere.'

Alnar's lip curled. 'You mean flee the country? Yes, Inspector, I'll let you know if I have plans to do that.' He pulled the towel more securely around his waist then walked over to the front door.

'A hunter are you, Mr Alnar?' Sener asked, nodding at the guns.

'I've got a license.' He avoided eye contact and closed the door immediately behind them.

'Have you time for a beer?' Os asked, as the two policemen made their way down the concrete steps.

'Why not? Fatima has her sister over - she expects me to entertain the kids.' Sener grinned. 'There's a new bar just down the road.'

When beer bottles and glasses had been placed in front of them, Os asked, 'What did you think?'

'Like you. He didn't do it.'

Os smiled. 'How do you know what I think?'

'I've worked with you long enough, sir. I'm right aren't I?'

Os nodded. 'I just needed to be sure. At the end there though, I thought I might be wrong.'

'You believe that he'd have got rid of Uludag, if she'd asked him?' Sener poured his beer then sucked up the froth. His eyes watched Os over the rim.

'Probably not.'

'I think he's daft but straight, sir. He loves that woman so he thinks he has to put up with her rules.'

They both sat in silence for a few minutes. Os found himself comparing his own relationship to the one they were discussing. In some ways, was not Roisin calling the shots? Was he like Alnar, accepting the situation because he had no choice? If it continued, would people eventually feel sorry for him, like he felt sorry for the man they had just left?

'How's the new Inspector doing?' Sener grinned. 'Some of the lads are thinking of going to Atak to offer their services as her sergeant.'

'And you're not?' He wasn't sure how he would react if Sener said that he was interested in being transferred.

The young sergeant shook his head. 'You're not as pretty, sir, but I prefer to stay where I am. I don't think I would be much good working for a woman. Fatima wouldn't like it either.' He made a face. 'She would give me earache every night, asking what I'd been doing and where we'd been.' He shrugged his shoulders in self deprecation. 'As if a woman like that would be interested in me!' Sener glanced slyly at Os. 'She might be interested in another Inspector though.'

Os didn't rise to the bait. For as long as he shared an office with the very attractive, flirtatious Inspector, he would have to expect such speculations.

'She's a colleague, Sener, who the boss has put in my office. It certainly wasn't my idea and I'm not happy about her working with me on the case. But,' and here, Os intentionally put an edge to his voice, '...I'm not going to be discourteous to her and there are times when her contacts in Istanbul and her sharp brain are proving to be very useful. So I'll just get on with it, as I expect you to do.'

His sergeant took the rebuke in silence and his facial expression told Os that his subordinate knew that he had overstepped the mark. Os relented, knowing that he was perhaps too sensitive about the subject.

He smiled, 'How are Fatima and the children?' They talked briefly about the problems of Sener's five children and then Os stood up. 'We'd better get back. Will your sister-in-law have left by now?'

Sener pulled a face. 'I doubt it, but the younger ones will be in bed so it won't be so bad.'

Os smiled and wondered whether Roisin would still have her headache when he got back. He decided to buy a pizza big enough for the two of them, just in case she might be persuaded to join him.

Chapter Eighteen

It was ten o'clock the next morning when Zelfa and Os set off for Lefkosa. Os drove and, as soon as they were on the road leading up into the mountains, he told her about the interviews with both Ali Alnar and then Maria in Karaman village. Zelfa stared out at the looming, grey, craggy mountains in silence. Then she laughed.

'Anyone of them could have done it, couldn't they? As you say, we can't prove whether the female skeleton was this Dovish or not.' Zelfa pointed up at a ten foot, metal soldier perched on a crag above them. 'What's that?'

'To commemorate the Turkish invasion of 1975. Every one asks that,' Os grinned. He nodded to the left where an enormous white house stood above a gully. 'That's where the generals stay. It's supposed to be five-star accommodation though I've never had the opportunity to try it out. The Commander gets invited there sometimes.'

'Do you like him?'

'Who, Atak?'

'Yes.'

Os overtook a lorry that was inching its way up the mountainside, its load of builders' sand dribbling onto the road. 'He's all right,' he answered blandly. The only person, who knew that he considered Atak lazy and in the pockets of the politicians, was Roisin. His view wasn't different from a lot of the men in the station but he chose not to join in when the Commandant was being criticised. There was always someone keen to make trouble and Os had no desire to make his meetings with the man any more difficult. Zelfa wound up the window as a fine surface of sand blew back from the lorry in front.

'Hang on 'till this car comes passed and I'll overtake,' Os said. 'There's a quarry back there - that's why this is so bad. They seem to be dynamiting the entire mountain range. This road never used to be so busy.'

'What are you hoping to get from this visit to Dr Pehlivan?' Zelfa was uninterested in the destruction of the Northern Cypriot terrain.

He sighed. 'I suppose I'm hoping that they'll have found something that will give us the identity of the other skeleton.'

'You don't think Uludag was blackmailing the two people thirty years ago and killed them because they refused to pay, do you?'

He heard the incredulity in her voice and the moodiness in his own when he replied. 'I just know that the two things are linked that's all.'

Perhaps picking up on his despondency, she changed the direction of the conversation. 'How long has this Team been around? I've never heard of them.'

'A few years. A large number of people went missing during the conflict. Most of their remains are just being discovered now.' Os's mobile rang; he balanced his arm on the open window ledge, his phone clamped to his ear. 'All right, mother,' he said, as soon as he had an opportunity. 'I'm on my way to Lefkosa at the moment. I can drop in if you want but I can't stay.' He ended the call and rolled his eyes. 'I've got to make a short detour if you don't mind. My mother had a suit made for my birthday and she collected it from the tailor's yesterday. If I don't go now, I'll have to come back another time.' He grimaced at the prospect of another weekend spent visiting his mother. There was no question that, this time, he would be travelling on his own.

Zelfa smiled.'No problem. I'd like to meet her.'

It would be interesting to see what his mother would make of the Inspector. Mrs. Zahir accepted that women, from what she called good backgrounds, now chose to work but she would be surprised that one of them had reached the same rank as her son. He grinned at the prospect of her observations.

Mrs Zahir was sitting on the covered veranda waiting for him. She stood up all smiles, which faltered when she saw he was not alone.

'Hello, mother,' he said kissing her. She smelled of lavender which always reminded him of his childhood. 'This is Zelfa Urfa a colleague of mine from Istanbul. She's seconded to the Girne station.'

She turned to Zelfa and kissed both her cheeks. 'Welcome to Northern Cyprus, my dear. You can both stay for coffee can't you?'

Two coffee cups and a bowl of sugar lumps were already set out on the low table. He groaned inwardly, knowing that refusing would only upset her but it meant that they would be late. 'All right, but we'll have to be quick. We shouldn't be here at all.'

Having got her own way, the older woman hurried into the house. Zelfa laughed at his expression. 'Don't worry - my mother would be exactly the same. We'll tell the doctor that we were held up in traffic.'

He relaxed. As Zelfa said, she wasn't behaving any differently from other mothers. If only Roisin could ignore her comments instead of always taking offence when the subjects of marriage and children were raised. He glanced at the various pots of flowers and herbs that were being cultivated on the veranda. His mother had always taken immense care with her house and garden but then she had given up work when she had married. Nevertheless, he felt a sense of pride in Zelfa seeing his childhood home.

As if reading his mind, Zelfa said, 'This is lovely. It's where you grew up?'

'I was born here,' he answered, memories of a happy childhood making him smile.

The coffee had obviously already been prepared as his mother now re-appeared in the doorway carrying the coffee pot, an extra cup and a small plate of Turkish Delight. Os wondered how quickly they would be able to drink it and get away without giving offence. Zelfa took her cup and smiled at Mrs Zahir. Os then watched as his mother fell under the Inspector's charm.

After fifteen minutes, Os stood up. 'We've got to go. Thanks for the coffee, mother. I'll fetch my suit.'

'It's in your bedroom dear,' she answered, as if he was still living in the house. She turned back to ask Zelfa a question and to press another sweet on her.

His bedroom was as he had left it four years ago, when he had moved into his new apartment a couple of kilometres away. His mother hadn't been able to understand why he wanted to live on his own but he had delayed the eventuality long enough. To be fair, she had never complained when he stayed out all night and she had always insisted on doing his washing and cooking. He had accepted her excessive mothering until, for no particular reason, he decided it was time to move out. But she still kept his room as it was - perhaps on the off-chance that since he was not married, he might come to his senses and return home.

His new suit was hanging, in its cellophane wrapping, on the outside of the wardrobe door. Os unhooked it, without bothering to glance underneath the plastic at the tailor's handiwork, and went back outside.

'Ready?' he said to Zelfa who looked as if she could have sat on the porch chatting all day.

She stood up and then bent over the older woman, kissing her on both cheeks. 'It's been lovely talking to you, Mrs Zahir. I hope that I'll see you again sometime.'

'I've enjoyed meeting you, my dear. Get Os to bring you any time.' She followed the two young people to the gate, holding up her face for her son to kiss.

'Bye, mother, thank you for the suit. I'll see you soon.'

She watched them get into their car and then waited until they drove off.

'What a nice woman,' Zelfa said, buckling her seat belt.

Os grunted as he manoeuvred into the main stream of the traffic. His mother had always been charming to his friends and colleagues when he brought them home - in fact she had encouraged him to do so. He knew it was one of the things she had missed when he moved out, the young people around the house. It had been different of course if he ever bought a girlfriend; then her obsession, with him finding the right wife, put a strain on any meetings. He knew his mother well enough to guess that she was now thinking how suitable Zelfa would be as the next Mrs Zahir.

He glanced over at his colleague. 'Let's hope that Dr Pehlivan hasn't gone off for an early lunch.'

He concentrated as he turned off the main road and took short cuts through the backstreets that he knew so well. Eventually, he pulled up in a space outside a low modern building. He suddenly wondered if he was wasting his time. What could the anthropologist tell him that he hadn't already written in his report? Probably, he would have been better remaining in his office. But he was here now.

Os gave their names to the porter at the front desk. The man spoke rapidly into the phone then walked them down a long corridor to a door that had the name, 'Dr Pehlivan, Missing Persons Team,' on a brass plate outside.

The doctor was a grey haired man in his sixties. He looked up from a desk covered with papers and smiled, revealing several gold teeth. Pushing back his seat, he came around the table to shake first, Os's then Zelfa's hand. He then waved them towards some comfortable chairs.

'So, how can I help you?' he asked, directing his question at Os.

'We're hoping that you might be able to shed some more light on the Karaman skeletons,' Os answered. 'Your report states that they'd been in the ground for about thirty years. The female had a dent to the back of her skull that had been created by a heavy object and the man had been shot through the heart. One of his front ribs had been chipped, as had the identical one at the back.' Os looked at the anthropologist for confirmation.

The older man nodded. 'That's correct. The bodies were Caucasian as you would expect in this part of the world, especially at that time.'

'You also found some remnants of their clothes?'

'Yes. There wasn't anything unusual there except that one of the garments was made out of American cotton. It could have been an import but most clothes sold here in the seventies were from Turkey or perhaps the United Kingdom. The remnant of cloth was found with the male skeleton but we can't be a hundred percent sure the article was worn by him – there had been a great deal of disturbance by the time my team arrived at the scene.' The doctor shrugged. 'But whoever had been wearing the T shirt might have been an American - or been given it by an American. I don't know if any of this is of any use to you, Inspector?' Again he addressed his question to Os.

Os wondered how Zelfa was taking the exclusion; he was surprised that she was being so quiet. 'And the jewellery? Was there was nothing unusual about that?'

'Only that the cross and ring were attached to the chain. The woman had been wearing them around her neck. I assume both items had a special meaning for her.'

'But the man wore no jewellery at all?' Os confirmed. He was not one for jewellery himself. He would wear a wedding ring when he married, if he ever did, but that was all.

Mr Pehlivan shook his head. 'But we couldn't find the right hand of the male. I don't know if it had been eaten by an animal or whether the hand was missing before the man died.'

'Nothing else?'

'There were segments of leather boots, which would add credence to it not being summer when they died, but that would make sense anyway. Between May and September the soil would have been far too hard to dig a grave and they were certainly buried, not left hidden under stones.'

'If you've finished with your tests, I wonder if I can take the cross and ring away with me, sir,' Os asked.

Mr Pehlivan shook his head. 'I can certainly show you them and I can give you photos but the artefacts have to remain here with the bodies.'

'This is a murder enquiry,' Zelfa interrupted.

Os's stomach contracted at her tone.

Dr Pehlivan turned to her, seemingly unperturbed by her attempt to bully him. 'I'm well aware of that, Inspector Urfa. I hear you are from Istanbul but here, in Northern Cyprus, my team has autonomy over any bodies that date back to the troubles of the sixties and seventies. We have our own detective as well as anthropologists and archaeologists.' He resumed his conversation with Os as if there had been no interruption. 'We will of course be looking into the American connection. I rang their Consulate on the Greek side this morning - they are normally very helpful.' He smiled as if to soften the previous criticism. 'They promised to go through their archives to see if there is any record of a young man or woman reported missing at the time. I'll obviously let you know as soon as I hear.' He stood up. 'Now, shall we go down stairs?'

As they were on the ground floor, Os looked at the doctor in surprise.

The man smiled. 'My team work in the basement. You wanted to see what was found with the bodies,' he reminded them.

As Dr. Pehlivan led the way down the stairway, Os could hear Zelfa's heels clacking on the tiles behind him. Then he stopped, opened a door and they stepped into the laboratory. His old colleague was not there but the anthropologist he had talked to, a few days ago on the hillside, smiled at him. The remains of the skeletons had been positioned on two tables.

Dr Pehlivan acknowledged his team then said, 'Inspectors Zahir and Urfa are here to examine what was found at the site. I know that you'll give them any help they need.' He turned back to his visitors. 'I must now get on with some work but you'll be well looked after. If you need me, I'll be in my office. I'll call you when I hear from the American Consulate.' He shook hands with them both and left.

Os stood for a few minutes staring at the tables. Unlike the plastic skeletons, he remembered in his school science lab, these bones were no longer attached but nevertheless were laid out in the correct positions. A little heap of spine bones were in the centre of the body and the skull rested on a padded ring of grey cloth. One of the bodies had only one claw- like hand, a bundle of grey material positioned nearby. Os assumed that it was the remains of the T shirt that Dr Pehlivan had mentioned earlier. Taped to each table was a diagram of the site before it had been excavated. Os suddenly realised that the drawings had not been produced by a computer but were drawn by hand. He moved over to the second table. By the side of the female body was the chain with the cross and ring attached, the silver, tarnished to a dull black.

'Could we have some photos of this, please?' he asked of no-one in particular, unable to take his eyes off the macabre sight. The flash of light made him look up into the face of the photographer, a young woman. Os moved out of her way.

'I felt invisible back there,' Zelfa said, as soon as they were outside. 'And how did he know I was from Istanbul?'

Os grinned. He had wondered how long it would be before she spoke her mind. 'Word carries fast. You're a bit of a celebrity at the moment.' They had reached the car and he handed her the poloroid photos before climbing into the driver's seat. 'Have a look at them and tell me what you think.' He edged the car out into the traffic while Zelfa examined the four pictures.

Eventually, she said, 'There's nothing remarkable about this cross. Thousands of them must have been bought and sold to Greek Cypriots in the seventies.' She paused, as if she had suddenly thought of something. 'This doesn't add up though. It's definitely a man's ring but it was around the woman's neck, along with the cross. To me that suggests that she was emotionally linked to someone else.' They had now reached the main road out of Lefkosa and Os was attempting to overtake an old truck belching out exhaust fumes.

The manoeuvre finished, he said, 'If that's the case who was the man and why were they buried together?'

Zelfa shook her head. 'What's your thoughts about the T shirt?'

'We don't know for definite who was wearing it. She could have had it on under a jumper or jacket.' Os returned to the point he thought Zelfa was ignoring. 'But why were they both found together?'

Zelfa narrowed her eyes, obviously perplexed. 'Are you suggesting that they died at different times and were buried there as an extension of the graveyard down the hill?'

Os shook his head. 'No, otherwise they would have had grave stones to mark the place. I'm sure they were buried by whoever killed them.' He sighed, 'But what does this all have to do with Uludag? He knew something about the deaths and I'm sure he was killed before he could tell me what it was.'

They sat in silence as Os lowered the gears to cope with the mountains ahead of him. They hadn't eaten and he wondered whether he should suggest they stopped off in the restaurant near Buffovento Castle. The kebabs were excellent, as were the views down to the sea. But no, it was more important that he had a meeting with Fikri and Sener. If he was going to Istanbul tomorrow then he needed to be in his office this afternoon.

As they walked into the police station the duty sergeant called out, 'I've got a phone message for you, sir, a Mrs Isler from Gazi Magusa.' Os took the scrawled note, his stomach tightening as he scanned the contents.

'Anything interesting?' Zelfa asked.

'She wants me to go over. Apparently, the young woman who works for them has got something to tell me.'

'Do you want me to come with you?'

He shook his head. 'I'd rather you delved into Gorus's background, see what you can find. He's got a few secrets, that one.' He dropped the crumpled note into the bin. 'This could be all or nothing but I'll ring you on my way back.' Os flashed a brief smile at her and turned to walk out of the station before she could think of a reason to join him.

He slipped in a Buddy Holly tape and reversed out of the car park. He felt a level of excitement as he retraced his route back out of Girne and on to the mountain road. Luckily, the heavy traffic had now disappeared and he was able to put his foot down, over-taking the occasional car. The new speeding cameras that had been in operation a couple of months were having an effect. Os wondered whether a fine would be posted out to him or if there was some mechanism in place that recognised unmarked cars driven by policemen.

As he reached the top of the mountains, he looked below at the Mesaoria Plain stretched out below. A shepherd slumped on his donkey, his hat pulled down over his forehead against the fierceness of the sun. The sheep nibbled on the yellow grass while a few goats huddled under the scant protection of a lone olive tree. There was such a difference in the colours when spring turned into summer. Os didn't understand how the shepherd coped with the boredom and the heat but presumably he was used to it. Again, he found himself thanking Allah that he was educated and didn't have to do such work.

When he reached the roundabout, he turned left to Gazi Magusa instead of continuing to Lefkosa. Again, the road was quiet, perhaps because people were having lunch. He remembered that was what he had been intending to do himself but it would have to wait. It wouldn't do him any harm anyway. Since he had lived with Roisin he had put on weight, eating together every night, as well as sharing at least one bottle of wine or a few beers. He decided that it would be a good idea to take her out that evening. They could go down to the 'Half Way House' and have a Meze. Perhaps he could persuade her to talk about what was bothering her. He was so absorbed with his thoughts that he almost missed the sign for Gazi Magusa.

The two Islers and the shop assistant stared at him when he pushed open the door. No-one smiled.

'We'll go up stairs,' she said as way of a greeting. She glanced at her husband, sending some kind of silent message, then called to the same assistant he had noticed the last time he had been here. Os followed the two women up to the apartment.

The living room was still cluttered and Os did as he had last time, cleared a chair and sat down. Nurten nodded to the young woman to do the same but she remained in the kitchen area, folding clothes that had been left in a heap on one of the surfaces. She appeared tense and glanced furtively across at the two of them.

Os kept his voice gentle as he asked, 'You have something to tell me?'

The young woman plucked at the material of her skirt. Os wondered if her agitation was due to her lack of experience in dealing with the police or whether she had something of great importance to tell him. He felt a twinge of excitement and smiled encouragingly at her. Her heavy eyebrows creased in worry but still she said nothing. There was exasperation in her employers' voice when she broke the silence.

'This is Ilkay Ozturk. She comes from the same village as my father. She went home on her day off yesterday and told her mother about how my father died. The village obviously knew about his death but not the details.'

Os held up his hand to silence Mrs. Isler and turned back to the young woman opposite him. 'Are you able to tell me yourself?'

She nodded, then began to speak in a voice much gentler than the woman she worked for. 'My mother told me she was glad because he'd been blackmailing one of the men in the village for years. She wouldn't say why but just that the man was now dead.'

The tiredness from the journey slipped away. Os leaned forward. 'Did your mother say what he died of and when?' he asked.

'Who? The man from the restaurant?' the young woman asked.

Os nodded.

She shrugged. 'A heart attack - I think it was a couple of months ago.'

Os sat back. He wasn't surprised when he thought about it. Disappointed, yes, but he had never held out much hope that the one unidentified name in Uludag's ledger was the murderer.

'Where is the village you come from?' Os asked.

'On the northern coast, a place called Malidag.'

At three o'clock, it was the last thing he wanted to do but at least it would save him coming back again. For a moment he considered sending Fikri or Sener tomorrow but that would take half of their day, whereas now, it was only a short detour for him. If he went himself he could also be sure that what the girl was telling him was true.

He wrote down the mother's name and address and then thanking them both, made his way towards the stairs.

The husband was busy dealing with a customer but, nevertheless Os felt his eyes on his back as he pulled open the shop door. He wondered what the husband was making of all this. Supposedly, the man had never met his wife's father but either way, these events were a terrible slur on the family.

The build up of heat leapt out at him when he opened the car door; summer appeared to be on its way early. He leaned across and pulled the glove compartment open, taking out the map. As he thought, the village was less than half an hour's drive away. He pushed a fresh tape into the recorder and turned on the engine.

Once he had left Gazi Magusa behind, he was able to put his foot down on the empty road. The terrain was flat in this area with huge expanses of farming land. Each village had its own mosque, some of a size much larger than seemed necessary for the population but he'd heard the ostentatious ones were funded by Saudi Arabia. A tractor pulled out of a side road forcing him to brake and it wasn't until they reached a straight stretch that he felt safe to overtake.

At last Os saw the sign for Maladag. He turned left, off the asphalt road onto a mud track, slowing down to avoid the tractor ruts created over years of regular use. He couldn't imagine existing out here; he had always lived in a town. Even there, the neighbours knew your business but in these villages it would be impossible to have any privacy at all. He glanced at his hand-written instructions on the passenger seat and then saw the local restaurant ahead of him. It was a basic affair with a few metal tables and chairs under a bamboo-covered awning. Three old men sat at a table, coffee cups in front of them. Os pressed a button and the passenger window slid down. He leaned across and asked where Mrs Osturk lived and was directed to a side road, four hundred yards further along. He thanked them and drove away, leaving them to speculate over his business with their neighbour.

He found the house immediately. It was a peeling, bright blue structure with a wooden balcony in front. Parts of old cars and unwanted household furniture cluttered the front area. A typical Northern Cypriot home but Os could never understand why the collection of useless items didn't bother the inhabitants. His parents had filled the front of their house with plants and trees but several of the houses in their street were as messy as this one.

A woman opened the door before he could ring the bell. Undoubtably her daughter would have somehow prewarned her of his visit. Mrs Osturk didn't smile but neither did she seem unfriendly. Her age was more difficult to determine. She had the appearance of a woman in her sixties but with a daughter as young as the one in the Gazi Magusa shop, it seemed unlikely, more like early forties. The climate out here was unrelenting and he doubted whether she wore face cream or ever visited a beauty salon. She asked him inside.

This was like so many houses he visited, devoid of any comfort. A wooden, Turkish sofa, covered in a faded multi-coloured, woven cloth was pushed against the wall. An old man, possibly the grandfather, lay on a day bed by an open window, his mouth wide open as he slept. She returned to her chair and picked up her crochet hook and thread, indicating that he should take the chair on the other side of the wooden table.

'Your daughter told me about the man who recently died here. I understand your need to be discreet but it's essential that you tell me everything.' Os smiled , trying to put her at ease. 'I'm afraid I also need to meet your friend.' A silence hung between them - no doubt she was already regretting having spoken to her daughter. When she did speak, Os was not surprised by what she said.

'My friend is dead. She died, giving birth, five years ago. Her husband and two children still live here in the village but they know nothing of what I'm going to tell you and must never know.'

Os sat back on the hard chair and waited.

'My friend married a good man but he worked away in Germany for two years. To make extra money, she helped out in the kitchen of the restaurant here. Enver, who ran the place was not married then and she was lonely.' The woman pursed her lips at the inevitableness of what had materialised. 'She discovered she was pregnant just before her husband returned. Everyone thought that little Turgay came a month early - except for the three of us of course. Uludag,' she spat at the mention of his name, '…found out one night when he was here visiting his old mother. He went to school with Enver so it was natural that they should have a drink together. One night, after too much brandy Enver told Uludag the story.' The woman took a sip of water then, remembering her manners, asked him whether she should fetch him something. Os shook his head - the last thing he wanted was to break the momentum.

'But why did Enver continue paying after your friend died?'

She reached for her packet of cigarettes. Os sensed a sadness about her as if it had all happened just a few weeks ago.

'He wanted to protect his son. What good would it have done if the child had found out who his real father was? Enver had married a woman in the village and they had their own children.'

Os watched the crochet hook dip in and out of the coarse thread. 'And now that the three of them are dead, you are the only person who knows the real story?'

She spoke quietly. 'And yourself - what will you do with it?'

Os stood up. 'Nothing. I've learnt what I need to know. I don't think I need bother you again.' She smiled and Os realised that once she had been very pretty.

He nodded farewell to the old man who was now watching him through cataracted eyes. The woman hadn't been quite honest about the number of people who knew about her dead friend; presumably the old man had heard the conversation. But that was her problem not his. When he got into his car she had already gone back inside, leaving the door open to catch the breeze.

Chapter Nineteen

Once he was back on the dirt track he keyed in Roisin's number. She picked up on the fourth ring.

'Shall we eat out tonight?'

There was a long pause.

'Where did you have in mind?'

'Anywhere you like.' He attempted to gauge her mood. He didn't think that he was imagining the edge to her voice.

'Fine. I'll book us in at the, 'Half Way House' for eight o'clock. You will be back by then, won't you?'

'Of course. I'll call in at the station and then I'll be straight home.'

He stared moodily at the road ahead - her present behaviour was so unlike her. Only a few days ago he had been thinking how easy she was to live with; but things had certainly changed, ever since he had asked her to marry him, he thought. The fact that this was his first homicide wasn't helping either. But marital problems were a common occurrence in this job. He ought to talk to her about it tonight but the prospect was unappealing. It was one thing to turn down his offer of marriage but then to be moody about it afterwards was going too far. And there was nothing he could do about the hours he worked. Annoyed, he attempted to clear his head and put on his music.

As he drove down from the mountain into the outskirts of Girne, he saw the new left turning onto the back route home. It was gone five. As he was taking the early morning, Istanbul flight he would have been in his rights to go straight home. He could easily telephone the station to see if there were any further developments. But the feeling of annoyance towards Roisin made him drive on into the town.

Zelfa smiled up at him when he walked into their office. 'How did it go?'

'Hang on a minute.' He keyed a number into the phone. 'I need you and Fikri in my office, now,' Os said. He then rang the porter's office. 'Tea?' She nodded, and he placed an order for four glasses just as the two sergeants appeared in the open doorway.

He indicated the hard chairs jammed against the wall; since the arrival of Zelfa's desk, there wasn't room for anything more comfortable. With three pairs of eyes focused on him, he told them about his afternoon.

'At least we don't have to waste time looking for him now,' Sener said.

Os looked at both sergeants. ' So what have you two come up with then?'

Sener answered. 'Nothing of importance, I'm afraid, sir.'

'You're lucky that some of us are making headway then.' His tone softened the implied criticism. 'Have you got Dr Pehlivan's photos, Zelfa?' She reached into her desk drawer and lifted out a plastic envelope. Os took it from her, examining for the first time the pictures they had been given that morning. He stared at the blue topaz stone which was still in its silver claw. 'There has to be a link with the T shirt and this First Nation ring. And if the man was from the States, why kill him with the Greek girl?'

Fikri eased a straining buttock, appearing uncomfortable in his cramped surroundings. 'Perhaps they were lovers and her parents didn't approve?'

Os nodded, 'It's possible but it seems a bit extreme to kill her as well.'

Zelfa cut across them 'The woman might also have been an American. We don't know for definite that she was this Dovish. We're only assuming she was Greek because of the conversation you had with the old woman in the village. The bones could be the remains of Americans who had come here on holiday.'

'Okay,' Os responded. 'But then why were two Americans killed and buried on a hillside in Northern Cyprus?'

'Drugs?' Fikri suggested.

Os shook his head. 'Unlikely in the seventies that they would have been killed, even if they had been dealers. Not impossible, of course.' Os always tried to be encouraging of any suggestions even when he thought that they were way off beam.

It was a very unusual ring. He had seen the same opaque, blue stones on sale in tourist shops in The States. Although the silver was scratched, it had not worn thin, which suggested that the owner had not had it long. And why had it been on a chain instead of on the man's finger. Pehlivan had been very sure that the chain had once hung around the woman's neck.

The cross was about three centimetres in length, a delicate thing with silver flowers encrusted on top. The two items seemed incongruous together, one dainty and feminine, the other bulky and very masculine. Could she have kept the cross and ring hidden under her clothing. Perhaps that was why the chain was so long. If Dovish's family had told everyone that she'd left to marry a mainland Greek, it would imply that they disapproved of her involvement with an American. But if that was the case how and why did she die? If, he reminded himself, it really was her remains in the laboratory in Lefkosa. He tried out his theory on the others.

'It could have been a suicide pact,' Zelfa suggested.

'Why didn't they just leave and go back to the States. If the man was an American, his family would have had money, otherwise how did he afford to come here?' Sener asked.'

'Aren't all Americans rich?' Fikri asked.

'Far from it,' Os answered, remembering some of the shacks he had seen while he had been on his six-month exchange. 'But I agree with you, Sener, I would have thought that an American, travelling here thirty years ago, would have been reasonably well off.'

'He couldn't have been a soldier could he?' Zelfa asked. 'I was only just born when all this was happening - I'm afraid I don't know much about the period?'

Fikri shook his head. 'There weren't any American soldiers here - there never have been. It was the British. Not that they did much to protect us. If the Turkish army hadn't moved in, the Greek Cypriots would have killed us in the name of Eoka.' Fikri went to spit and then, as if remembering where he was, stopped himself. 'The world has forgotten that now - they only support the Greeks, accusing us of taking their land.' Os, Zelfa and Sener stared at the older man whose narrowed eyes seemed to be reliving the horrors of his youth.

Os suddenly realised that it was seven o'clock. 'I've got to go, I'm afraid.' He stood up and handed the photos back to Zelfa. 'Give me a call tomorrow you two, if you find out anything.' They nodded and he wondered how they felt about the change in the team dynamics. Before Zelfa, one of them might have gone with him to Istanbul. And she appeared to want little to do with them, preferring to deal directly with Os, as if they were a two - person organisation. Well, hopefully, it wasn't going to be for long. If they could only solve this case then she would have no excuse but to take on her own work load and they could all get back to normal. He suddenly remembered something.

'Did you find out how regulary Gorus visits Istanbul, Zelfa?'

She nodded. 'At least once a month, sometimes more. But we haven't any proof that it's anything but business and we know he has family over there.'

'But if he does have a tendency to indulge himself in young boys then he has the perfect opportunity.' Os hovered by the doorway aware that he would prefer to stay and discuss the case further. But it was late , so he said, 'Right, I'm off. You three go home too.' He left, leaving the office door open behind him so that they could follow him out.

She sat outside reading a book, a full glass of wine on the table beside her. She smiled up at him as he bent over and kissed her. It was a good start he thought, considering he was so late.

'I'll just have a quick shower and then I'll be ready,' he told her, disappearing in the direction of the bathroom.

On the drive down to the restaurant, he started to tell her about his day but she interrupted him.

'I know, you've been to Lefkosa - your mother rang to say that you forgot the two shirts to go with your suit.' She paused as if replaying the conversation in her head. 'She also told me what a very nice colleague you've got working with you. Presumably, that's the reason I can't go with you to Istanbul tomorrow?'

Os inwardly cursed his mother, while at the same time, was puzzled by Roisin's reaction. He was not sure whether to be flattered or annoyed. He had never considered her the jealous type - she was far too independent.

Preferring to keep on neutral ground, he asked, 'Are you hungry?'

'A little.'

'I've not eaten since breakfast. I've also done nothing but run around all day, so let's just have a nice evening, shall we?'

He pulled into the space in front of the restaurant. The owner came out to greet them and Os kissed the middle - aged woman on both cheeks. Roisin made a point of admiring the large collection of patio plants then led the way up to the roof terrace.

There were only two groups of people eating but Roisin chose a table as far away from them as possible. She sat down facing the mountains, her back to the rest of the diners. Os stood for a few seconds staring out at the black, distant sea, the lights of Girne and those of the small settlements nearby. Then, after ordering wine and water, he pulled out a chair opposite Roisin.

She had made an effort with her appearance. Without makeup she was very pretty but when she dressed up he thought her stunning. She had on a turquoise sun dress in some crinkled material that shimmered like silk. He took her hand across the table and was pleased when she smiled. Relating the events of the day, he omitted any further reference to Zelfa and their visit to his mother. Roisin listened intently to his description of the jewellery and segments of clothing that were now being held in the Lefkosa laboratory.

'So you think the man was an American?'

Os took her left hand and squeezed it. 'I don't know - it's just a theory. We won't be sure for definite until Dr Pehlivan gets back to us. And he's waiting on the priority that the American Embassy gives the request.'

A waiter began to unload a tray of Meze onto their table. Soon, twenty small dishes covered their red and white checked tablecloth. Os loved eating here. The restaurant was in a renovated village house. For most of the year the tables were set out on the roof but, in winter, they ate inside by a roaring, log fire. The building could not be called anything but rustic but that was, beside the excellent food, its great charm. Everything was always home-made and there were dishes here that you remembered one's grandmother making. He recognised houmous, fresh beetroot, cheese in flaky pastry, bean stew and fresh cabbage but he always enjoyed Roisin's expression of wonder as she tried the different tastes. Tonight a new dish of flower heads fried in batter, made her stop the owner and ask her about the dishes she had prepared that morning. Os hoped this meant that they could now forget their differences and enjoy the evening. He poured them both a glass of cold, white wine and for a while neither of them talked.

'You've got your appetite back I see.'

She grinned at him, the kind of grin that lifted his spirits. 'Are you saying that I'm greedy?'

'Not at all.'

'So tell me again why you're going to Istanbul tomorrow?' Her voice had lost its accusatory tone of the previous evening.

'At this moment, Gorus is the most likely suspect. He's got the contacts and motive but because he's so well connected, we've got to do everything by the book.'

'I think I know that name.' Roisin screwed up her face as she tried to remember. 'Wasn't he one of the candidates for the mayor of Girne?'

Surprised, then realising she had read it in the local English paper, he said, 'He doesn't have an alibi for the evening of the murder. He says that he was in the office on his own, until about eight, and then he went home to an empty house. His wife and children were visiting his father-in-law - which was either fortuitous or unlucky for him, depending on whether he is innocent or guilty.'

The waiter started to clear away the empty dishes. Silver - foiled parcels and a plate of roast potatoes were placed between them. Os peeled back the foil. The aromatic steam, which rose from the knuckle bone of lamb, made Os realise that perhaps he could still manage a little more.

'This really is delicious,' Roisin said. 'We've got to learn how to use the wood oven at home.'

Os was about to say that he would ask his mother to show them, next time he spoke to her, before he checked himself. Now would not be the best time to remind Roisin of his mother.

'But why go to Istanbul? Couldn't you find out everything you need by phone?'

'I want to interview the young man who said that he was assaulted by Gorus when he was fourteen. Remember, I told you that his family withdrew the complaint. But it's likely they were pressured into it because the father worked for the family.' Os took a sip of wine. 'The boy will be in his twenties now. He might be persuaded to tell the truth this time if he thinks we're not wanting to renew charges.' He picked up the half-eaten knuckle and tore off the remaining meat with his teeth.

'Make sure you leave something for Tramps.'

Os grinned. 'You'd rather I went hungry instead of your dog?'

'You've just eaten a huge Meze and he's our dog not mine,' Roisin bantered. 'Anyway, carry on.'

'We're waiting to hear whether Gorus's name is linked to any other paedophile cases. It's such a potentially explosive situation - Atak doesn't want any of the information exchanged over the phone.' He wiped his greasy hands on a paper serviette. 'He's worried about it all back - firing and Gorus's father-in-law making trouble for us. You know how terrified he is of politicians.'

'I'm thinking of going home for a couple of weeks.'

Os put down his wine glass and stared at her. 'Why?'

Her eyes didn't quite settle on his. 'I haven't been back since I came out to sell my aunt's house. I only meant to leave my flat for two weeks. Mary's been watering the plants ever since.' She paused, then added something which caused Os's stomach to contract, then harden. 'I have to decide what I'm going to do. If I'm to stay out here permanently, then I have to either rent, or sell the flat in Liverpool - I can't just leave it empty.'

What she was saying made perfect sense if it hadn't come on top of the problems of the last couple of days. Was she thinking of leaving him? He had noticed that she called England home instead of Northern Cyprus - where he was.

'And when were you thinking of deciding what you're going to do?' he asked coldly.

'I've been thinking about it for the last few days.' Her voice faltered.

Despite his growing anger, he reached across and took her hand. 'What's happening here, Roisin? We were getting on so well?'

She stared out into the night. The other tables were now empty and the waiters' voices drifted up from below. At last she looked at him and said, 'I suppose it started when you asked me to marry you.'

'And was that so terrible? Am I such a dreadful prospect?'

She smiled at him but there was no joy in her face. 'No, I'm the terrible prospect. I've gone into my usual self destructive mode. I'm frightened the relationship won't survive, so if I end it before you do, I feel I'm in control.' She paused but he chose to say nothng. 'I know it doesn't make sense to you. I'm not sure it makes any sense to me either - I just can't help myself.'

Now his anger was replaced by a frustration that made him thrust his clenched hands into his pockets. 'I love you,' he said at last. 'It's ridiculous to think that marriage would destroy what we've got between us.'

'Your mother doesn't agree.' She spoke the words simply, without spite.

Os frowned. 'I know she's difficult but all she wants is to see me married with children.' Os held up his hand as he saw the expression on her face change. 'I know, I know, you never want to get married. But you're making your decision for the wrong reasons and now you seem happy to just walk away.'

Perhaps knowing herself how ridiculous her argument sounded, she took a different tack. 'I also need to see my friends and sister.'

'That's understandable. But can't you wait till this murder enquiry is out of the way? Then we can talk properly - I don't want you going back to England until we've sorted this thing out.'

She sat still for a few seconds then nodded. He leaned over the rail and called down for coffees and brandies. Intuitively, they both moved on to other, less explosive subjects. Os encouraged her to talk about the book she was writing. Although he was proud of what she did, it wasn't something that they discussed a great deal. English language books for school children was not the most fascinating of subjects. Perhaps that was why they spent so much time discussing his job.

He drove home with her cuddled up beside him. At least he was able to talk to Roisin about their relationship. Previously, girlfriends had always complained that he skirted around his feelings but perhaps that was because he hadn't cared enough about them. He found his thoughts turning to the new Inspector. She had a ruthless streak but perhaps she was different in her personal life – he was probably unfair to judge her so soon. But he could never become seriously involved with another police officer. With Roisin, he could discuss his work if he wanted to, but otherwise they would talk about other things. They rarely discussed his colleagues. Sener was the only person she had met and that was only once. He suddenly became aware that she was staring at him.

'What time are you going tomorrow?'

He grimaced at the prospect. 'I'll have to set the alarm for four. Do you want me to sleep in the other room?'

She shook her head and the look she threw him gave him hope.

Chapter Twenty

At five o'clock, Zelfa was standing outside her apartment, as glamorous as if it was ten in the morning. Os didn't feel quite so bright. He had turned on the radio so that he could listen to the news rather than talk. Fortunately, she was not feeling as good as she looked or she sensed his need for silence, but neither of them spoke during the forty-five minute drive to Ercan airport.

Already there were queues of tanned tourists forming but as officials they were dealt with quickly. Os took her through to Customs where a friend, who was finishing the night duty, offered them coffee. Again, she was uncharacteristically quiet. He and Hassan talked about mutual friendships and a trip to Ankara that the Customs man had recently made in pursuit of a drug trail. At one time he had toyed with the idea of transferring to Customs but since he had moved over to homicide he felt differently; piercing together the clues in a murder case had renewed his enthusiasm.

At the muffled call for their plane departure the Inspectors made their farewells and crossed the tiled area of the departure lounge towards the boarding station. The plane was half empty. Zelfa had bought papers, so Os spent the ninety-minute flight browsing the news and drinking three cups of coffee. Zelfa was proving to be a much easier travel companion than he had imagined; he suspected that if Roisin had been with him, he would not have got off so lightly. They were greeted by a plain-clothed policeman and given priority through the terminal to a black Mercedes waiting outside.

Zelfa spent the journey chatting easily about what had been happening in her absence while Os stared out of the window at a city coming to life. It occurred to him that his presence was probably superfluous. Zelfa had proved herself more than capable of managing this end of things but it had been Atak's idea that they come together. For once, money had not seemed a problem to him; his worry over this investigation into the son–in-law of a government minister, overrode any of his natural parsimoniousness. Perhaps he should feel flattered that his presence was deemed neccessary when Istanbul was obviously Zelfa's turf. And it was good to get off the island, if only for a day. Sometimes the insularity of the country got to him.

He recalled the previous evening's conversation and his attempt to think positively about his and Roisin's future together. She'd been enthusiastic about visiting the lunar landscape of Cappadocia in the centre of Turkey. The idea of their staying in one of the houses or hotels, built into the rock –face, was appealing but for this they would have to wait a few months until it was cooler. Early October would be a good time, before the snows of winter. They had also discussed hiring a private gullet and spending a week drifting from bay to bay, stopping off to swim whenever the fancy took them. When the case was over, he would look into it. Though he couldn't help but wonder if they would ever prove who killed Uludag.

They were now travelling through the middle of the city. The shops' metal shutters were up and many of their wares were either stacked in plastic boxes outside the windows or hanging from wires across the shop frontages. Men and women in business suits hurried along the already busy pavements, seemingly uninterested in the leather jackets and fresh fruit and vegetables. Then, through the windscreen, he caught his first sight of the Blue Mosque. The gold of the spinnerets glinted in the morning sun and next to it, competing with the beauty of its neighbour, was the dome of St. Sophia. A line of horses and carriages waited patiently for the first tourists of the day.

A few minutes later the car came to a halt outside the uninspiring modern block of a police station. It was not so dissimilar to the one in Girne, except that it was five times the size. Os sensed the sudden tension in Zelfa and it occurred to him that she might be worried about meeting her ex-fiancé. He was sure that today she had made even more of an effort with her appearance. Despite the fact that they had been travelling for several hours, she still appeared as fresh as if she had just arrived from her apartment in Istanbul.

They crossed the entrance hall to the row of lifts. People swarmed from all directions, creating frenzy unimaginable in Girne. They pushed themselves into the crowded lift and Zelfa pressed the button for the fifth floor.

Os wondered whether the tall man, who stood up when they entered his office, was the person she had come to Northern Cyprus to forget. It was obvious that he was attracted to her but then, Os reminded himself, that was how most men looked at her. He came forward, kissing her on both cheeks, his hands hovering a little longer than necessary on her shoulders. He then turned to Os and shook his hand. Halil indicated that they should sit down before asking Zelfa how she had settled in her new job. Yet again, Os felt superfluous. He was beginning to think he should have spent the day back in Girne, talking to people in the jewellery trade. There were several people he knew who had been around thirty years ago. But when the coffee arrived, they got down to business.

'We've got nothing definite as such,' Halil now included Os in the conversation. 'Gorus, is head of one of the new, wealthy families that have appeared in Istanbul over the last few years. The old man's got three sons, the youngest who you've met in Girne, and the other two now run the businesses here.'

'So nothing suspicious about them?' Os asked. He wasn't sure what he had expected.

'I didn't say that, I just meant that we didn't have a police record on any of them.They've done inordinately well for themselves.' Halil leant back in a chair that equalled Atak's in stature. 'Gorus senior came to Istanbul in his early twenties from a village near the Iran border. Started off with nothing - like most of these country people, hoping to make their fortune in the city. They usually pick up low paid jobs and move into basic housing in the poorer areas - the majority of them are barely educated.' He paused as he stirred his coffee. 'However, Gorus Senior went on to do very well for himself. He got a job in a large painting contractors and eventually married the daughter. The company is now highly successful - dealing with many of the five star hotels here. He then expanded into car hire which again has done well.'

'So money laundering is a possibility?' Os asked.

'More than likely but if so, they're good at it. I wouldn't be surprised if the family's linked to the Turkish Mafia - it would make sense why they became so wealthy, so quickly. It would normally take two generations at least to do what he's done legitimately - most people from his origins can only dream of the money he's made.'

'So Erim Gorus would have the necessary contacts to kill an old man?' Zelfa asked.

The Turkish policeman sighed. 'I'm sure that would be no problem at all.'

Os wrote down a date and passed the paper across to Halil. 'Any chance of you checking the whereabouts of any likely candidates around that period? They could have gone through Ercan Airport, or used one of the ferries.'

'No problem,' he said and left the room.

Os turned to Zelfa who now appeared a little more relaxed. 'Glad to be back?' She shrugged then picked up her coffee as if to hint that this was a subject she had no wish to discuss. Os glanced at Halil's unoccupied seat. 'And is he the fiancé?'

She shook her head again and gave a thin smile. 'He's not here today, I've already checked.'

Halil reappeared in the doorway. 'I've got someone dealing with it. Now we can either bring in the young man, who initially brought the charges against Gorus, or we can go out to his bar and interview him there.' He sat down behind his desk and waited for their answer.

Zelfa's voice was breathy with excitement. 'So you've found him?'

'He manages a small bar in the gay part of the city. Again, we've checked his background. The only documented dealings he's had with the police was that time when he was a teenager.'

'Have you already talked to him?' Os asked.

Halil shook his head. 'We thought we'd leave that to you. I didn't want to scare him off. Better to surprise him.'

'Thank you,' Os looked at his watch. It was ten thirty. He had been up for five and a half hours but suddenly he had the energy for anything. 'Could we go now?'

Halil raised his eyebrows but stood up immediately. 'Of course. We can talk further in the car.'

As they travelled through the city, Os no longer noticed his surroundings. His mind churned over the information. Everything he had heard suggested that Gorus could easily have got rid of Uludag. The family was suspected of having criminal links so it would be natural for his brothers and father to help the younger brother to solve his problem. After all, he had played the game and married well like his father. The fact that he was now trying to get into politics would benefit the extended family further. Os felt a renewed sense of purpose and for the first time since they had arrived in Istanbul, he felt glad that he had come over and not left everything to Zelfa. It was going to be very interesting, meeting the young man and getting his side of the story. But it was a pity Halil's investigations hadn't found anything more inflamatory on Gorus. If the businessman was continuing to indulge himself, he was presumably being far more careful.

The police car turned into a small, side street and a few seconds later the driver pulled into the kerb. There were bars on either side of the narrow road; some were shuttered and it suddenly occurred to him that they could be unlucky. This was an area that obviously stayed open until the early hours and as it was now only eleven o'clock, the man they wanted to talk to might still be in bed. The three of them climbed out and scanned the street for the bar called Zeus. It was a hundred yards away and as Os had feared, the shutters were down.

All the buoyancy that Os had felt earlier began to deflate but then Halil nodded to the window above the bar. 'He lives up there - that's if he's in.' The Turkish policeman strode over to the shutters and after failing to find a bell, proceeded to bang on the metal strips.

Os stood in the middle of the road looking up at the windows. There was no movement behind the glass. He sighed. They would have to wait until the man returned from wherever he had spent the night. He looked up and down the street. A few doors away, a modern café already had a few customers sitting outside. He turned back to his two colleagues, to suggest the venue, when the top window opened and an unshaven head poked out.

Halil held up his badge and the man withdrew.

He glanced back at his colleagues, 'We're in luck.'

There was a clanking sound and the shutters began to move upwards. A few seconds later, the young man joined them on the pavement. He finished buttoning the fly of his jeans but left his shirt hanging outside. His hair was cropped short and his moustache clipped to just above his lip. Despite the need for a shave and a wash, he was a good looking man, not much taller than Zelfa. However, he had the appearance of someone who spent time in the gym. According to the records he was in his early twenties but in this stark, morning light he might have had difficulty getting a drink in any other of the bars on the street if they hadn't known who he was. Possibly, that had been another reason for Gorus finding him so attractive; it was likely that as a child he would have looked a lot younger than his fourteen years.

'We'd like to speak to you inside, if that's all right, Mr. Songur,' Halil said.

A tired expression flicked over his regular features and Os wondered if police harassment was a regular occurrence in this area. He turned and walked back into the bar, the three police officers following him.

The smell of stale smoke and alcohol was overpowering. Songur went behind the chrome-fronted bar and began to fiddle with the expresso machine. He used the mirror behind the glass shelving to speak to his unwanted visitors.

'Coffee anyone?' When all three shook their heads, he replied, 'Well, I need one if you don't mind. This is early for me. If you're after my books, they were only looked at last week and everything's in order.'

Os eased himself onto one of the tall, chome bar stools, keeping his elbows away from the overflowing ashtrays stacked on the stained counter. 'We're more interested in your relationship with a business man called Gorus.'

Songur's back stiffened and his hands ceased momentarily in their task of spooning coffee into the machine. 'I haven't got a relationship with any Gorus.'

'I'm talking of ten years ago. We need to know why your family withdrew the case against him.'

Songler turned to Os, his face showing his curiosity.

'Why? What's he done now? That was all finished with years ago.'

'Just answer the question, sir.' Zelfa said, moving forward to stand by her colleague.

Songur's blue eyes flitted over the policewoman but there was no lust in his gaze.

'And if I don't, I suppose you'll find a reason to turn this place over.' It was a statement rather than a question.

Os gave the nod that was expected though he had no stomach for such tactics.

'I've had nothing to do with him since my father left the business. They're not a family you want dealings with if you want to keep out of trouble.' He poured thick coffee into a glass and raised it to his lips. 'I've seen him on the street a few times in the last couple of years. He even came in here once but, luckily, I had someone helping me behind the bar and I went into the back. I'm not sure he'd recognise me now, but he still looks exactly the same.'

'Who was he with?' Os asked.

'No-one. He's always on his own.'

'What do you think he's doing here then? A married man - I wouldn't have thought that this would have been an area that would attract him.'

Songler smiled. 'Gone down that route has he? Well, it doesn't surprise me. His family were none too pleased when they found out what he'd been doing with me. I suppose now he looks respectable, he can get up to what he wants - as long as he's discreet. Probably accounts for the fact that I don't see him here very often.'

Songler appeared to be unaware that Gorus was no longer living in Istanbul.

'Perhaps he's just coming for a quiet drink away from his family?' Os continued.

A sneer appeared on the handsome features. 'He wouldn't be down here if he wasn't looking for something. You can get anything you want, if you've got the money to pay for it and know who to ask. No. He'll be after a young lad for a few hours - no ties that can get him into trouble. He would have learned his lesson with me.'

'They paid your father off?' Zelfa interrupted.

Songler shrugged, appearing to have no opinion on the subject. 'My father was furious when he found us together but then, after he had reported it to the police and Gorus was arrested, it all got a bit out of hand. The old man offered money and by then my father had realised how much it would cost him in legal fees. He didn't have an option but to take the money and get himself another job.' Songler turned to refill his cup. 'It was enough to buy our apartment and the subject was never brought up again - one of those taboo subjects.'

'You don't think he just comes here for a drink, away from his family?' Os persisited. They had come a long way to intereview this man; they could not afford any misunderstandings.

Songler snorted. 'No middle-aged, heterosexual man comes here to drink- he'd be too scared of being propoisistioned. I told you, he'd be after a young lad for a few hours.' He screwed up his face in disgust. 'He might have got himself a wife but nothing changes.'

'I'll have some of that coffee of yours, if you don't mind now.' Os glanced across at Zelfa and Halil and they both nodded. Songler turned back to his machine and Os cleared a space on the counter in front of him. Above the hissing of steam, he asked, 'Can you tell us what happened exactly? We've only got the police report to go on.'

Songler sighed but continued to operate the coffee maker. 'For years my father had been the foreman of the paint warehouse. When I was thirteen, he had me working in there after school and on Saturdays. He was determined that I would be taken on after I left school.' Songler turned around and placed three cups on the counter. 'I was good with numbers so my father had me checking the stock and helping with the books. I liked the work.' He sighed again. 'Anyway Erim started to call in more than usual. He then offered to take me to watch rally-car racing. I think my father was surprised but our families had known each other for years - because of dad's job, we'd been invited to their house a few times. He had a Lamborghini and would take me for rides. And then he tried it on.' Songler shrugged at the inevitableness of it all. 'I knew even then that I was not interested in girls. He was too old for me of course but,' again he shrugged, '…he gave me money, a lot actually.'

'How did your father find out?' Os asked.

'Gorus and I were at the back of the warehouse - he wasn't able to keep his hands off me. Anyway my father saw us. Perhaps he was beginning to suspect - who knows. But he found us both with our pants down.' He pulled a face. 'I took the easy way out. Said that I'd been forced into it.'

Os pushed his coffee away, suddenly no longer attracted by its aroma.

'My father went mad, called the police. But the next day, old Gorus came around to the apartment and made a deal with him - everyone has his price.' Songler's eyes slid over to Halil. Halil stared back, his brown eyes blank. 'My father got a new job and he bought our apartment from the landlord. I didn't see Erim again until last year. It was a bit of a shock as I said – he hadn't changed at all.'

'This place – is it yours?' Halil asked.

Songler shook his head. 'Wish it was. I just manage the place.'

Os looked at both of his colleagues then slid off the stool. Zelfa flicked her notebook open to a blank page. 'We'd like your mobile number in case we need to talk to you again.'

Songler reached up and took a card from a pile on the top shelf and placed it on the counter top. A young, female voice broke into the tense atmosphere making them all turn in the direction of the door.

'Can I come in and get started,' she repeated. A tall woman in jeans and T shirt stood staring at them. Her face showed no interest in whom her boss was talking to, only in how it would affect her work schedule.

Songler looked at Os who nodded. Songler had been fair with them and he could understand that the man didn't want his cleaner knowing his business. The three police officers went back into the street.

As they climbed into their waiting car, Halil asked, 'Do you two want to drive out and have a look at the Gorus family house? We won't go in but you'll get an idea of how well they've done from the outside.' They both nodded, their minds still processing the last interview.

Chapter Twenty-One

Os pulled the safety belt across him and closed his eyes. It had been a very long day. He hadn't been surprised when Zelfa had told him that she was going to stay in Istanbul until the early morning. Her boss wanted a meeting with her and then she intended to have a few drinks with friends. The hotel room had been booked and paid for anyway, as was the early morning return flight. She had tried hard to persuade him to stay so that she could show him the night life of her city. For a brief moment he had been tempted but something in her eyes made him realise that he wanted to get back.

But he was surprised that they had allowed her to move to Northern Cyprus. She was obviously very good at her job and, even in the city of Istanbul, she was the only female Inspector. Perhaps tomorrow she would tell them that she had decided to go back. He thought about how he would feel if that happened and surprised himself when he realised that he would be sorry, even though it would mean having his office to himself. As the plane began to move, he leaned back in his seat and closed his eyes.

Frustration gnawed away inside him. If the Gorus family had hired a hit man he would have travelled on a false passport or come ashore on a quiet beach. The Karpas was a perfect place, providing numerous deserted beaches and a reduced police force to equate with such a sparsely populated area.

Once on land, he would have passed as a migrant worker, employed by one of the many building contractors in the area. It would take someone less than a day to travel by bus to Girne - for someone experienced it was an easy task.

Os refused the drink and sandwich from the air hostess. He was still sated from his late lunch, courtesy of the Istanbul police. The Meze, followed by a large fish cooked in a casing of salt, had been delicious. Zelfa, Halil and himself had sat at window seats, overlooking the Bosporus, in what must have been one of Istanbul's best restaurants. At times, he had found it difficult to concentrate on the conversation while watching the ferries and ships pass by only a few yards below them. The atmosphere of Istanbul and perhaps Zelfa had affected him but he was happy with his decision that in a few hours, he would be driving himself home from Ercan Airport.

He was nudged awake; passengers were unbuckling their seat belts and standing up to get their hand luggage. Os took down a large box of Duty Free chocolates and several packets of Dutch, filter coffee.

As he strode out of the terminal he keyed in Roisin's mobile number. He would be home by eight o'clock, thirteen hours earlier than planned.

Running up the steps to their house, he felt the anticipation of someone who had been away much longer than the early hours of that morning. Roisin was sitting outside and stood up to throw her arms around him. He breathed in her familiar scent then sat down on one of the pool chairs and pulled her onto his lap.

She snuggled into him. 'How did it go?'

He searched for a word that would best describe his day. 'Fascinating! But I doubt that they'd have been so helpful if I'd gone on my own though.'

'Did you talk to the man you wanted?'

Os nodded. She seemed so relaxed, like her old self.

'So, what was he like?'

Os wished he had a cigarette. He would have loved to have lit up while he told her about his day. He couldn't face another stick of gum so he just answered her question.

'He's done well for himself, considering his age. But I'm not sure he's quite the victim I envisaged.'

Roisin twisted in his lap to look up into his face. 'What do you mean?'

'Maybe he just doesn't want to appear a victim but he certainly gave us the impression that he did well for himself out of the situation. Gorus is definitely still into young boys from what Songler told us. He seemed quite certain about that.'

Roisin remained quiet for a while as she thought about what Os had said. 'So after the whole thing had died down, Gorus was sent over to expand the family business in Girne?' She finally asked.

Os reached across the table for his beer.

'Presumably they didn't want to risk it happening again. But he got married and had children so he must have redeemed himself.'

'Perhaps relieved,' Roisin suggested. 'But you were right about him going back to Istanbul,' she made a face. '… for his boys. The family can't be too keen on that.'

'If they know about it. I would imagine that he says he's going out with friends and as long as he doesn't rub it in their faces …….'

Roisin picked up Os's beer and took a few sips before handing it back to him. 'What are you going to do now?'

'Istanbul are looking into a few things but I'm not holding out that they'll find anything.'

'How was the gorgeous Zelfa in Istanbul?'

Os didn't respond to the sarcasm. 'Very useful in the end. She's coming back in the morning.'

'So why didn't you stay?'

Os grinned. 'I preferred to come home.'

They sat silently for a few moments and then pushing her temporarily off his knee, he stood up and went to fetch two more beers. They talked for another half hour while listening to the sounds of the cicadas in the undergrowth. Just as he was going to suggest another beer, she took hold of his hand and he found himself, not unwillingly, following her into the bedroom.

He was at his desk at nine o'clock the next morning and, soon after, Zelfa walked through the door. She wore a brown, silk suit that rustled as she moved.

'Have you come straight from the airport?'

She nodded as she picked up the phone and ordered coffee for both of them.

He watched her move papers around on her desk. 'So what did your boss want to talk to you about?' She looked up at him but he couldn't read her thoughts.

'He wants me back. There have been several murders in the section of the city, predominantly Kurdish. He wants me in charge.'

'Sounds interesting?'

'I thought about it but decided to turn it down – at the moment, anyway.' She attempted a smile but now he detected sadness in her eyes.

'Does Atak know?'

'My boss spoke to him before he talked to me. I'm sorry,' she wrinkled her nose, '... it means I'll still be sharing your office.'

Their coffee arrived and her phone rang. He sipped his viscous drink and listened to her side of the coversation.

She replaced the receiver. 'That was Halil. They've cross checked all the registered entries into Northern Cyprus and nothing has materialised.'

Os didn't even feel disappointed - it was what he was expecting. He made a decision. 'I'm going back up to Endremit to talk to the barman.'

Her eyes widened. 'Why?'

'I'm not exactly sure but I've got to do something and we can't arrest Gorus with what we've got on him.'

'Should we interview the neighbours again? Show them a photo of Gorus? Someone might remember seeing him that night.'

He shook his head. 'Maybe later on today. I'll give you a ring.'

'You're sure you don't want me to come with you?' she repeated.

'It would be a waste of time. I don't even know why I'm going, except that I'm sure he knows everything about everyone in that village. Whenever I talk to him it's like he's not telling us something.'

'I'm thinking of going to see Gorus again.'

Os stared at her but she looked back all innocence. 'Why?'

She shrugged, as if implying it was no big deal. 'He's lied to us and I want him to know that we know. He might drop his guard.'

'Be careful. You know how nervous Atak is about it all.'

She grinned impishly. 'Don't worry, I'll handle him.'

He had no doubt that she would but, nevertheless, he felt uneasy.

A young woman sat at the bar reading the Vatan. She looked up as Os crossed the floor to join her. 'What can I get you, Inspector?'

'A coffee, please.' He slid the newspaper towards him and glanced over the front page. The coffee machine hissed and when he looked up he saw that she was watching him in the mirror.

'Any further on to finding out who killed Uludag, Inspector?'

Os wished that he could be lying when he shook his head. Instead he answered, 'We're following a few lines of enquiry. Is Hassan around?'

She turned and placed a small cup and saucer in front of him. 'He went into town to do some shopping.'

Os sighed. What was he hoping the bar man would tell him anyway? He glanced down at the newspaper again but instead of taking in the words, his mind ran over the faces of the people he had interviewed in the last few days. Was he making a mistake concentrating on the businessman? Was there something he had missed? Was it because the other three victims had been women that he had decided that they couldn't have been capable of Uludag's murder? He rubbed the top of his nose, trying to ease the tension that had built up there. His mobile rang.

'Yes, Sener?'

'I thought you would want to know sir, that we've had a phone call from Dr, Pehlivan. The American Embassy has got back to him but there's no record of anybody reported missing during the period we're interested in. And the results from the walking stick are back. It's Uludag's blood and there are strands of his hair stuck to it. It's definitely the murder weapon. '

Os was aware that the woman could hear every word. 'All right, I'm coming back in. Get hold of Fikri and we'll have a meeting straight away.' Os avoided her eyes, placed a note on the bar and left.

Sener was hovering in the entrance to the station when Os walked in.

'Did you get hold of Fikri?'

'Atak wants you first, sir.'

Os sighed. 'All right, wait for me. I shouldn't be long.'

'Inspector Urfa is already up there, sir.'

Os stopped and looked more closely at Sener. 'And?'

'She's been in there since she got back from talking to Gorus. I don't know anything else except that I was in the corridor when she returned and she looked pretty fired up.'

'I see.' Os didn't like what he saw but he had no alternative but to do as he had been ordered. What had Zelfa discovered and why hadn't she talked to him first?

Atak's secretary looked up from her computer and nodded to the door that divided her room from her boss. As usual her face was devoid of any welcome.

'Go straight in, Inspector.'

'Thank you,' he answered, already pushing open the door. He saw the look of triumph in Zelfa's eyes as soon as he entered the room. 'You wanted to see me, sir?' He remained standing, not particularly wanting to be part of this cosy meeting but knowing that he had no option.

'Sit down, Osman. Things have developed since you've been out.'

Again, Os glanced at Zelfa. Some emotion flashed across her face and he wondered whether it was embarrassment or something else. He hoped it was the former - they were supposed to be a team.

Atak dabbed his perspiring face with his handkerchief. 'We've brought Gorus in for questioning and more than likely going to charge him with murder. We're waiting for his lawyer to arrive from Lefkosa now.'

Os stared out of the window for a few seconds before answering. He included only Atak in his question. 'On what grounds, sir?'

'He's admitted to Inspector Urfa that he did visit Uludag on the night of the murder. He says he didn't kill him but Inspector Ulfa thinks that he's lying.'

Still Os directed his question at Atak 'What reason did he give?'

The ringing of the Commandant's phone stopped him from answering. A few seconds later he replaced the receiver and stood up. His bulk increased as he shrugged on his jacket.

'Now you're here, Osman, we can all go down to the interview room. Mr Gorus's lawyer has arrived.'

Os said nothing. If they could prove that Gorus was guilty, he hoped he would be man enough to congratulate Zelfa, however badly he thought she had handled things. But he was surprised that Atak had agreed to this interview. Unless he was missing something, he doubted that they had enough on the businessman to charge him.

But Zelfa looked jubilant, seemingly unable to contain her excitement. Os stood back, allowing both of them to go in front of him.

Zelfa had booked the largest interview room. Gorus and his solicitor were already seated at the table and two uniformed men stood behind them. Two empty chairs had been placed opposite the table, so Os picked up one that was pushed against the wall. He was tempted to sit there, distancing himself from his two colleagues then wondered whether he was being childish. Zelfa turned on the tape recorder then read Gorus his rights. A cloying perfume dominated the stagnant air; the room had been sprayed overzealously with an air freshener. The combination of sweat, smoke, after shave and now this, made Os stand up again and open the window. He took several, deep breaths before returning his attention to the dynamics of the group.

Had Atak been aware that Gorus would employ the top, criminal lawyer in the country? Os had seen the man operate in a Lefkosa court where he had successfully destroyed all the police evidence against a well known thief. He now sat relaxed next to his client, an air of arrogance about him. Os knew then that Zelfa didn't stand a chance.

Zelfa glanced at Atak and when he nodded said, 'Mr Gorus, we've brought you in for questioning because we believe that you were the last person to see Mr Uludag alive.' Gorus sat further back in his chair and folded his arms.

His lawyer answered, 'I think my client has been more than helpful, informing you that he visited the deceased on that evening. But he left him in the same manner as he found him - alive and well.'

'I'm afraid we have a difficulty with that version of events, sir,' Zelfa smiled, all charm. 'You see, although no-one saw Mr Gorus arrive at the house, no one saw him leave either. He's admitted that he purposely left his car outside the village and then walked around the back of the houses so that he wouldn't be seen.'

Although his face was blank, Os sensed that the businessman was nervous. The lawyer adjusted himself on the hard chair, his voice still calm but with an edge that screamed out a warning.

'My client has already told you the reason for his visit. He wanted to talk about the extra money Uludag was demanding. Although the case in Istanbul never came to trial, Mr Gorus naturally did not want his family and friends to read about it in the newspapers. As I'm sure that you're aware, with the elections for Mayor, it's a very sensitive time for him.'

'But if the case had been dismissed all those years ago, why was he so worried that Uludag would go to the press now?' Zelfa asked.

The lawyer's smile reminded Os of a crocodile.

'Oh come, Ms Urfa, none of us in this room are that naïve. If this story hit the newspapers - despite the fact that my client is innocent - his political career would be over before he has a chance to show what he can do for this town.'

Despite himself, Os felt a twinge of sympathy for Zelfa. He cut in. 'You can see our difficulty, Mr Gorus. If you'd been honest with us from the beginning, then we wouldn't be in this situation now. We could've dealt with this privately - in your office.' The lawyer's eyes slid across to settle speculatively on the young, male Inspector. 'And, if you'd come to us for help when Uludag began his demands, then perhaps you wouldn't be in this embarressing position at all.' Except for the rattle of Atak's breathing there was silence. Os watched a pink tinge spread up from Gorus's neck to cover his face. He continued. 'You can appreciate our problem, Mr Gorus. As far as we know, you were the last person to see our murdered man alive and we have no evidence to prove that you didn't kill him.'

Gorus leaned forward. 'But I didn't. I admit that I was tempted to use that stick of his, when he said how much more money he wanted - but I made myself leave.'

The lawyer's eyes narrowed as he glanced at the man next to him. 'Let me deal with this, Erim.'

'It is interesting that you should say that, Mr Gorus,' Os said, ignoring the lawyer. 'It's been confirmed today that Uludag's walking stick was the murder weapon.'

Now the lawyer put a restraining hand on his client's arm before smiling himself; a smile that moved his thick lips but not his eyes. 'As you say, Inspector, interesting but hardly proof that would be accepted in court. Again, my client has merely been honest – perhaps too honest for his own good. He would have liked to have got rid of his Blackmailer - a natural reaction in the circumstances, but he restrained himself. I'm assuming that you haven't found any thing on the murder weapon that would compromise Mr Gorus?' The lawyer looked at the three police officers opposite him; he already knew the answer. Os felt fresh frustration over the situation he had been forced into. They were going to have to release the man and now it was going to be far more difficult to bring him in next time.

'I'm sure that I don't have to remind you, that if any of this is released to the press, I will put in a charge of police harassment. It would be my civic duty to inform the newspapers and the officials who make public appointments,' here the man paused and stared for a moment at Atak, '…that incompetence is rife in the police force.' Again he spoke softly but the message was crystal clear.

'Is that a threat?' Atak's voice carried the same weight as his ample frame. Os experienced a rare feeling of admiration for his boss. Knowing Atak as Os did, the lawyer's comments could not have been more pertinent.

'Not at all, Commandant,' he answered.'I'm only dealing with the facts. Now if there is nothing more you want to ask my client, we are both busy people.'

The screech of wood on tiles, as Atak pushed back his chair, brought a glint to the lawyer's eyes. Os followed his colleagues out of the room.

'We'll have to let him go,' Atak sounded weary. 'Unless you've anything else you can throw at him - he's not going to confess.'

Zelfa looked at Os but he had nothing to say, she was obviously furious. 'Not this time. His lawyer has him well under control.'

He wondered what she had expected. Someone in Gorus's position was not going to turn up at the station unrepresented. But why Atak had agreed to the interview in the first place, he had no idea.

'Unless either of you have anything else up your sleeve, I'll tell him he can go for now. But we'll have to have something very definite if we're ever to bring him in again.' Atak looked at both Inspectors and when they both shook their heads, he sighed and went back into the room.

Barely able to control the volcano of anger building up inside him, Os strode off down the corridor. She didn't call after him so he didn't have to make a decision whether to ignore her. When he reached the stairs, he paused. He had no desire to return to his office and it was too early to go home. As if Allah was aware of his plight, a voice called his name and turning around he saw Sener walking towards him, a sheet of paper in his hand.

'There's been a phone call from Dr Pehlivan, sir. He wants you to ring him back.'

Chapter Twenty-Two

Sener agreed immediately to his Inspector's request. In the privacy of the moving car, Os told him what had happened. For once he had no intention of being professional, choosing to criticize both Atak and Zelfa. When at last he fell silent, Sener handed over a packet of cigarettes and a lighter.

'So what happens now, sir?'

Os placed a cigarette between his lips. 'I don't know but at least we're out of the place. I doubt that Pehlivan has anything of great importance to tell us but I'd have said something I'd have regretted if we'd stayed.'

Sener backed the police car into a parking-bay of the hospital. The sergeant had driven faster than usual but whether that was because he had been affected by the stress emanating from his passenger or because he wanted to get home again, Os wasn't sure. But for once he wasn't complaining.

Standing outside the Foreign Office it occurred to Os, as it had the last time he had visited, that it was strange that the laboratory was in the basement of this building. As far as he was aware, there was no obvious link between the two departments but perhaps it was the only government office space available.

A different porter was on the desk. It was only as Os made his request that it occurred to him that the anthropologist might not be there. His need to leave the station immediately, instead of ringing ahead, meant that he could have a wasted journey. But for the first time that day Os's luck was in.

They were met by Dr. Pehlivan's secretary who immediately showed them into the man's office. He came out from behind his desk, shook both their hands and waved them to seats.

'I'm sorry - I hadn't meant for you to come out here, Inspector Zahir. I could easily have told you the new development on the phone.'

'It was no problem, Doctor.' Os smiled. 'What was it you wanted to tell me?'

Dr Pehlivan perched himself on the edge of his desk. 'I don't know whether you're aware that we now have a machine that determines the DNA of bones?' Os shook his head. Dr. Pehlivan continued, 'It's been generously funded by Argentina. The downside is that we share it with the South but nevertheless, it's allowing us to make huge advances.' He paused, perhaps for effect. 'Something quite interesting has come to light.' For the moment Os forgot about his previous irritations and leant forward to catch every word. 'It seems that your young man had a hereditary bone disease called Legg- Perthes. It affects the hip joints, eventually causing the person to walk with a limp. Of course the deterioration varies considerably but the unlucky ones end up in wheel chairs and even the least affected would expect to use a walking stick.' The doctor smiled. 'It's not much I'm afraid, but I thought I'd let you know straight away.'

The memory of Uludag's stick flashed into Os's mind. But then it didn't make sense that the skeleton could be related to him. There had been a son who had died but he had been a member of the 'Turkish Cypriot Resistance'. So why bury him next to a woman? And Uludag's leg had been damaged in a car accident; that was why he had been pensioned off from the station. It could, of course, be a mixture of both. The accident could have made the genetic-deformity worse. However Os twisted the facts, nothing really made sense. He spoke his thoughts out loud.'We could do tests on this man, Uludag. Of course we would now have to dig him up, which means making an application to the courts.'

The doctor moved back behind his desk. 'I believe that there was a daughter? It would make more sense to take her DNA.'

'I can't see there being any problem there,' Os answered. 'If this turned out to be her brother, she'd want to bury his remains next to her father.'

'She'd have to come here. But with having to share the equipment, it would mean waiting for at least two weeks. I'll let you know.' The doctor sighed. 'Perhaps you could contact her - see if she knows about this disease. Not that it would necessarily have been diagnosed years ago. People often suffer pains in their hips and do nothing about it - they just accept that it's part of getting old.'

Os felt none of the usual euphoria when a new piece of information came to light. He caught Sener's attention and they both stood up. 'Thank you for your time, Doctor, and, as you say, we'll keep in touch.'

It was not until they were in the car and on their way back to Girne that Os said, 'If nothing else, it got us out of the office. If it was Uludag's son, then I can understand him wanting to keep the identification secret all these years. Being buried next to a Greek woman is very different from being killed fighting with the Resistance.' Os paused while Sener overtook a lorry. 'But all this doesn't make sense. He wouldn't have hinted that he knew something if it was his son up there in an unmarked grave. He wouldn't have asked about a reward.'

'So there's no point questioning the daughter then, sir?'

Tiredness suddenly overwhelmed him but he made an effort to answer. 'We'll go over tomorrow - see if she knows anything. It's not that we've got anything else to do.'

They stopped talking then and Os leaned back and closed his eyes. It was six thirty when Sener dropped him off in the police car park before heading off in the direction of home. Os walked over to his own car, climbed in and turned on the engine.

He attempted to feel positively about the evening ahead as he drove up the hill. He could open that bottle of Australian red that he had bought the previous week and perhaps persuade Roisin to go to bed early. The thought brought a smile to his face and some of the tension in his shoulders eased.

Wild barking made him look up. Tramps was at the top of the stone steps, his tail rotating in excitement. Then Roisin appeared next to the dog and smiled. Suddenly the day didn't seem so disastrous faced with the pleasure of such a home coming.

'I tried to ring you,' she called.

He remembered that he had turned his phone off at the start of Gorus's interview and then forgot to turn it back on again. He reached the top of the stairs and pulled her into his arms. She pushed him away. He looked back at her puzzled; he thought things had improved between them.

'What did you want?'

Her voice bubbled with excitement. 'We went back to Endremit. The barman was wearing a ring very similar to the one found on that body.'

Os stared at her.

Irritation crept into her voice as she repeated, 'You know, like the ring that was on the skeleton.' He continued to stare at her. She sighed. 'Shall I fetch you a beer?'

He recognised the hurt expression on her face as he moved away to sit down on his usual chair by the pool. The beer bottle was placed on the table beside him with more force than he felt was necessary. Roisin started to speak but it was with less enthusiasm than a few minutes ago.

'You told me a ring was found on one of the skeletons and you described it when we were having dinner in the 'Half Way House.' Well, I think that I've just seen one like it on Hassan's finger.'

'Are you sure?' Even as he spoke, he knew that the question would infuriate her.

She glowered at him.'As much as I can be without seeing the original. He wasn't wearing it when I had coffee there the other day.'

Os pictured the bar owner in his mind. He couldn't remember Hassan wearing any kind of ring, never mind one that was as flamboyant as the one that was still in the laboratory in Lefkosa.

'And you say he was wearing it this afternoon?'

'Wake up, Os. I don't know how I can say this more clearly.'

'Describe it to me.' He was not being slow, it was just that his mind was hurtling around all the possibilities her statement had thrown up.

She peeled a beer mat apart and then drew the ring on the plain inside. He went into the bedroom, fetched copies of the lab photographs and spread them out on the plastic table. Roisin picked up a photo of the ring which was attached to a small cross on a fine silver chain. The excitement in her voice had returned.

'It was exactly the same as this. He wasn't wearing it before - I would have noticed'

Os took the photo from her. It couldn't be the original that Hassan was wearing – that was still in the lab in Lefkosa. But why did the bar owner possess the duplicate of such an unusual piece of jewellery? Perhaps there was a logical explanation but he would go and find out. He picked up his discarded jacket and kissed her.

'I don't think you should go on your own, Os.'

The concern in her voice surprised him. He thought of Zelfa and knew he wasn't going to ring her and really, at this stage, there was no point bringing his sergeants out again. This was nothing more that routine questioning. If anything came of it - they could follow it up tomorrow.

'I'll be fine,' he answered, shaking his head as if to dispel her worry.

Fresh excitement fluttered in his stomach as he drove down the hill. There were all manner of reasons why Hassan should have an identical ring to the one found on a skeleton. It wouldn't help him prove that Gorus murdered Uludag, but if he discovered the link between the two rings it would be a small triumph in a day that could not have been more infuriating.

Os studied the bar from over the top of his parked car. Hassan's mother stood framed in the doorway; unaware of his scrutiny, she stepped down into the road. As she made her way up the street she leaned heavily on a stick, a shopping basket in her free hand. He was glad she was not going to be around; he wanted to speak to Hassan on his own. He waited a few seconds longer then went in search of the owner.

The bar was empty but then he noticed the open door leading into the kitchen.

Hassan was stood at a table chopping onions. It took a few moments for him to become aware that someone else was in the room, and by then, Os had seen that Roisin was right, the ring was identical. Hassan made no attempt to smile.

His voice was curt verging on rudeness as he asked, 'Can I help you, Inspector? I'm not sure that Health and Safety would be too keen on you being in here.'

'I'm sorry to bother you again, Hassan. I was passing so I thought I would call in. I'm hoping you'll be able to throw light on something that doesn't make sense to me.'

Hassan reassumed his chopping. When he eventually spoke, he made no attempt at geniality. 'If you've something to ask I'd prefer that you were quick - this is a bad time - I'm behind this evening.'

Os ignored the man's blatant attempt to get rid of him. 'You must have heard by now that Uludag had been successfully blackmailing people for years?' Hassan didn't say anything though his eyes flickered from his chopping to the Inspector and then back to his knife and onions. Os continued. 'What I can't understand is why he was considered so threatening. People paid him a small fortune over the years.'

Still Hassan remained silent and Os wondered what the man was thinking. He was about to repeat the question when Hassan spoke.

'If people have a secret that they think will ruin their lives if it becomes common knowledge, they'll pay anything to keep it quiet. Uludag knew that.' There was contempt in his voice. 'It wouldn't have mattered how old he was, he still had a tongue in his head. You know what it's like around here, people love to gossip.' Hassan glanced up at Os. 'What I find strange is that I never saw him spend any of it.'

Os nodded, as if in agreement. 'That's an interesting ring, Hassan. I've not seen you wearing it before.'

Hassan glanced down at his hand. 'My brother sent it from Chicago, years ago. I haven't had it on for a while - it wore thin at the back so it's been in the jewellers.'

'The brother who died in the troubles?'

Hassan shook his head, his earlier impatience returned. 'No, my oldest brother - he went to Chicago in the early sixties. He used to send us presents before he died of cancer.' He lifted his ring hand. 'This was one of them. Now, is there anything else, Inspector?'

'So you and your younger brother both had identical rings?'

'Yes, he sent us one each. But why are you interested? He lost his a few months after they arrived - swimming in the sea.'

'Presumably this older brother sent American T shirts as well.'

Hassan nodded, this time more cautiously. A nerve in his right eye started to twitch. As if the only reason for his being in the kitchen was to chat with his new friend, Os pulled out a stool and sat down.

'What I can't understand is why you have an identical ring to the one found by the skeletons?'

Hassan's knife clattered onto the table and then a silence, charged with energy, filled the room. For the first time in Os's short acquaintance, Hassan seemed lost for words. Os expanded on his theory.

'It was your brother buried up there, wasn't it Hassan? He hadn't lost his ring in the sea - he'd given it to his Greek Cypriot girlfriend - Dovish. She was wearing it on a chain next to her Christian cross when she died. And he was wearing his American T shirt. Did you kill him and his girlfriend?'

Hassan's lip showed his disgust at such a question. 'Don't be stupid. Kill Saffet, my own brother?'

'You know that we can find out the truth by taking your DNA. Why don't you make it easier for yourself and tell me how it really happened?'

Hassan looked towards the open doorway. Os wondered whether he would try to run; he found himself tensing in expectation. But when Hassan did open his mouth, his voice shook as if it had all happened yesterday.

'My brother killed himself. It was a Saturday night in February 1971. I'd been out. It was gone midnight when I got back and found a letter on my bed. I hadn't known that he'd been seeing a Greek girl from the village,' Hassan nodded up in the direction of Karaman, '...the old Greek village, Karmi. Apparently, the girl was pregnant and went to tell her family that she wanted to marry Saffet. They thought that her father would agree since there was a baby on the way.' He glowered over the top of his black glasses. 'If they had talked to me about it, I would have told them there was no chance that she'd be allowed to marry a Turk. But he wrote that Dovish went into the house and he hid in the bushes outside. It seems he wanted to go in but she wouldn't let him. She told him that she could persuade her father to allow the marriage if she was on her own.' Hassan began to re-chop onions with an increased ferocity. Then he leaned over and spat on the floor. 'I knew the father. He had his own building company - a bully but he was a member of Eoka so he got away with it. People were scared of him and his connections.' A pile of onion slivers grew by the side of the flashing knife. 'He wanted Cyprus to be all Greek so he was not going to allow his only daughter to marry a Turk - even if she was pregnant. How could he explain that to his cronies? He wouldn't be able to hold his head up again.' His anger was suddenly replaced with sadness. A tear ran down his face and he wiped it away with the back of his hand. 'My brother wrote that the father hit the girl and she knocked her head on something and died. And do you know what those bastards did? To their own flesh and blood?' He glared at Os but when the policeman didn't answer, he continued. 'It was the middle of the night but her brothers rolled her up inside a carpet and then took her in the back of their truck to that hill.' Hassan waved widely in the direction of the burial ground. 'My brother followed and watched them dig a hole. They were lucky that there'd been a lot of rain, otherwise the earth would've been too hard.'

Os's memory flashed back to the same comment made by Dr Pehlivan. It seemed a long time ago. Hassan wiped his mouth with a handkerchief then continued.

'He came back here, got my gun, wrote me a letter and then killed himself. When I got there he was already dead. I buried him as the sun was coming up and then told our mother that he'd left to fight the Greeks. She had to have something to be proud of. That's why his name's on the stone outside.' He glared again at the Inspector. 'What would you have done?'

Os ignored the question; he didn't know the answer. Instead he asked something that had always puzzled him. 'What happened to his hand?'

Hassan's shoulders slumped. 'I hacked it off with my spade. He'd lost his little finger when he was a child. I wasn't thinking straight. I was terrified that if he was dug up, he would be recognised by his hand and people would think him a coward. Stupid I know.' He sighed, the air rushing out like a burst valve. 'But then I had to get rid of it. I buried it here in the village. After the Turkish invasion it was my idea to build a monument for the dead men. The bones of the hand are underneath it.'

For a few seconds Os felt lost for words. He shook his head, amazed, that in his line of work, he could still be shocked by human behaviour.

Then, recollection of the information they had been given that morning made him ask, 'Did your brother walk with a limp?'

Hassan stared at him.

'Dr Pehlivan mentioned something. I take it you don't have problems with your legs but your mother uses a stick.'

Hassan shook his head. 'No, I'm fine. But yes, my brother had trouble walking. The doctors gave him a built up shoe. He wouldn't have been any good going away to fight - he wouldn't have been able to move fast enough.'

'And where does Uludag fit into all this?'

Hassan shrugged his shoulders. 'I've told you all I'm going to, Inspector. What do you want me to say? That I killed Uludag?'

Os crossed over to the back door and looked out into a deserted lane, then turned around to face Hassan. 'But you did kill the old man. He knew it was your brother up there, didn't he? Was he asking you for money to keep his silence?' The bar owner walked over to the sink and held the kitchen knife under the running tap. Os continued, still using the voice of a puzzled friend. 'You weren't in his book, so presumably you hadn't yet made a payment. The old man was meticulous with his accounts.'

Hassan dried the knife on his apron. 'I told you, Inspector. I've nothing more to say.'

'Os!' Roisin's tentative voice pierced his concentration. A mixture of annoyance that he was being disturbed when he knew that he was about to get to the truth and concern for her safety, now that he was convinced that Hassan had killed Uludag, flashed through him.

Still facing Hassan he called out. 'Stay where you are, Roisin.' But she had already come into the kitchen.

She spoke in gasps. 'I had to know that you were all right.'

The moment was broken. All he could do was arrest the man. But although he knew that Hassan was Uludag's last blackmail victim, unfortunately he had no proof.

Os indicated with a jerk of his head that Roisin should leave the kitchen. Then he turned to Hassan. 'I need you to come down to the station in Girne.'

For a middle-aged man, Hassan could move very fast. Suddenly he was stood next to Roisin, his left arm around her neck. The knife was in his right hand and he pointed it at Os.

'Don't come near me, Inspector, or I'll hurt her.' His pupils had shrunk to pinpricks but there was no madness there, just pain and desperation.

In the ten years of being a policeman, this was the first time Os understood the true meaning of feeling terrified. His brain seemed not to function. Then a stream of words rushed out in a voice he didn't recognise.

'Don't be stupid, Hassan. Where do you think you're going? You won't get off the island.' Os grappled for the words that might bring the man to his senses. 'If you stop now, the law will be sympathetic to you. Your only crime is not admitting to the identity of your brother. But kidnapping is another matter.' Os forced himself not to focus on what could happen to Roisin.

Hassan spat out the words. 'You're going to put the old man's murder on me - you've said as much.'

Os held up both hands in what he prayed was a placatory manner. 'If I've made a mistake then I'm sorry, Hassan.'

He watched the knife twist up against Roisin's neck. Shots of their life together ran through his head - them laughing, making love. The idea of losing her now was something he knew he would not be able to bear. And it would all be his fault. He lunged forward to grab the knife. Hassan's eyes rolled. Letting go of Roisin he slashed out at Os. Os heard a scream before he felt the deep pain in his side. Instinctively, he touched his shirt. His hand was covered in blood. He backed up against the wall and slid slowly down to the floor.

'What are you doing, Hassan?'

The old woman stood in the kitchen. Her basket had fallen to the floor, its contents of loaves spilled onto the tiles. Os watched her limp over to her son. She grasped the knife from a hand that was now hanging by his side; he let her take it from him. And then Roisin ran to Os and he reached up and grabbed her hand and squeezed it, knowing that any other contact would hurt too much.

He tried to smile. 'Ring the station.' This time she did as he asked.

Hassan had collapsed on a stool while his mother hovered over him.

'Did you think that I didn't know? You think I'm stupid?' Hassan stared miserably at the floor. 'I knew that night that you lied to me when Saffet disapeared. He'd told me his girlfriend was pregnant. When you said he had gone away to fight the Greeks, I never believed you - I thought they must have run away together. But when he never wrote, I knew he was dead. I saw you come back late that night carrying a shovel and your gun.' She seemed to have difficulty with her breathing, taking in great gulps. 'I knew you were lying when you told everyone that Saffet had joined the Resistance. Now what have you done?'

The woman's voice had reached a high pitched wail. Hassan appeared strangely cowered, as if he was a little boy again.

'Did you kill Kutlay Uludag?' she screamed. 'Is this what the policeman is saying?'

She grabbed hold of her son's chin and thrust his face up to her. If she had been wary of him before, she showed no sign of it now. Her right hand clung onto her walking stick and the wood shook with her frailty. Os wanted to move over to support her but he didn't have the energy. Despite the pain, that had turned to a deep ache, he knew that this old woman could get more out of her son than he could ever hope to. He strained his ears as the mother's voice dropped to a whisper.

'So tell me,' she repeated. 'Did you kill your brother?'

Os watched Hassan's haggard face. He shook his head.

'No. He had already shot himself with my gun when I got there. I buried him so no–one would know the shame he had bought on the family – killing himself over a Greek woman.'

The old woman now spoke in a whisper. 'And Kutlay Uludag?'

Her son's voice was flat, as if aware of the futility of lying. 'Yes, I killed him.'

Then no–one spoke. Os could hear laboured breathing - perhaps his own -perhaps the old woman's. It was as if no–one dared to speak. Os felt, rather than saw, Roisin crouch down on the floor beside him. He wondered, fleetingly, what had taken her so long. Her arm then slipped around his shoulders. He wanted to close his eyes and sleep but he had to listen and watch. He lip-read, rather than heard the old woman.

'Why did you kill Uludag?'

'The old man told me that he saw Saffet hiding in the bushes that night. He heard the shouting in the house - the windows were open. But the next day, his Greek girlfriend said that Dovish had left the island to get married - so he believed my story about Saffet going away to fight.' As if remembering the treachery of the man, Hassan's voice became more animated. 'But last week, when the bones were found, he realised things had happened differently. He said that he was going to talk to the Inspector again in the morning - if I didn't give him money.' Perhaps aware that Os was still in the room, he turned to him and said, 'I knew that with DNA it could be proved that he was my brother. I've been following in the paper what those people in Lefkosa have been doing. I knew that, one day, the bodies would be found.'

A wail brought Os's attention back to the old woman. Hassan moved to take her hand but she snatched her wrinkled claw away. Hate had aged her face further. Os wondered how she had managed to keep her feelings hidden all these years. His voice seemed to stay muffled in his head but he had to ask now, before Hassan decided that he wasn't going to talk any more.

'But why did you kill Uludag? What does it matter now how your brother died? It happened over thirty years ago.'

The bar owner looked up at his mother. He spoke so calmly that an outsider, unable to understand the language, would think that he was talking of mundane things.

'I lost my temper – I'd done a lot for the old man over the years and now he was demanding money for his silence. I hit him with his stick. I didn't mean to kill him but...' Hassan shrugged at the inevitability of it all.

The old woman, as if suddenly blind, felt for a stool with her left hand and then sat down. She was crying but the tears fell silently, running down her face and sliding onto her dress. She kept repeating the words, 'My son, my son,' over and over until her voice had become a chant. It was as if she wanted to block out anything this other son might say. Os could only assume that she was referring to her youngest and presumably her favourite.

He glanced at Hassan and saw the pain in his eyes. Uludag had been a tic, sucking at people's need to hide their past, but killing him was not Hassan's right.

Os made an attempt to get to his feet but Roisin's protests stopped him. Instead, in a voice even he didn't recognise, he said, 'I'm sorry, Hassan, but I'm arresting you for the murder of Kutlay Uludag. Anything you say might be held in evidence against you.'

Hassan lifted up his head and stared at Os, as if noticing for the first time that the Inspector was sitting on his kitchen floor. Os knew that, if the bar man decided to make a run for it, there was nothing he could do. He was having difficulty forming the words in his head, never mind getting to his feet and making a physical arrest. He felt himself slipping away.

The private clinic was the same one that could be seen from Atak's office window. Os leaned back against the starched pillows, staring out at the garden. He was unable to hear the birds that he could see in the olive trees because of the gentle hum of the aircon. A vase of flowers had been placed on the table at the far end of the bed. A card showed that Zelfa had sent them in that morning. It was a kind gesture which made him feel more amiable towards her. That is, if he didn't already owe her for reacting so quickly to Roisin's phone call. She'd even collected Sener and Fikri on the way, so it had been a team effort. Hassan had been sitting on the stool as if waiting for them. When they first saw Os on the kitchen floor, his head on Roisin's shoulder, they had thought that they were too late.

He closed his eyes against the ache in his side. The doctor had said that his chest would have to remain bandaged for a month and that he couldn't return to work for at least two. But he had been lucky - it appeared that Hassan had lashed out with very little enthusiasm. If it had been otherwise he would have been dead.

He heard the door to his private room open and he opened his eyes to see Roisin staring at him. She was frowning with worry but when he smiled at her, she responded. She crossed the room and bent over to kiss him. He told her his plans.

Printed in the United States
210102BV00001B/93/P